Girl on a Bar Stool

Girl on a Bar Stool

Tim Roux

To order additional copies of this book, contact:
Xlibris Corporation
1-888-795-4274
www.Xlibris.com
Orders@Xlibris.com
36250

This book is dedicated to the memory of my niece, Clare, and to my friend, Max, who insisted that I should write a book on brand marketing.

Further brand management materials

The techniques referred to in this book are described in more detail on the Mud Valley™ strategy and brand marketing community site, to be found at http://www.mudvalley.co.uk.

Specific topics referred to in this book include:

- the brand development process
- market segmentation:
- brand definition
- brand proposition testing & tracking
- advertising development
- advertising tracking research
- scenario planning
- naming a brand
- creating a brand identity
- brand architecture
- second brand strategy
- designing focus groups
- re-branding
- brand revitalisation
- creative problem solving techniques

Part I

Chapter 1

Hi, I am Adam Melton. "The Ad," my friends call me, because of that ad. My enemies call me something altogether less pleasant but, to be honest, I am not very bothered about them. The greater your income, the more miserable sods there are who whinge on about you and all your dastardly deeds, like not giving them more attention than they deserve. When you're a star, people want you to love them, they really do. Sod that. I'm not a star, and I'll love whom I like. It will do me in in the end, I know, but until my tragic demise I'll be as carefree as a monk in a knickers factory.

You've seen the ad, although you can be forgiven for not realising that I was the guy who was responsible for it, from creative glimmer to industry awards and mega-sales. Apparently the ASA got more complaints than they have ever had about any ad before. The TV broadcasters refused to run it at all, until it gained such a buzz that Channel 4 adopted it as a social statement, not least to attract viewers to its flagship programmes. They even advertised when the ad would run. There's an irony for you. I calculated that I could have got laid about twenty times on the brass of that ad (but, with admirable restraint, I only sampled a couple). "What yer 'aving, darling? Petrovsk, of cosk" became an instant catchphrase, running on looptape in every bar in the country, or possibly whenever anyone anywhere offered anyone a drink.

I became the overnight hero of marketing, taking Petrovsk Vodka, Czar of all the Russians, from seventh place to brand leader within weeks, and attracting the ominous envy and enmity of a few penis-threatened big-hitters within the company who quietly hissed revenge for being temporarily outshone by a ginger-haired smart-arse.

Even though I am well acquainted with the theory of marketing which, let's face it, isn't that difficult ("give them what makes them feel good"), it still always amazes and delights me when the theory marches off clutching promises in both hands, and returns glorious and triumphant. You get so used to people telling you what the latest guru says, and it turning out to be totally phut-all useless, that you are wide-eyed and gormless when the man from Head Office gets it right. "I'm the man from Head Office, and I am here to help you," used to be the standard cynical joke among the salesforce. I was the man from Head Office when I got the Brand Manager role for Petrovsk, and the salesforce thought they had better shit all over me before I did it all over them. If I had cared, it would have been a strung-out tear-fest for me, and a jabbering jamboree of apes for them, but they soon realised that I wasn't about to let them get the better of me, and that I would seek them out for individual punishment however long it took me if they didn't get back into line, so they pretty rapidly did.

Power is about letting the other person know that there are no limits to what you are capable of doing, no precipice you will not readily hurl yourself from, that your recrimination will be agonising, relentless and endless, and that it will be so much more peaceful to stand back and let this pathological lunatic through. It is all about energy. If you can out-pace them, you are in charge. I am always in charge.

When I told the sales team that we were going to run a TV ad, they said "Good luck to you, Adam," thinking I would never get the budget in a million years. Petrovsk, supposedly Peter the Great's favourite tipple, was just not considered in the TV class. All advertising money would be wasted. But I had studied the market. All the other brands were peddling the line that vodka was such a smart drink doing such wonderfully sophisticated and amazing things to you, when I knew that on the street it was knocked back by ladettes out for a rowdy, raucous evening, determined to hook a guy, shag him, and to wake up without a hangover. Their voice, their outlook was not being reflected by any of the major brands. They were all tuxedos, private yachts, and it-girl floozies.

Don't sell your product to your customers, sell your customers to your customers. That's the bottom line.

So it had to have a naked girl in it, didn't it? It was not immediately obvious how, but which vodka-toting ladette has not dreamt of being cool, naked and mysterious in a bar, fatally alluring to her choice of guy? It's like perfume. Girls wear perfume not because men like it, but because it makes them feel irresistible, and therefore powerful. And how much easier it is to feel irresistible when you are half-sloshed and partying. So, take a colourless, tasteless, yet powerful drink, add a few Ben & Jerry flavours, give it a brazen attitude, and watch it roll. "Red Rasputin" for the one with raspberries in it. "Blue Babushka" for a hint of blueberry. "Molotov Medley" for a mixture of mango and lime. The girls love it; the ad makes them famous, at least in their heads. They aspire to be the girl at the bar who turns to the tough hunk and asks him "What yer 'aving, darling?" Those that ask for anything else get the cold shoulder (and the actress playing the girl was indeed absolutely frozen by the time we finished shooting). Those who say "Petrovsk, of cosk!" get it all, we assume. Blokes all across the country converted to vodka on the off-chance of the girl in the bar turning naked, and that vodka was mostly ours (there was something of a spill-over onto some of the other brands too).

I know that you can recall the ad because Nielsen tell me that 76% of the population can quote "What yer 'aving, darling? Petrovsk, of cosk" in its word-perfect entirety, and then laugh. For some reason it is only 47% in Devizes C1 women over 60, but that is about the only cloud out there. In London it is around 87%, even among teetotallers.

That's the great thing about stats. You can spend an hour patting yourself on the back congratulating yourself then, in a final act of showmanship, you pick up on one tiny detail of some interest but no relevance, and everyone thinks you know what you are doing. Of cosk, in my case, I do. I don't suppose I shall ever have to prove it again, in this company or anywhere else.

OK, I am being a bit flip about statistics. They really are beautiful. Some people literally see them in all the synaesthetic colours of the rainbow, and as shapes formed to entice. I don't do that. But I look at numbers, and sometimes I laugh alongside them in our joint exhilaration, as if they have told me the most comprehensive joke in the world. Sometimes my eyes swell with emotion as they confide their hidden truths. Mathematics are magic—Magical Realism—because everything they say is a bold reflection of the world, even when they are abused and contorted. I think anyone who falsifies statistics is either the most despicable, sneaky and cowardly vermin one could ever encounter, or a maestro of wizardry and arbitrage, depending on the end in mind. Numbers are the abstract song of mankind, even of the universe. They tell the tale as it could never be better told.

And when they tell everyone that you are a fucking genius, they get even better.

✳   ✳   ✳

My predecessor (I'll skip the illustrious bit) is George Grice—GG, as you would expect. You also expected me to say "was", didn't you? Predecessors are usually past, presumably because they are often dead. This one is very much in my present.

Let me describe him. He is an identikit corporate climber. He looks good in a suit, without being either remarkable or handsome. He appears comfortable in it, without seeming complacent. He is pleased to see you. He has an appeasing, inclusive smile that covers his face as he greets you. He is never quite at the heart of anything, and never very far off.

He vacated my job to become Marketing Director for the Snacks Division, which is doing surprisingly well of late, up 23% in sales; surprising given its history, and surprising given George's presence which has never been known to inspire a bonanza before.

I would like to give him some credit, but the truth is that the food wholesalers are forever rationalising their supplier base and, until recently, we at United Victuallers, were cast into a remote orbit. However, the runaway success of Petrovsk puts us back in the game. We are eligible for the full range of categories that we were previously excluded from, so a number of divisions are suddenly doing rather well. Unsurprisingly, none of the directors has had the decency to thank me for their good fortune. I wouldn't expect it, I have to say. They are too busy peddling the line that they have turned around their respective businesses through a balanced programme of planned measures including driving down factory costs, more effective allocation of the A&P (advertising & promotional budget), improved relations with the wholesalers and retail multiples, fewer supply outages, and solid, competent leadership, to cite just a few dead fish strategies that they fry up for the board. Boards feel comfortable with explanations describing "balanced portfolios", "rigorous cost cutting", "relentless quality improvement", "proven leadership". Even more, they appreciate their officers praising the exploits of non-commissioned staff. They resent the lower ranks grabbing hold of wasted opportunities, and being inspired with visionary insight. That sort of thing frightens them. They haven't the talent to do anything like that, nor the courage. Anyone who has is a threat.

So there is George, smiling serenely, surreptitiously slipping a blade between my ribs with all the admiration he declares for my achievements. I am a hero (therefore I am a loner, not a team player), I have charged the barricades (I am a rebel), I have shown great daring and ingenuity (I am the unshaven, scary-eyed wild man of the woods).

"Well done, well done, Adam. We need people like you. Tell me, George . . . ." said our Chairman, Lord Fullbrow.

He does need me. Especially if he listens to George.

You probably think I am being catty and unnecessarily immodest. That is also what the members of the Board think of me, without ever having heard me utter a single word of criticism of them in general, or of George specifically, in their presence.

The telling sign is that when I mention George's name in front of my team, everyone goes silent. They know that he ran this business for nearly five years and nothing ever happened. He had his explanations. It is a highly competitive, crowded market, and the market leaders (Smirnoff, Absolut, Vladivar) were outspending us 3:1. Vodka sales are all about the bottle, and ours was rated the consumers' favourite, so if we only threw money at the market, we would be successful. Unfortunately, UV was not prepared to invest in our sector, so we were reaping the harvest we were sowing, so to speak. Also, there were a few novelty vodkas around, like the one with the bottle that talks to you, and while they were not making any significant inroads into the market, they were disrupting it. We were also having supply problems, and our supermarket key account teams for Tescos and Sainsburys had gone off the boil. The future offered us mild cause for optimism, but the past was understandably flat. Etc. etc.

All of which totally rational and credible explanations were blown apart when I was appointed to give it a shot, and I did my maverick thing. I half suspect that they gave me the money because they thought I would fall flat on my arse, and prove that gung-ho marketing strategies would fail to move the dial on sales, and succeed in sinking the needle on profits. In other words, they were setting me up for a costly disaster so that they could justify their steady hand on the tiller. Beware of corporate executives proffering high-roller budgets. Accept them, and you might as well be taking heroine. It is a long, slow corporate death from there. Board Directors have not got their seat at the table because they are either generous or fair. They are killers; brutal extinguishers of any up-and-coming careerists who do not demonstrate total obeisance to their command and deference to their virtues.

George will do well, without ever achieving anything. I am on warp-speed headed directly for the sun; I am Icarus. I need a new job in a new company. Luckily, they also seem to need me. I am already in talks with several of the top food and beverage brand owners for a lucrative transfer fee, and I have no political choice but to go. The Board will be relieved.

❄   ❄   ❄

So what do I do all day? How does a branding guy spend his time?

Well, he spends some of it in bed with branding girls, or the shy virginal types from Customer Service or Logistics. Every year we have our own version of the Derby. It starts when we begin interviewing for next year's placement students. The ones who are going to get the jobs are, inevitably, those whom we want to nail. There was a time when we used to go for marketing talent. Luckily, nowadays, the best talent normally has at least sufficient competence in marketing too. So, by Christmas, next summer's hares are all lined up, and the greyhounds are already baying. Just before they arrive, we talk sternly to our teams. "This year's placement student is extremely attractive. If I catch any one of you displaying inappropriate behaviour, I'll be showing you the door before you even get the chance to show her anything you have in mind. Understood?"

"Yes, Adam."

They have indeed understood. The managers get the handicap start. They can have a go at the leftovers come November/December.

So the race is on between us, the atavistic brand managers. Funnily enough, the students are much more interested in our sales performance than the Board. The better your sales growth, the greater your chances. Weird, isn't it? They appreciate business skills, and are prepared to pay their dues.

Mind you, that is not all we do. A depressing amount of the time we are chasing up orders and trying to tame megalomaniac, and every other sort of maniac, buyers. They get to screw us too, royally, and virtually every day.

I was brought up with the idea that being a brand manager was all about creative, compelling and effective marketing strategies, and that you spent all your time accordingly with a gifted multi-disciplinary team which would give you your breakthrough. As it happens, I still believe that, but reality necessitates rather a lot of something else.

Take today, for instance. There is a new set of Internet traders attempting to break into the market. What do we do about them? The e-channel is getting ever more significant, albeit from a low base, and nothing yet to have any sort of impact on the supermarkets and the other high street multiples. Nonetheless, everyone assures me that they are worried shitless, and so should we be. One of these start-ups is going to make it really big, coming from virtually nowhere. But which one? We have backed a few, and they have yet to get beyond impersonating the proverbial signposts in the desert. This lot today are reputedly a bit of a joke, singularly unimpressive as individuals, no real investment, a bunch of enterprising 20 year olds having a laugh, and getting to be taken nearly seriously by the biggest brands in the country. This makes me nervous. Never underestimate the quiet determination of apparent airheads.

We had a meeting in our offices. Four of them turned up, Harry, Barry, Geoffrey and Susan. Harry, Barry and Geoffrey were clearly mates from university, or something. Susan was quiet, and attentive. The boys alternated between larking around and impersonating businessmen. However, one or two things that they said jolted me upright. They were not all angles and presentation, and they weren't planning on drinking the stuff themselves and, believe me, we have had our share of those. "Just send me some samples. A couple of cases will do it."

We looked at their business plan. It ran into the tens of millions as a projection for next year, their profits were no doubt grossly optimistic, although they did not actually show us those figures, and they had no really dramatic new ways of stimulating demand. That is what really worried me. You can spot the likely losers a mile off. They are smart people with incredibly creative ideas of how they can corner the market and, when the heat hits the kitchen, they will evaporate. These guys were dimmer (if that is the opposite of brighter), but they had a disguised ruthlessness about them. They might be prepared to do anything it takes, or they might not.

An old boss of mine once met Martin Sorrell when he was running WPP (Wire & Plastic Products) as a supermarket trolley business. Martin is not especially tall, even in high heels, but he still seemed to dominate the room. He told my old boss, Peter Brunel, that he might be nothing extraordinary today, but he would be the owner of a communications empire in ten years' time, as indeed Lord Sorrell is. My advice for spotting winners is don't pay any notice to anyone's veneer of professionalism. Most people can pack together some numbers that both add up and sound cautiously optimistic. The thickest corporate executive is adept at that. Feel their aura. I cannot see their auras any more than most people, but I can feel the colour it glows from the energy it generates. The angrier and the more steely the aura, the more attention you should pay them. Don't tell me what colour that is, it doesn't matter. It is an augury of the potential of success.

I think we will back these people. They will probably have split up within nine months, but I would bet that one of them will make it, possibly two of them together. I would back my hunch for Geoffrey and Susan. Geoffreys are always tough, and Susans are never simple. Actually, their business plan did not add up exactly. There were several glaring discrepancies which I got the impression they had already identified and could not be bothered to correct.

My colleagues who met them, Lucy, Spencer, Mark and Jilly, thought I was mad. They even laughed at me. Then they saw that I was serious, and came on board. They are a very good team as lawyers, accountants, forecasters and sales people go. There is absolute trust between us. Our Director, William Cranwell, doesn't like that either. He doesn't have an in to our team. He is an outsider, and big bosses detest that. He has been tempted a few times to play me off against some of his other brand managers instead, just to cut me down to size, but he realises by now that I only slice them to shreds, which boosts both my confidence and my power. Instead, he confides in me, treats me as his favourite, and awaits his moment. They say that 75% of all head-hunter calls are commissioned by your boss. I am pretty sure that 75% of mine are. Thanks, William, I am thinking Diageo.

✳   ✳   ✳

While I would like to suggest that the naked girl on the bar stool was pure inspiration on my part, I have to admit that it wasn't. It was art modelling life, or almost. The advertising agency folks at MDH hated the idea, or rather they resented its provenance. Clients are meant to appear with tight briefs they can flout or otherwise flex, no brief ever being precise enough in their judgment to be worthy of actually being followed to the letter. Rumour has it that Procter & Gamble is about the only company in the world that is so prescriptive in its briefing that agencies are obliged to comply absolutely. It sounds stultifying, yet constraint theorists argue that the more restrictive the limitation, the greater the urge and the scope for creativity.

Anyway, I marched in on a roomful of sheen-skinned advertising gods, bejewelled and bedecked in shirts worn with studied casualness, and costing three times anything I might consider buying, and I lay down my idea splat in front of them. They all stopped talking, which added to the tension in the room, and perused me as if I were a dead fish someone had wantonly tossed into their circle, until they remembered that I was the chief client of the day.

"Excellent idea, Adam," announced Henry. "It gives us a solid base to work from. It is always good when a client throws in some of his own thoughts. It lends us a reference point."

Remember, I was new to the job. Everybody knew that I had been recruited from outside the drinks industry, from the world of insurance indeed—loads of money, puff-ball of a product, the relentless (and duplicitous) "I'll be your friend" pitch—"negative reassurance", as we used to call it.

I think I was being told to back off. I might understand how to sell fear, but I knew nothing of greed.

I explained why.

"Have you researched this?" inquired Ginny.

"Actually, yes."

"Focus groups?"

"Two rounds of qual and quant. Incontrovertible, I am afraid." I smiled disarmingly.

"Could we see it?"

"Of course."

"Just a minute," said Paul. "I'll go and grab a couple of our research specialists."

There followed something of a bait-the-bear circus. I, naturally, was the bear. Provocatively, I sat there with absolute confidence born of the fact that I had done more intense research in three months than they had done in five years. Advertising agencies do not really understand market research, in the way that talkers do not understand or appreciate listeners as people, only as an audience. They prefer brushstroke research they can adapt to mean anything they like. It fits their purpose but it never stands up to the real thing when challenged.

The research specialists set off on their extended fishing trip, trying to find a naivety in the agency, a flaw in the methodology, a lack of representation in the sample structure, ambiguities in the questions, or a contention in the analysis, but they realised that they no longer stood a chance from the moment they asked me who conducted the research and I replied "Research International." Finally they sat back, opened their hands, shrugged, smiled and declared in synchopation:

"It looks solid to me."

"And to me."

Henry, Ginny and Paul grimaced, but it was already game, set and match. Almost . . . .

"Where did you have this idea, Adam?" Paul inquired.

"In a bar in Reading."

"In Reading?"

"It's our target audience. Lads and lasses partying the night away."

"In Reading?"

"Believe it or not."

"Well, I am not sure I would have done."

"Then come to Reading and find out."

They did. We had a very boozy night out in Reading, the agency team and my lot. We were surrounded by our target consumers, we bonded, and everyone came around wholeheartedly to my point of view. Vox pop. You cannot argue with it, especially when it is screaming down your ears.

"So who was the girl, then?" asked Matthew from the agency.

"Yasemin, my girlfriend."

"Really?"

"Really."

"This may be an indelicate question . . . ."

"No, she wasn't." Matthew smiled conspiratorially. "Not then, anyway."

"Ah." He looked awkward.

"But that is the point," I shouted at Matthew over the crowd. "That is what the blokes hope for."

"And the girls?"

"They are there for the attention, and the adventure. For the exercise of control and its abandonment. It is not exactly PC, but PC never sold products. Believe me. I am from the insurance industry, where wealth and cunning always outmanoeuvre middle-age and angst. Our ads all look PC, but underneath the surface they are plain pocket-stuffers. We insurance companies never believe that it is in our interests to pay out. We have got your money; what on earth are we going to hand it back for? Our motto is delay until doomsday. Deferment is profit; only the most determined get paid, and we don't want customers like that, if we can help it. That is why we introduced the no-claims bonus, to shoo off the financially astute, and to lure in the gullible who believe that by not claiming their due they are saving money." You can tell I was really drunk and prancing all over my soap box.

"Is that why you left the financial world?"

"Actually, yes. I eventually decided that the pickings were lucrative, but the money arrived via the toilet."

"So you turned to 80% proof alcohol instead?"

"A much more traditional form of corruption. No misrepresentations, no headaches next day when you realise that some ugly great institution has turned you over the night before and left you destitute. Vodka is pure pleasure. That is why we call our Division of UV the Joy Division. Everyone knows exactly what is at stake. No small print. No disguised exemption clauses. Just the bottle and you, and what you choose to do with it."

"Are you a poet, Adam?"

"No, just a piss artist."

"And what is Yasemin doing tonight?"

A very good question, Matthew, my friend. She wouldn't tell me. After we had spent some time at the bar chatting each other up, and it was obvious that we had decided to go to bed together, Yasemin gave me a simple ultimatum. "I have one rule, Adam."

"Shoot."

"You must obey it if you want anything to do with me."

"I will." I was looking at her body under her tapered black dress. I would have sworn to anything.

"The rule is this, Adam. You can try to do anything you like with me, but I do as I like."

"Sounds fair."

"I will tell you only what I want to tell you. I will see anyone I like whenever I like. I will sleep with anyone I choose (and if you cannot accept that, you are free to go). I will spend my money wisely or unwisely. I will not have children. And you will call me 'hunnybuttons' in our most intimate of moments."

"OK."

"Adam, you are pathetically in love. No-one has ever agreed to the hunnybuttons bit before."

"It might just be lust, and I don't care what I say."

"No, it is love. I can tell."

"And you? Do you love me?"

"Far too early to tell, hunnybuttons." She laughed at the face I pulled. "Maybe in my own way."

❋　　❋　　❋

Chapter 2

At UV, the planning cycle kicks off in September, for programme implementation the following September, underpinned by a three-year strategic outlook. We need to agree where we are headed mid-term, but we don't identify the specific path to get there. Conversely, the programmes we select for implementation next September will, at least initially, be executed to the letter.

As with most consumer goods, 50% of our Petrovsk vodka sales are made around the Christmas period, between late October and early January. What has not been sold into the wholesalers by the end of September has missed its slot. So, our busiest time is either side of the summer holidays, and we go completely bonkers from late August.

I take a long sun-based holiday over Christmas and the New Year, and a one-week snow holiday just before Easter, with whomever I am with at the time, so that I am in the office to oversee any crises during July and August.

Some groups don't start their planning until January, but that is slap bang in the middle of my three-week vacation, and wastes the back end of the year when nothing much happens other than snap disasters, nervous breakdowns, stoic resignation, or wild exultation. I think that it is best to counterbalance the excess emotionality of the ups and downs of the Christmas season with some cool, dispassionate thinking, although it does mean that some of my planning sessions are sparsely attended in body, and especially in mind, as we hurl ourselves into more pressing remedial actions.

The sequence we follow in our planning is:

- **October-December**: short, medium and long-term market assessment
- **January**: review last year's results and future corporate expectations; amend topline deliverables for the next three years
- **February**: develop and prioritise strategies
- **March**: develop and prioritise programmes within the strategies

- **April onwards**: resource re-allocation, recruitment and programme implementation

I regard my primary role in the business as being to harmonise a bear pit of expectations: of the corporate executives, of my Divisional Director, of the retailers, of the wholesalers, of my sales people, of my marketing people, of my customer service people, of my logistics people, of the marcomms suppliers—the advertising agency, the PR agency, the sales promotions agency, the direct marketing agency, the merchandising agency, the sponsorship agency, and so on. That is a lot of expectations to reconcile, everyone demanding the same more for less. The profit is in the squeeze. It is not entirely a zero-sum game, but it can run pretty close if you do not manage it properly.

In principle the people I have to please first and foremost are members of the Board. For years they required George Grice to maintain sales and profits from a platform of a reduced level of investment. In other words, they treated him as a cash cow. Now that I have battered down the competition and seized the brand leadership, they want more of the same in a market which is unlikely to grow significantly. In my more paranoid hours I suspect that it is an act of revenge for breakthrough performance, but perhaps they are just stupid, or greedy, or cannot work out where else to get it.

"Yeah, no problem", I normally end up saying to William. "I can promise you anything you like, so long as you do not expect us to deliver it".

"Of course I expect you to deliver it," he replies each time, crushing me with an intense stare in which his eyebrows meet in the middle and ripple like waves. How does he do that?

"Come on, William," I reply. "You know as well as I do that the only three ways to get growth are to increase prices, increase market consumption, or to take share off the competition. We have already taken 37% share off the competition over the last two years, and the market is growing at 2.7%. I can offer you 4% growth, that is it, and then only if you ring-fence our budgets."

William leans forward in the negotiating equivalent of a half-nelson. "I need 5%," he declares. "How are you going to get it for me? Ricky won't wear anything less."

Ricky (Brabant), our MD, always punches for aggressive targets, which he subsequently discounts to the City. In principle, failure to meet them is never tolerated; in practice he pardons defaulters so long as the over-performers over-compensate for the under-performers. Ricky promises the City solid, reliable growth, no investment jitters, no profit warnings, no nasty surprises. His multi-million earnings depend on it, therefore, so do my £70,000 salary, company 5-series BMW, generous expense account, and extra-curricula bedding and bawling, although that particular pastime has dropped off significantly since I hitched up with Yasemin. Not entirely. After all women are still attractive and attracted to me, and Yasemin makes me no promises.

In the forecasting and targets game (a forecast being when you look down the barrel of the rifle, a target being when the barrel of the rifle looks straight at you), the one thing you never want to get caught by is what we call "the eunuch's bind" where you commit to achieving accelerated growth on the basis of existing or additional resources, and you find yourself lumbered with the growth target while your resources are whipped away from you. Closely related to that is the predicament where your recruitment plan is put on ice but your targets are not.

So my other key task is to ensure I get the resources and budget I am promised. Twice that has meant my buying in contract staff in flagrant defiance of recruitment freezes, which William only discovers after the results have been announced. On both occasions, William helped me bury the bodies, demanding that I never repeat my capital offence again. He knows that I have not the slightest intention of keeping my word. It will only matter if I miss my targets, at which time he will get the opportunity to stage at least my mock execution. Sorry, Billy-boy, it will never happen.

So, Step 1, market assessment. One of the most valued members of my team is the man we call The Wizzard, indeed that is now his official job title. I argued that if Microsoft could have one, so could we. Gerry is what I otherwise call our Marketing Accountant. Spencer, the real accountant, counts financial beans, pointing out where costs are rising and falling infinitesimally, and working up draft P&Ls (profit and loss accounts). Gerry does the same thing for markets. Day-in, day-out, he settles himself into a chair after three cigarettes and five cups of coffee, all before 8:00 a.m., and revs up his SPSS statistical package. Then the real world begins to spin, at least to the extent that it is represented by market data. Gerry turns the figures this way and that way, chortles and harrumphs, and then tells us nothing.

"What was that about, Gerry?"

"Nothing."

"Come on, Gerry. You noticed something there, I heard you."

"Nope."

"Gerry, we don't pay you to be impenetrable."

He puts on his sweetest, nicotine-teethed, coffee-stained broad-lipped smile. "Yes, you do."

"Will we ever find out what it was?"

"Not this time, Adam. It didn't check out."

"What didn't check out?"

"Nothing. It wasn't there. Now can I get back to my job?"

In the early planning sessions, Gerry is the star, addressing multiple data files like Rick Wakeman plays the keyboards. "The Home Audit says . . . .", then "According to the TGI," followed by "If you triangulate the Nielsen data with the Panel findings and the latest omnibus research and build in a two month time lag, you get . . . ."

"Is any of this useful, Gerry?" challenges Spencer, who is never accorded this degree of rapt awe for any of his insights.

"You tell me, Spencer," Gerry replies.

"I don't know," Spencer parries. "I am just an accountant."

"You want the bottom line?"

"Always."

"Then the bottom line is that our core customer base is dying of both alcohol poisoning and the effects of underlying demographic shifts (the upwards average age drift), while it is statistically less likely to read a newspaper than for any time since 1953, spends 1.73 hours a week in a supermarket, 5.6 minutes in an off-licence, and now buys 0.32 bottles of vodka a month from a garage forecourt."

"Meaning?" we all chime.

"Meaning Petrovsk + petrol is a winning combination if only we can extend our core age range, which is a problem because Petrovsk in a word stands for debauchery which is typically something not aided and abetted by a car."

"So we need a second brand?" I venture.

"Could be."

"So we have to do it all again?"

"Could be."

I look around the conference table. "Did anyone meet their girlfriend on a garage forecourt?"

"You could try the line "Petrol, of cosk"," suggests Jilly.

"We could try the brand name 'Petrol'," observes Jim, my wiry old marketing exec.

"'Petrol', 'Diesel', could we get away with it?"

"Until the day you decide to sell fashion accessories," counsels Lucy.

"We could say that Petrol is for a more refined audience," chips in Spencer, eager to join in a branding discussion.

"Very funny."

"Jim, could you look into it?"

"I'll set Tasha onto it straightaway. I have always wanted to sell petrol."

"Could she work with Mark on this one?"

"Mark will think that it is Christmas."

"Tasha will think that it's Good Friday."

"Just tell her to get on with it," I insist. "She is a placement student, for Christ's sake, here for job experience, not borderline discrimination."

"Doesn't "Petrol" connote disgusting fumes?" asks Lucy, breaking into the conversation.

"That may be the joke," I reply.

"I'll set up some focus groups while I am at it," volunteers Jim.

"And please not the Beaded, Bearded Guru of Wapping, this time. We want market research, not chakra cleansing."

"Too right."

"There you are, you see, Spencer," Gerry declares. "Some people like my statistics. They even know what to do with them."

"Good work, Gerry," I add. "What else?"

"You want more. Could you cope?"

"Try us?"

"Car ferry sales appear to have had a sudden surge. I can't account for that one."

"Well, Petrol would work there too," Jim comments. "They always smell of the stuff."

"We have just run a big promotion on ferries," says Jilly. "I am delighted it shows through to the stats. Thanks, Gerry."

"Nice one, Jilly. Now back to planning. Segmentation."

"Can't it wait for next time?" Jim counters. "I have a three-thirty."

"At Newbury or in the office?" quips Spencer.

"See you guys later. I have a horse to catch. She is called Margaret Bains."

Definitely not Newmarket. Margaret Bains is about sixteen stone: too light for a horse, too heavy for a jockey.

❋   ❋   ❋

If you don't know about segmentation, it is what a marketing god created to make brand managers feel better about having a puny market share. Instead of confessing that you have only 1.63% of the market, you can claim to have 25.9% of the teetotallers serving vodka to attendees of bridge nights market, segment #43.

If you are a market leader you are probably not going to be overly worried about segment-based micro-marketing, unless you believe that the no. 2 in the market is chipping away at one of them.

In marketing theory, a segment is a group of people who cohere around a set of attitudes / needs / values, behavioural characteristics, or demographics (broken down by age, sex, status and geography).

If you want top marks in your CIM (Chartered Institute of Marketing) marketing diploma, you spend all your spare time triaging for segments that are large enough to be profitable, and where a mutual love affair could be ignited. It is the marketing equivalent of gluing yourself to the rear view mirror during a driving test.

In real life, segments tend to be "people up north", or "men over 50", or "home owners", or at least they were in the insurance company, although we did have two other key categories: those who read the small print, ennobled to the title of "discriminating buyers", and those who don't, whom we nicknamed the "cash machines"—you just go up to them, proffer an insurance certificate, and withdraw as much money as you need at the time. In consumer sales, cash machines outnumber discriminators by about three to one, fortunately.

"Ladettes" is an example of a combined demographics (women between 14 and 30), behavioural (who go out on the piss) and attitudinal (they want to be like the lads) segment, so I was proud of that one, and it was an insight that thrust me to brand leadership, so my previous take on segmentation is unduly cynical and belies my own experience.

So, I'll re-phrase my observation. Segments are wonderful things if you happen to stumble over them, and then recognise them for what they are, but devilishly difficult to identify if you are merely looking for them. Both in the insurance company I worked for prior to UV, and the industrial conglomerate who employed me before that, we spent years in search of them like intrepid Victorian explorers, but we could never find one that would provide us with the up-draught we needed to seize the market, and nor did anyone else.

Anyway, we do segmentation because it is fun, and allows us all to have a laugh, which is what we will do all day next time. Which reminds me, we need a facilitator. I must ask Ralph from Corporate. He takes it so seriously as to keep us amused all day. He tried to hijack the credit for the "ladette" segment by claiming we developed it in one of our work sessions, whereas I actually ushered it in fully-formed, so he'll certainly come back for more.

❅   ❅   ❅

I have found myself inadvertently backstage in the theatre of the universe, and that would frighten anyone. It scared the shits out of me.

I remember once, at school, Josh Hartland jumping in the air to kick a door open, only for it to be opened by someone coming the other way. Without the door there to impede his trajectory, Josh sailed straight on, and smashed his head hard into the lintel. He lay unconscious for a few seconds, came round, and his friends eased him solicitously into a half-seated position. "Who hit me?" he said.

I want to ask the same question. "Who hit me?" I also want to ask why, because I know that no-one hit me as such. I am making no sense.

I was in the Barbican, attending a conference on retail optimisation. I was giving a speech, God knows why I get asked. I am not much of a speaker, I have very little to say, and you don't even get paid, but I get this urge to perform from time to time. I have watched many conference presentations over the years, and one thing I have learnt is never, never attempt to teach anyone anything. No-one is there to learn, yet they are subjected to one earnest how-we-don't-do-it-but-would-like people-to think-we-do lecture after another. There comes a time in the day when anything at all entertaining is riotously rewarded by the audience. I am that turn. It gives me the chance to be a stand-up comedian for

40 minutes, and I play it for laughs. Somehow, if you manage a vodka brand, you have the licence to tear the place down.

So I was unduly pleased with myself after a fun time bouncing off the audience and a few walls, and I was making my way down to street level, when I heard someone behind me say "I thought that was excellent too, Minister."

Naturally, that caught my attention because I doubted that the speaker was addressing a vicar. There must be a member of the Government nearby. Would I recognise him?

I turned round, and I did recognise him immediately with such a jolt of horror that my insides nearly landed on the floor.

The Minister saw me, and immediately smiled. "Hello, again."

"We have met before?" I asked.

"Many times, but you don't know it yet."

The civil servant, I assume, who was accompanying him, was watching us with amazement and confusion.

"You will get used to it, Adam, and learn to accept it. What were you doing today? Ah yes, the retail conference. Good, wasn't it?" He leant over and whispered into my ear "I enjoyed that one, although we have done many even better ones since."

I could not say a word.

"Sir William," he said, introducing me to his aide, "this is my younger self, also called Adam, naturally."

"Named after you, sir? I thought I could see a family resemblance. An absolutely remarkable resemblance, in fact. Are you in politics, Adam?"

"Only local stuff," I replied.

"That will change," the Minister reassured me. "You are in for a meteoric rise, I can assure you. Enjoy your good fortune."

"Yes, sir," I said.

He held out his hand. "The next time will be easier, Adam. Must move on, I am afraid." They both walked briskly off in front of me.

I stood there wishing to sink to my knees, but too self-conscious to do so.

I had just met myself.

Chapter 3

GG has just come over to invite me to lunch with some of his fellow Marketing Directors: William, Eleanor Barrett from Chilled Foods, and Seamus Sissons from Frozen Foods.

What is going on?

GG treats it as if it is a great privilege and honour for me. I view it as more likely to be a trap although, about what I cannot quite work out.

Everyone is fulsome in their welcome. They must, at least, be after something.

"Adam," officiates William as my boss and therefore the initial spokesman for the group, "we wish to thank you for all your wonderful work with Petrovsk. We have all benefited from it hugely, and we have realised that we have not accorded you the gratitude you deserve."

"Thank you."

"UV is having a record year, and it is in a large part thanks to you."

"Thank you."

"But you are forecasting far less growth this year," Seamus comments.

"Yes," I reply. "Inevitably. We have got most of what we can get with the Petrovsk brand. However, we are investigating a second brand to access other niches."

"That is the first time I have heard of it," William objects, the aggrieved victim of a presumed lèse majesté.

"It only popped out of our initial planning meeting last week. We have no research to assess whether it is a viable option or not at this stage. I promise to keep you informed."

"Have you a name for this new brand? It will be treated as a second brand, I presume?"

"No, we haven't settled on a name yet . . . ." (pray God none of the team has mentioned "Petrol" to him, perhaps in jest). "We have some options which we are investigating shortly."

"How are you generating the names? Through a naming agency?"

"It depends on how the names we have already brainstormed check out, and what we consider the market potential to be. We will probably do some random generation of possible names to supplement the ones we already have, before we go into research."

"Please, no silly names," advises William.

"Second brands are expensive, and a dilution of focus," observes Seamus.

"I assure you, William, that you will be fully consulted before we go ahead and do anything. Obviously, the name, or names, we will recommend to you will have been chosen as giving us the greatest possible likelihood of success." I hold up my hand as Eleanor looks about to speak. "Sorry, Eleanor, I wanted to answer William's other question. I do not believe in second brands as such, if you mean by that secondary brands. All brands must play at the top of their game if we are to get the best results. So, if we decide to propose a second brand, I will also be recommending the setting up of a second brand team to compete directly within the market, even with Petrovsk, no holds barred, so long as they remain within their brand definition."

"You also get a lot of cannibalisation, if you are not careful," Seamus adds.

"Which won't matter if we have the same underlying profitability in the business model. That is the typical pitfall of second brands. The second brand is designed to be less profitable than the first, so it is used only as Plan B. This limits its potential, demoralises the team, and ensures marginal performance. If that is the only option, I won't do it."

"I think that depends on what William decides," Eleanor cuts in.

"No. That bit is non-negotiable from my perspective. I don't play to lose."

William coughs uncomfortably, having received his second dose of lèse majesté in under five minutes. "We will talk about this offline. However, Adam, while you are still with us, I would appreciate your thoughts on another problem I am facing. What does George do about gluten-free in the Snacks Division?"

"Good point, William," George declares. "I am glad you raised that one."

"Certainly not eat it, or the lack of it," Eleanor responds.

"It is coming up on us in Frozen too."

"The trouble with gluten-free is that it is a worthy cause everyone aspires to, and nobody actually wants to eat," GG expostulates. "Nobody would kill for a bite of gluten-free, I know. It is worse than decaffeinated. Sales are driven either by dietary necessity or neuroticism. We are increasingly being forced to produce gluten-free products by the retailers to fill a gap in their range, and to boost their image, then we sell about two packs a month, one in Aberdeen, the other in Barnet. It's ridiculous."

"I know what you mean, George. We face the same dilemma."

"So you are caught in the old Lucozade trap. Lucozade is for sick people. Don't buy it if you are not sick."

"Exactly, Adam, exactly."

"So you need to give it a face-lift . . . ."

"I thought it was in existence to avoid one," quips Eleanor. Do I get the impression that she is getting all ready to have a go at me behind my much-stabbed back?

"It would have to be one hell of a plastic surgeon," adds George. "I think it is intractable. It might be more a question of how we avoid the pressure of Tescos and Sainsburys to market the disgusting stuff."

"Upsetting Tescos is not a smart idea," I comment. "I don't know anything about snacks beyond the habit of eating them, but I am aware of the whole problem of projecting healthy food as fun food. However, there must be an angle. You could use some well-funded research to act as a delaying tactic with Tescos. It might work, but equally a competitor might simply grab your facings, which you don't want."

"I agree with Adam," Eleanor interposes. "Thwarting Tescos is not an option."

"If in doubt," I continue, "a play on words generally goes down well. What about 'gluttony-free'?"

"What about gluttony-free?"

"Well, everyone likes the idea of gluttony without the consequences. You would clearly have to research it, but I would go at least that far. You can have your cake and eat it, you can binge to your heart's content, and you will never get fat. I doubt that your claim could be as specific as that because they almost certainly would get fat, but you could offer something suggestively in that direction. Sort of the opposite of 'naughty-but-nice'. With this delicious delicacy, you can eat your head off and not succumb to a moment of guilt. You would have to get the recipe right, of course. It would have to taste really good."

"Which is simply not possible with gluten-free, in my opinion," George pronounces.

"Well, if the product really tastes revolting, you are inevitably niche. There aren't so many people in the world who eat shit, whatever the reason."

"Delicately put, Adam." I think Eleanor is developing a nice little bee in her bonnet.

"Talking of the which, let's eat," Seamus suggests.

I look around the group. I have absolutely no friends here. What do they want to do, to provoke me into some careless suggestions they can ridicule? I have a sixth sense for trouble, and it is definitely rattling its tail, gaining pitch all the time we are talking.

"Adam, you never stop having ideas, do you?" Seamus comments. "They should give you a stint in the labs for a bit, thinking up new things to do with béchamel sauce."

"I'll take that as a threat, then," I riposte.

"Heavens no," Seamus replies, squeezing my elbow. "Just a friendly warning." Another smile. "Only kidding."

I hate that phrase.

And that is that. Everyone settles into their plates, making sporadic listless conversation, interspersed with moans about having to attend a Board Meeting at 2:00 p.m. Either they have what they came for, and have now switched off, job done, or they are depressed.

"Just you wait, Adam," beams George.

Yes, but for what? Methinks he hath a flabby and gluttonous look.

✻   ✻   ✻

I sometimes speculate that Yasemin is some kind of a revenant, a corporeal ghost, returned to earth to expiate my sins.

I have just looked up "expiate". It doesn't mean what I thought it did. It means to "pay for", from "expiare", to appease. So perhaps I mean "intercede" instead.

However, I can imagine that someone might need to appease on my behalf. That is not an action that is prominent in my repertoire. Sociologists argue that human beings are unique among all animals in that we have no concept of appeasement. Whoever thought that one up hasn't met the people I know. Appeasement is rife in the companies I have worked for. There is always that implied threat of retribution if you do not sell your soul to the management, if you do not continuously doff your cap to the hierarchy. People live in fear, and appear, at least to me, to appease the source of power and wages whenever they are confronted. They would say that they have to keep their job, that they cannot afford to be unemployed, but I doubt that that is really it. I think it is merely that appeasing a higher social force is built into our behaviour, as it is with an ape or a dog.

And we cannot shed our recognition of hierarchy. If someone calls himself a Managing Director, we immediately place him above us, and start to laugh at his jokes, even though it might only mean that he has shelled out £80 and set up a marginally trading company, at least in England. And the weight of tradition tells us that our superiors are our betters, and that it is a form of treason, of sacrilege, a betrayal of the divine order, to question their commands, a mutiny, a violation, a basis of reprimand, not only within your organisation but within the wider world.

I feel that pressure, but I resolutely defy it. I, rare among human animals, resist the safe passage of appeasement. I do not believe that those who are of a higher social rank are better than me. My bosses are there usually because they are older than me, or got there first, not because they are more talented. Older and more senior, does not mean wiser. It normally means more pompous, fatter, lazier, and closer to retirement and death.

So, Yasemin can indeed appease for me, if there is a divine requirement that each human being appease.

With her black wavy hair, and amused, defiant, dangerous eyes, I don't think she is appeasing anyone on her own behalf either.

She comes and goes in my life, in my house, like a shadow in the light and in the dark. Just because you cannot see it, does not mean that your shadow is not there. Yasemin is always there for me, but much less often visible or present. I have learnt, over several months, virtually nothing about her. She talks about "my brother this" and "my mother that", but I cannot get any grasp or any taste of these people, and I doubt that I shall ever meet them, if they exist at all. I almost get the sense that Yasemin's world is entirely made up, a mirage dreamed up to give her substance, a reality.

In the flesh, Yasemin is definitely substantial, which is not to suggest that she is padded, only that she is immediately and silkily beautiful. Her body is like a human thong, skinny and temptuous. She moves like a dancer, and talks with the ghost of an Irish accent, despite being Kurdish in origin. She has Celtic sapphire blue eyes, and an enticing mouth I cannot help zooming in on.

She just turns up, then she just leaves. I do not even know where she lives. I have her mobile phone number. I tried to follow her one night, along a dark windswept, stormy journey into the countryside, and she simply disappeared on me. She rounded a corner, and was gone.

I ask her questions to reassure myself that she exists, that she is not some kind of incorporated ghostly plasma. She laughs at me, and calls me weird. "I've never met a guy like you before", she keeps commenting. "You've a little more than met me," I keep replying. "Yes," she says, "but I don't know you."

"You don't know me?" I declare incredulously.

"You keep yourself very hidden. You don't disclose much of yourself, of your emotions. I do not know what would make you cry."

"You sometimes make me cry."

"That is ridiculous. I have never seen you cry, and I do nothing to make you cry about."

"Perhaps the word is 'weep', then. You make me weep."

She observes me with a still seriousness. "Why would I make you weep?"

"In frustration. Trying to get my arms around you."

She laughs. "You have had your arms around me quite often enough."

"Not around your soul. I haven't contained you, even for an instant."

"What, are you a devil, that you want to possess my soul?"

"No, I am a man wanting to possess a woman. Wanting to possess you."

"No, I am not a possession, you are right. You cannot own me, any part of me. And I cannot own you either. You are what you accuse me of being, evasive to the grasp. Quicksilver. We are two of a kind, unique to the world. We stand apart from it, and we see it all."

"We stand apart from each other too."

"You think so. I would have said that we were inextricably linked."

And I think that is the most beautiful sentence that has ever been said, even in mathematics.

"Will you stay the night?"

"Certainly, but I must slip away before morning. I have so many things to do."

She never explains what, and I don't think it is drying her hair.

❉ ❉ ❉

I am standing in my room at home. My parents have lived in the same house all my life. They are lovely people. Tim is now 58, greying, dignified, kindly. Joyce, my mother, is 56, calm, warm, all-accepting. She must also be one of the youngest Joyces on earth.

"Can't you change your name to something else?" I have asked her since my late childhood. I have always wanted to re-brand her.

"I like 'Joyce'. It has a friendly feel to it. It means joy, rejoicing. What is wrong with that?"

"It means a 70 year old, with a blue rinse, slippers and curlers, doing good to the next door neighbour."

"And what is wrong with that, Adam? You have such extraordinary prejudices. Do you like 'Adam'? Have we messed that one up too?"

"You haven't messed up being called Joyce. You didn't choose it. No-one in their right minds would choose it. I like Adam, though. It is a simple, authentic, classless name. Classy in a niche sense."

"Adam, I sometimes wonder whether you are speaking English. And what about 'Tim'? Is that good enough for you, for your father?"

"No, Tim is a nice name, mother, although there has never been anyone very important called 'Tim'."

"There is Tim Rice, Tim Piggott-Smith, Tiny Tim."

"Precisely, if that is the best you can do."

My mother considers it for a moment. "I think it is."

I am standing in my bedroom. I am watching a small boy there. He is playing with his soldiers on the bed, making "squwth" and "shoom" noises, as the cannon balls land, and the swords swish. He is engrossed, and oblivious to me.

He is me. How have I entered his world of 17 or 18 years ago? Why?

I exit the bedroom and walk onto the landing. When I rejoin my parents downstairs, I don't know whether they will be in their 50s or their late thirties, forty. I scrutinise the grain on the banister, the slope of the stairs, the brush hair encapsulated in the paint on the wall high above me as I descend.

"Adam," my mother greets me, 56 after all. "Your father wants to know whether you would like a beer with him. I think he wants a man-to-man chat with you, before lunch."

The Sunday roast is smelling sweetly.

❊   ❊   ❊

Our segmentation work is much advanced. Gerry has established that the "ladette" segment is actually growing at around 6%. "Don't tell William," I instruct him. "He will raise our forecast. And the segment for Petrol?"

"20-30% and rising, we reckon. Smart, sophisticated, slightly rebellious and alternative. Virgin territory."

"I am not sure that is very reassuring, given Virgin's history."

"History need not repeat itself. It is there to be learnt from, and we are not Virgin," counters Jim.

20-30% and rising, That is good enough to go for.

Tasha and Mark have been checking out the name Petrol.

Most people misunderstand naming, even marketers. They ask what has that name got to do with that product? They assume that a brand name needs to be descriptive or suggestive.

"What has Shell got to do with petrol?" I counter. "What has Ford got to do with cars? What has Marks & Spencers got to do with retailing? They are now synonymous with them, but they do not inherently mean those things. It is simply a question of long and significant usage."

The most important thing about a name is that you can own it. Nowadays, that means can you get the .com, .co.uk or whatever, although all the new suffixes, .biz, .eu., .info etc. have opened up the possibilities a bit. However, any kosher brand should really have either the .com or the .co.uk.

The other aspect is that legally you can retain it exclusively in your category, and any other category you might extend into. In continental Europe, this means registering your trademark first. In the UK and the US, this means that you have to have first usage, whether you registered it first or not. It is still worth registering it, but it is not sufficient.

The least protectable names are purely descriptive, e.g. Cars for selling cars. You could have got cars.com if you were quick enough, but it is virtually impossible to protect Cars in the real world, if it is for an activity relating to cars. How can you prove you were the first to use it? Anyway, the trademark office (the Intellectual Property Office in the UK) would not allow you to have it on public policy grounds.

However, you can misspell it, as in Ford's Ka, and there is always a dodgy area across languages. "Car" is generic in English, but not in Spanish.

"Ka" is an example of a name that is suggestive rather than descriptive, because of the spelling. That is slightly better. Better still, is an existing word irrelevant to the context. Car brands usually fall into this category—Ibiza, Laguna, Scenic, Corsa, Monza.

The most legally protectable trademarks are those that coin a new word. There you clearly have first use because you invented the word yourself. Xerox and Kodak are classic examples of these. There is a funny story about Xerox. The person who originally registered it, actually wanted the name Xerex, as a palindrome. However, the registration clerk could not read the guy's writing, so it was registered as Xerox.

Most of the horror stories about brand names are where they mean something absurd or offensive in another language. The famous one is the Vauxhall Nova, because "no va" in Spanish means "doesn't go." In its first design, it should have gone all right, straight into the bin. What an ugly looking car. There was a Japanese car (Nissan?) they wanted to call the "Little Bugger". One of my favourite inappropriate names is not to do with a brand at all. The ex-President of the Philippines, Cori Aquino, means in Spanish, with a liberal translation, "Do you want to fuck? No, not here." Mind you, the Philippines have some splendidly dodgy names. They also produced the church man Cardinal Sin.

Petrol is checking out well. A search of the UK Intellectual Property Office shows that it has not been registered in any of our product categories, a search on Google suggests that there are no prominent Petrol brands other than brands of petrol, and the petrol.com site says "inquire about this domain." It is going to cost us money. We have money.

Tasha has run her first focus groups. Before going in, she used an online random name generator to suggest some additional names, and came up with Tort'aio, Etasy and Vorchai (some connection to Russian tea?). Petrol easily screened the best. Everyone liked the joke about going to the garage to buy some petrol, except for the slightly cantankerous guy in the second group in Manchester who said that it deprived petrol of its natural meaning in the English language, as had happened with "gay". Is it the same bloke who turns up in all these sessions, or is there always one person somewhere who thinks that whenever you do a random trawl of people?

Tasha and Mark are delighted. They know they are onto a winner. I saw them almost hug each other yesterday, then stand back rather embarrassed. Mark walked away, bending forward slightly. I think he had a hard-on.

Chapter 4

I enter the sitting room, and immediately pull back.

I am there on the sofa with Sylvie Clarke. I must be around seventeen, and about to have my first real kiss and grope session.

I am there; I was there. I am seventeen; I was seventeen. Time is as confused as I am.

I want to watch them/us, but there is nowhere really in the room to hide. I do not know whether they can even see me, but I fear some cataclysmic universal disaster if our alternative worlds should collide. Then I remember that I have already come face-to-face with another myself without any noticeable damage to the order of things.

Still, I don't want to be seen. It only takes one of them to glance up and catch my outline as I dodge back behind the doorframe. Then the realisation strikes me that I did not in fact see myself conclusively standing there when I was seventeen groping Sylvie Clarke. So, unless this is an alternative world, or unless this world will take a different course, it did not happen. And if it did? Then, in a few seconds I will remember seeing myself standing in the doorway, because the memory will have changed both instantly and across eleven years, culminating immediately in the present. It is not easy exploring so many aspects and permutations inherent in the complexity of space and time when you are hovering in a doorway watching yourself experience a very wet kiss.

I remember that kiss. It was like sucking jelly, all wobbly and slimy and wet. Then her tongue entered my mouth with the gauche enthusiasm of an uncertain girl doing what she thinks she is expected to do to be a sport.

Sylvie is ripply in her overweight frame, her skin ceding to my fingers like a cushion filled with gel. Nonetheless, I have never done this with a girl before so I am determined to force through the experience, to get it over and done with—first base, second base, third base etc., although that is American, and I was not using those words in my mind.

I was strategising how to get my right hand under her bra to touch her naked breast. Would she stop me? I ease my mouth away from hers. "Sylvie, you are very beautiful."

"Really? Thank you."

Apparently she will not stop me now. Sylvie is a quarter French, which makes this a considerable coup for me. I am not succeeding in touching up a fat girl, but a French one.

My hand is under the rim with some twiddling of the fingers. Blancmange. I cannot see them, yet I know that they are white and unused to being exposed to the light. I have them both in my hands. Now where? Should I start to stroke some irrelevant (at least to me) zones in order to distract her from my next target which I can already visualise without knowing in detail what it looks like? I have heard that girls get turned on by that, the caressing, barely without touching, of non-erogenous skin.

It is not long before my hand is creeping up her leg, initially moving up the outside, then crossing the street to the sweatier inner thigh. Sylvie disconnects to say "I like you too, Adam," then returns to kissing me, condoning my upward progress. The higher my hand rises, the more berserkly her tongue flickers in my mouth. It is a sort of ticklishness associated with nervousness.

She stiffens. "What was that?" she asks.

"What?" I reply, defensively.

"There was a noise."

"It could have been my parents turning round in bed."

"Could they come down here?"

"No. I am sure they will leave us well alone."

"Could they be doing what we are doing?"

"I hope so, for their sake."

Sylvie grins.

I return to the rim of her panties. My knuckle has already accidentally caught the spring of her pubic hair beneath the cloth. Can I finger my way inside? I can. I am there, three or four fingers at last flat against the centre of her sexual being. I cannot remember whether it felt wet or not. Probably. Everything about Sylvie's body was wet.

Her hand moves across the trousered surface of my crutch and rubs a little. She does not venture inside.

"I must go now, love" she announces sweetly. "My parents will wonder where I am."

"I will drive you home."

"Thank you. I must find my coat."

And I am out of there, shaken by my memories of that first conquest.

I never went out with her again. I wanted somebody slimmer next time, even if she were English.

❋   ❋   ❋

Yasemin is sitting on the bed, cutting her toenails directly onto the carpet. I cannot say that it is a habit I approve of, but I tolerate it because she dutifully collects up all the clippings afterwards.

She is in her bra and panties, dark and slim and firm—her underwear and her body.

She looks up at me. "You were a bit of a bastard really, weren't you? Deceiving her just because she needed to make herself available to someone to feel she belonged."

"In that case we were both serving a purpose for each other. Almost the same purpose, in fact; to be known to have consorted with the opposite sex."

"'Consorted'? Does that word still exist?"

"Only when coupled with 'the opposite sex', and only in a certain sort of mock-dispassionate report."

"Heavens. I am caught up in the middle of the social sciences." Yasemin's ironic eyes glitter.

"Are you saying that you never took advantage of someone just to have the experience?"

"Not men, no. I got them anyway. It was more a question of stopping the flow. With another woman, yes. I pretended to be interested in exploring being a lesbian once to find out what it was like with an attractive woman."

"Really?" Yes, really. "And . . . ?"

"Yeah, it was all right. It was quite interesting, in fact. I got to know a lot more about my own body and how it worked. Indeed, how it looked. I am not flexible enough to go to that level of detail on my own body."

"What part of a woman's body do you like the most?"

"Funnily enough, the bum hole. I can't tell you why. It's the way it puckers up, and is otherwise entirely useless in the course of sex between two women. It is about the only bystander, so in some way it asks shyly for attention. And you?"

"I like it all."

"Not very discriminating."

"No, I don't mean that I like every bit equally. I mean that I love the overall impression rather than any specific part. I love it as you are now, leaning over your knee, playing with your toes, leaning back to talk to me because I am standing slightly behind you. I love the composition of your body in its many poses."

"Well." Yasemin raises an eyebrow appreciatively.

"So you don't think I should go to see a psychiatrist?"

She frowns. "You particularly want those little plastic tumblers with blue and red pills in them?"

"No, I do not necessarily need pills, or do I?"

"What do you think is wrong with you?"

"I don't know. I really haven't a clue. Apart from these weird flashbacks and flashes forward, I feel perfectly normal. It must be some equivalent to an electricity discharge or something; a dream even. I do not even know if they last as long as they appear to. It could be that they only last three seconds, or something. I am just frightened that I cannot control them, that I fall into them, more and more frequently, like people get epileptic fits. Will they just repeat and repeat and repeat, until that is all there is left?"

"I don't know, Adam. Not necessarily."

"I wish someone could at least give me a clue."

"I have never heard of anything like that before. You could try Oprah. She might have come across it."

"And I must admit I am rather nervous to go and see a shrink. If these episodes really are predictions, then it is rather awkward for a Cabinet Minister if he is known to have been treated by a psychiatrist, or a psychologist, or some other variety of therapist for suffering from delusional states. I could be blackmailed, and I doubt it would wash if I said they were all true because I had indeed become a Cabinet Minister."

"I think you are in a bit of a delusional state at the moment. You are only the local Labour Party branch secretary because nobody else can be bothered."

"I agree with you, Yasemin, I promise you. It seems an incredible leap to me. But Ken Livingstone did it. He just turned up in Norwood, or wherever it was, and became almost the entire constituency party—Chair, Secretary, Treasurer, the lot."

"But he is a bit more interesting than you are, Adam."

"Thank you, darling." I screw up my face and protrude my tongue. "But nothing like as handsome."

"So what is the answer? Go with the flow?"

"Do you think I am mad?"

"Not mad enough to be a Cabinet Minister."

"Perhaps I will see how it goes. Keep an eye on it. Will you keep an eye on me too?"

"I shall do nothing else, Adam. I want to be well away from here when you blow. There may be a narrow line between madness and genius, but the one between madness and government minister is probably even thinner."

"What do you think it is like to be a minister?"

"Lonely, busy, stressed and corrupting."

"Yes, you are probably right. I like the corrupting bit. I think I'll apply."

"Don't expect me to stick around. Us angels only recognise one source of power, of the invisible kind. The rest have smelly feet."

"Perhaps I should focus on how to avoid being lynched by George Grice and his pals at UV first. It will be an excellent training ground for real politics."

"You only need to skip the country, don't you, or at least their country. With your track record, tons of people will have you and, as you will arrive already billed as a hero, you will be quite safe so long as you repeat your success."

"So you think I should leave UV?"

"Definitely."

"I would like to finish off a few things first."

"Yes, but you will be wasting your time."

"I am only 28."

"And I am already 26. I have things I need to get going with."

"Are you proposing to me?"

"I did that long ago, when we met, in fact."

"You said it was too early to tell."

"I have to pretend to be human sometimes."

"So you can see the future too, can you?"

"Yes, but I can see all of it. That is why I am here."

"To save the world, I suppose."

Yasemin engages me with a steady intensity, and pauses for a long time. "Actually, yes. I am your chaperone. We will save the world together. I am here to make sure that you actually want to, and have the courage to go through with it."

I have a sensation of coldness suddenly, of remoteness from the room, yet of fusion with Yasemin. I have begun to be afraid that she is not joking. Perhaps for the first time in my life I am learning fear. Yasemin is still scrutinising me with her laser-blue eyes. She is not exactly smiling at me with affection or amusement, rather with both of those—the inclusive 'or'.

✻   ✻   ✻

Mark phoned Ralph in Corporate the other day, and told him that we no longer needed him to lead a segmentation workshop because we have all that mapped out and under control already, but we will need some facilitation for workshops on scenario planning and building the brand definition for Petrol. Would he mind? Would he ever?

So here he is. The full team is assembled, there being no crisis yet today. We had a disaster yesterday when Petrovsk the Great, our premium product went into backorder just as the shelves emptied throughout the country, so we were all required to do some shouting at the source of supply. Tasha was voted the most convincing, and gets the Order of the Mars Bar and the Freedom of the Coffee Machine for today. She is still young enough and enthusiastic enough to appreciate the gesture. When Jim won it a few months ago for landing a massive catalogue coup with Dinky Drinks (they even published his home-made vodka mix recipe), his only response was "Are you trying to fucking kill me? Have I been around too long?" We explained patiently that it was an honour accorded to very few. "I thought that the death penalty had been abolished entirely, at least in this office," he retorted.

By the way, did you know that vodka can, and is, made from virtually anything (not including the rendered animal fat Mars Bars are made from)? In fact there is a war going on as we speak. The traditional bases for vodka are barley, grain and potatoes, but the big western manufacturers prefer grapes, beets and citrus fruit. We briefly considered manufacturing our vodkas from the ingredients featured in the flavours, so raspberries, blueberries etc. We thought that this might hit a chord as a truly authentic novelty—"Made from raspberries, tastes of raspberries. Only from Petrovsk." We got the raspberries all right, from the research respondents when they saw the price, raspberries being somewhat more expensive as a base ingredient than, say, sugar beet. Nonetheless, I personally still believe that there is a nice little niche out there for an outrageously priced elite vodka range for London clubs via Berry Bros & Rudd. I even designed, in my kitchen one night, an elegant aluminium tray to contain twenty-four shots of this Petrovsk Boyars range, so that Berrys could ship them off to their clients on their yachts in the Med on a daily basis. William warned me not to push my luck. By the way, have you noticed how the floors at Berry Bros & Rudd in Piccadilly slope so treacherously that everyone appears to be lurching around drunk, except the sales staff who have learnt to accommodate this peculiarity? They just walk à la Quasimodo along the flat pavement outside. There again, the old codgers who stagger into the shop from their biblical lunches are almost invariably sloshed out of their skulls anyway, so it is a kindness to provide them with a generous excuse for their unsteady gait.

We start the meeting with a discussion of which we do first, the scenario planning or the brand identity development for Petrol. Mark, Jim and Tasha are arguing that the Petrol brand definition is really urgent. Jilly and I champion the scenario planning, as a basis for the Petrol brand positioning. Eventually Ralph tosses a coin. Scenario planning wins. I could have foreseen that.

We don't do a heavy version of scenario planning, or "fantasy planning", as Jim belittles it. That would spoil the fun. Nevertheless, it takes 2-3 days. The step most people hate is writing the newspaper reports. It is my favourite bit.

We start by defining the timescale. 10 years it is. We then describe the market as it is today. Very few disagreements there, and the market of ten years ago—not many changes, except for the rise of the ladette segment that we so brilliantly exploited, and the explosion of disposable credit, and the rise of the do one IVA (Individual Voluntary Arrangement, for debts), and get one free culture. Going back ten years before looking forward ten years encourages the team to be a little more realistic as to what can happen within the blink of ten years.

Then we are encouraged to go and live in ten years' time, as Ralph introduces an intervention. Think of the most ridiculous prediction you can. Lucy suggests that the licensing laws will reduce the minimum age of drinking vodka to three, but that you won't be able to buy an aerosol room freshener until you are 21, for health reasons. Spencer thinks vodka will be given away free to old age pensioners in a desperate attempt to bump them off before they become a ruinous drain on the state's resources. Tasha, fresh from her triumph, believes that there will be Mars Bar and KitKat flavours. Jim thinks that it will become fashionable to snort it. I never get my go. The more practical takeaways we draw from this are that we should probably consider an entry into the alcopops sector to groom the youngest female drinkers to become ladettes, that there will be a massive OAP market (we are not quite sure what to do with that), and that the mid market will be cheapened by gimmicky, kitschy flavours that will ultimately undermine the price base. We aren't so sure what to do with Jim's snorting. The best we can come up with is that cocaine might be declassified as a drug in 10 years, and there might be some bundling opportunities. A distant gaze of enchantment enters Jim's eyes as he fantasises about packs of free samples piled head high (just the right height) in the office.

Ralph admonishes us to be more serious. Consider the Political, Economic, Social, Technological, Environmental and Political implications for the vodka market in 10 years. Too serious, Ralph. That particular framework is better suited to Snacks.

OK, so now it is time to become intrepid reporters from the future, describing in 200 words what the world associated with vodka will look like in 10 years. I go for a rose-tinted scenario where scientists discover that vodka contains a heretofore undiscovered ingredient that extends your life expectancy with moderate intake for up to 20 years, thus helping us crack the 50+ market. Fortunately, only Petrovsk contains this ingredient in sufficient quantities to be reliably effective, and we have the patent.

The rest of the team find my prognostication "unhelpful", which is a negative criticism banned by the rules of creative brainstorming, I remind them.

The trends—ageing population, greater disposable wealth, shortage of pure, safe products to ingest, increasing urbanisation, the threat of terrorism. We decide that is a highly favourable environment for the steady growth of the vodka market.

Now the miracle has to occur. Ralph clowns being nervous. There is no known way to reduce this mass of information down to three major, alternative scenarios. It just has to happen.

"Well, one must be a puritanical backlash against products potentially harmful to your health, with severely limited advertising, and mounting litigation (I never realised that vodka contains alcohol)", champions Jim.

"I'll buy that," I respond. "I am not sure where it came from Jim, but you may well be right."

"Just a little thought I cooked up earlier," grimaces Jim.

"Alcohol-free vodka," slips in Lucy. "I bet it will taste disgusting."

"What about vodka spreading its reach to become a base ingredient for many products, given that it is tasteless and odourless, therefore adaptable to almost anything?" Mark speculates.

"What sorts of products?"

"Preservatives, medicines, tonics, a massive range of flavoured vodkas, and so on."

"Can we build that thought bigger?" prompts Ralph. "Perhaps the major expansion of the vodka market technologically, geographically, socially, that sort of thing."

"Big vodka!"

"Russia is going to rule the world. Big oil. Big vodka . . ."

". . . . big women," adds Jilly, who is a formidable presence.

"Don't go on the diet yet, then, Jilly. Your time is almost come." Spencer may be getting rather too far into the swing of things. Jilly does not appear to wholly endorse his proposal, and the rest find something to do momentarily.

"Then there has to be the steady as you go option," Jilly suggests. "Modest, incremental market growth, no big changes in legislation, increased disposable income, new market opportunities such as the older market."

"Well, that is three," I conclude, beating Ralph to the punch. "The New Prohibition, Big Vodka, and Steady As You Go."

"Any more suggestions?" interjects Ralph.

"Yes, that we all go home. It is four o'clock," Jim recommends.

"OK. We will pause it there. Thanks, Ralph for some excellent facilitation. What is next?"

"Next, if those are the three scenarios we want to explore, we should do event strings for at least the two more adventurous ones, not to belittle your 'most likely' scenario in any way, Jilly."

"What are event strings?" Mark asks.

"Event strings are where you try to map out how the scenario will develop and when. So, as an example, and not wishing to anticipate the outcome, if we start where we are now, and we end up in the New Prohibition, or Puritanism, or whatever, what has to happen to get us there? It could be that the government will start a scare campaign against alcohol to try to contain a dramatic rise in instances of sclerosis of the liver, and that vodka is the spirit worst effected, and that will happen next year, that sort of thing."

"Thanks. I now understand."

"Thanks everybody. We continue in two weeks. Spencer, have we got the sales flash yet?"

"From the sublime to the pitifully short term," Jim admonishes me.

✳ ✳ ✳

Yasemin has agreed to come along to a branch meeting, despite being neither a Labour Party voter, nor much interested in politics in general. She says she has time on her hands, and she would like to spend it with me.

I try to discourage her. "You cannot imagine how dull they are. They are like Alcoholics Anonymous without the angst of alcohol. We mostly sit there nodding at each other in complete agreement. We have an aggravated brawl about every third week because someone has bothered to read The Sun, and is worked up about immigrants, or Muslims, or the French cheese mountain, or whatever, but that happened last week."

"Let's hope for a statistical blip, then."

This year, as for most recent years, there has been an "unseasonable" Indian summer. Yesterday the weather plummeted into autumn with cold, damp fog to greet us as we park our cars outside the local Labour Party branch office. Yasemin hangs back slightly from the door as an inhabituée, and delivers a nervous smile. "Come on in. Nobody will mind. You might liven things up."

"Well, Mr. Secretary, I see that there are strangers in the house," Walter declares, making the traditional political joke.

"Caucus politics, Walter. I always like to enter a vote with an advantage." I introduce Yasemin.

"Anyhows, welcome Yasemin." Walter marches forward with outstretched hand.

"Walter Crump," I prompt.

"I've heard lots about you, Walter," Yasemin lies.

"All of it good, I hope."

Yasemin winces. "Not all of it." Walter's smiling face falters.

I expect Yasemin to effect a recovery. She doesn't. I will have to ask her about that later. We cannot have Walter upset.

"I think I told Yasemin about our death penalty discussion a few weeks ago. Yasemin is violently opposed to the death penalty."

Walter is not entirely in a forgiving mood. "Each to her own."

"I was a death watch volunteer in the States for two years. Pick up a random black person on the street, charge him with a heinous crime, torture him for fifteen years, move him to the holding cell, execute him. I had twenty of those in two years. It is not funny, I promise you."

"No, I can understand that would be very traumatic," Walter concedes, warming slightly. "Did you get anyone off?"

"No, just a longer wait to die."

Walter shakes his head in sympathy. "Still . . . ."

"Oh yes," declares Yasemin, "they are certainly that."

Walters expression returns to shock. How would I cope with her as a Minister's wife? She doesn't let up. I am beginning to take my destiny seriously.

Marion struggles through the door with her ruffled umbrella, immediately followed by Mike. "Evening all."

"Yasemin," I say, displaying Yasemin to them with the palm of my hand. As she is clearly not European, I do not need to add her family name, Kiram, although it could introduce an interesting, if diverting, discussion point that Yasemin is not allowed, by law, to use her Kurdish family name in Turkey.

"Good to meet you, Yasemin. Welcome to our happy band."

"Do you plan to be a regular?" Marion enquires. Walter is listening carefully.

"No, I don't think so, I am afraid. I invited myself along to get an insight into a different aspect of Adam, that is all. I hope I am not disturbing you. I can go if you like, now that I have met a few of you, and have a feel for the place."

"No, no, no" booms Mike. "Stay by all means. Especially if you can get Adam to shut up about fundraising. I didn't join the Labour Party purely to walk around rattling a collection tin in Reading on a Saturday morning, beaten into fourteenth place by the jazz band."

"Oh, I don't mind collecting for you," Yasemin volunteers. "I enjoy chatting to people. I couldn't tell them much about Labour Party policy, though."

"In that case, you will be very popular. Nobody wants to know anyway." Mike turns to me. "You don't know any more Yasemins do you? A few more like her would come in handy."

"I think I'll stick to the one,"

"A life-preserving choice," Yasemin adds.

I am about to say that I thought that Yasemin did not believe in exclusivity, when I realise how inappropriate that would be. Yasemin smiles as if she has heard me anyway.

"OK, to order," I commence. "Here is the agenda. Last time we discussed . . . ."

I have to stick rigorously to the agenda. Otherwise I am instantly coshed with a point of order. We have a quaint level of routine formality in the local branches of the progressive party. Depart from it, and a bitchy remark will soon appear in the middle pages of the Reading Evening Post.

Yasemin manages to remain by all appearances lively and fascinated throughout. I am not sure she has won over Walter again, though.

❀　　❀　　❀

Chapter 5

John has called round to my workaday three-bedroom home in St. John's Road.

People ask me why I, as a single person have three bedrooms. I reply that to have two bedrooms is sad (you are always waiting for a friend to want to stay with you), and one bedroom is worse. So I have three bedrooms kitted out as if at least two people are living here, which, at this precise second is more or less true. For the moment, Yasemin is more often here than out there. I am beginning to envisage it; Yasemin and I in the master bedroom, a child in the second bedroom, and all his favourite toys in the third. How conventional is that? Is this what I am reduced to, the common (statistically speaking) aspirations of about 20 million people out there in the UK alone. I am glad that IKEA is a long, long way away from us. Nonetheless, I know now that I am doomed to their chaotic collection point in the Wimbledon store one day.

John was made redundant five months ago from an industrial distribution company, which is where I first met him, marketing industrial products which he bought. In elapsed time, I have known him a few years. He is one of my best mates. In billable time, I have known him a few weeks. Come to think of it, most of my friends are like that. I would even bet that if a married man were to calculate his relationship with his wife into billable hours, he would have talked to her, in total, for 35 minutes on Monday, 14 minutes on Sunday (she spent most of her time talking to the female half of the couple), a whole hour on Saturday, because they were in the car together, and a mere 11 minutes on Friday.

In compressed hours, our partners are absolutely right. We never talk.

Yasemin and I do not say much either. With Yasemin, communication is all about the other senses—touch, smell, sight, sound, silence. She will come up to me gently and hold me for several minutes, sniffing my skin, running her lips against mine, smiling, but not speaking. I am getting used to living this trappist life to the point that I am not sure that I could ever go back to the wasteland of practical conversation again.

"Where's the cheese?"

"Where you put it."

"Where's that?"

"How should I know?"

Those are the sorts of conversations I used to have with previous girlfriends. Now, steeped in silence, I simply cannot be as irritating.

John is railing about his PPI. "They are total bastards!"

As he has not actually told me he is referring to his PPI, I am forced to ask "Who's that then?"

"Insurance companies."

"Well, yeah. I know that. I used to work for one."

"They just rip you off."

"Most of the time, anyway."

"They haven't the slightest intention of paying out. When I signed up, all they said was that if I was made compulsorily redundant, they would pay my loan premium for a year . . . ."

"Is it a big loan?"

"£23,000 still outstanding."

"Ow!"

". . . . then, when you have been made compulsorily redundant, it is suddenly 'You need an ABI1', 'Have you ever left the country?'."

"What's an ABI1?"

"It's a form you can only get if you apply for a Job Seeker's Allowance."

"Sounds reasonable. You'll want one of those anyway, won't you?"

"My pay-off takes me above £16,000 in savings, so I am not eligible for Job Seekers Allowance, and the insurance company won't pay out."

"You had better get spending, then."

"No, they ask you all about that too. And if you go abroad for a day, you have to start again. I don't think they understand the concept of personal environments."

"Being . . . . ?"

"That you need your environment to support you in order to achieve your goals. So, if you are looking for a job, you should hang out with people who have jobs, and avoid those who haven't. You should celebrate life, and keep yourself positive, rather than mope around feeling unemployed. You should go out and achieve things. You should travel. You shouldn't just sit there waiting to sign on every two weeks, or go into a Job Centre where all the down and outs hang out. God, it's depressing down there. They are trying to be all cheery and helpful, but within two minutes you are into queues, rules, procedures, second, third, fourth interviews, and general bureaucracy."

"Don't worry, John. Something will turn up. You are sitting here in your personal environment with a guy who still has a job. How lucky for you is that? It's in the bag."

"Oh, I'll get a job eventually, I am sure. It is not as if I am forty, or anything. Then it would be a lost cause. Hi, Yasemin."

"Hi, John."

"We are just discussing John's next job."

"You've got a job then, John, have you? That's great news! What is it?"

"No, not yet, Yasemin."

"Oh." Yasemin shoots a baffled look at me.

"Adam is merely trying to provide me with a supportive environment so that I'll walk straight out of this door into a £100,000 a year job."

"I'll have one of those."

"What do you do, Yasemin?"

"Nothing. I am looking, just like you."

"Perhaps we can get together and read the jobs sections over a cup of coffee, then."

"Yeah, sure. When do you want to meet up?"

"Hang on, hang on, hang on," I interject. "This isn't an 'excuse me' relationship."

Yasemin studies me hard. "Yes, Adam, it is."

"I'm not comfortable with this."

"And I am not comfortable with your exclusivity. Why shouldn't I meet up with a friend of yours to discuss jobs? What could be wrong with that?"

John has turned sheepish. "Sorry, guys, I didn't want to cause any trouble here."

"Of course you don't, John. It is Adam simply being pathetic. And he knows the rules between us. I do what I like. Savve?"

"Oh, OK then. I'm sorry. I'm a conventional guy. I haven't expected my best mates to start dating my girlfriends until this moment. Now that I re-consider my prejudices, I agree that they are ridiculous."

"They are," Yasemin confirms emphatically.

"Off you go then. Send me a postcard."

Yasemin stands up. "Give me a call whenever, and we'll meet up. OK?"

"OK," John replies, unsure of how hot the water is that he has found himself in, and of whether I plan to turn up the heat.

Yasemin turns on me. "Adam, I am very disappointed in you." She walks out of the room, and maybe out of my life. I have obviously committed a major transgression which I had better not repeat, should Yasemin allow me a second chance.

John opens his palms bare. "I'm really sorry, mate. I thought you two were cool. If I had guessed my offer would cause a fight, I would never have made it. Sorry."

"That's all right, John. It is something Yasemin and I are going to have to sort out between us."

Not so easy. I do not see or talk to Yasemin again for eight days. She disappears off my map. And as I haven't met any of her friends yet, and she doesn't work, there is no-one I can ask.

Sales are down. Spencer phoned me at 06:30 this morning from the office where he had just completed the analysis. I might want to get in quick and summon a council of war before William demands an explanation as soon as he gets into the office at 09:00.

This year, we are committed to a 10% sales growth, and a 12.5% contribution income growth (the 5% sales growth I negotiated with William a few weeks ago is for next year). Currently, from the off of the Christmas season in early October, we are down 4% on last year.

I feel the air of freedom being sucked from the room around me. The corporate monster is preparing to asphyxiate me. From 330% growth over the last two years to -4%. I have obviously got too cocky, with my smug, arrogant ways. I need an almighty kick up the arse. This makes finding another job imperative, before the February post-mortem exposes my commercial inadequacy.

I arrive at my desk at 07:45 and grab Spencer. "Any thoughts, Spencer?"

"Not really, Adam. The market is not really my territory. It is happening in the heart of the product range. Premium sales are holding up. Tescos, Sainsbury's and ASDA are all down, especially Tescos. The off-licences overall are up 3.6%. I would guess it is a competition thing, shaving margin off us, rather than consumers as a whole turning their backs on us. You tell me. You are the expert."

14% below target. That is one hell of a shaving. I cannot go into William declaring that we are the victims of some excellent competitive marketing, and that we should really applaud them, like the sporting people we are, for their cunning, if limited, comeback.

There is always a tension in brand marketing between branding and marketing. Branding works on a 5-20 years horizon, building underlying equity and momentum for a generation. Marketing works in months, and sometimes weeks. The problem is that some of the things you do for marketing, to get sales brought forward to meet your targets, are believed to damage the longer term value of your brand to the consumer. At least, that is the theory. If you do some quick fix, like money-off vouchers (Smirnoff), or bundling together a bottle of vodka with a Father Christmas teddy bear (Vladivar), or 10% off your next purchase (Absolut) etc., the belief is that you discount your brand for years to come. The equal and opposite view is that if they bought you last time, there are more likely to buy you next time too, and that consumers know to treat each buying occasion on its merits. With everyone discounting everything nowadays, and with shops offering permanent sales, no-one believes any more that promotions equate to desperation, except perhaps your granny, who is way outside our target market. Statistics show a downwards spiral in price in real terms for many established commodities, and ours is no exception. While, indubitably, some of this price erosion can be blamed on price promotions, you also have to give due weight to other factors, such as increased global competition, a reserve vodka lake which is becoming a sea, retail buyer pressure, and smarter consumers who are fully aware that any brand of vodka is pretty much the same as any other. They'll pay a few pence more for the brand they have the greatest affinity to, and that is it. Draw up your price curves and start calculating how much more you will sell if you reduce the price by ten pence below your reference competitor, and how much less you will sell if you charge significantly more.

However, as market leader, we are in a different position. We could start an all-out price war. All the other brands peg their prices to ours. It is a sort of like the automatic tracking system you get with shares. If we discount by ten pence, so do they. If we discount by 10%, so do they. They do not have the brand credentials to sell at a premium to us. Whatever we do is reciprocated. If we keep cutting our prices, so will they. So, as market leaders, we need to find another way.

Mark comes into the office, swiftly followed by Jilly. We have a quorum.

"Meeting everyone!", I announce.

"Meeting? Now?"

"I'll buy you coffee."

"That incentive is as old and stale as the coffee itself, Adam."

"OK, I'll buy you lunch,"

"Now we're talking. Business must be good."

I get Spencer to explain the stats as we know them. Jim joins us. "Well, they aren't making much of a dent given that they are promoting and we are not. I would say that we are holding up reasonably well."

"The problem, Jim, is our 10% growth target."

"Yeah, but you should never have agreed to that, Adam. It was always going to be a bit iffy."

"Well, Jim, we are stuck with it. Now, how do we meet it?"

"Can we come up with a value-raising promotion? Do some deal with Police glasses, or something?"

Jim looks up at Mark, and dismissively turns away again. "Not enough time," he grunts over his shoulder.

"I know that you are not going to like this, Adam, but we could join the crowd and discount too."

"You are right, Jilly. I am not."

"08:45, and William will have seen the stats by 09:00," Spencer observes. "We still have fifteen minutes and thirty seconds either to think up a great campaign or to escape from the building."

"I can do both in one," I declare. "Good morning, Tasha."

"Good morning, Adam. Good morning, everybody. Have I missed something?"

"Tasha, could you please inform MDH that Jim, Mark, you and I will be at their offices in two hours, and that we need to get a new ad out in two weeks? OK?"

"I can try."

"If they sound at all doubtful, tell them that I have instructed you to call a couple of other agencies as well. First come, first served."

"Wow!"

Yes, it is one of those moments."

"And that gets us out of the building too?" laughs Jim, admiringly.

"You bet. We are leaving now. Tasha, you follow on when you can. I think we'll use the fire escape. Spencer, when William asks, tell him that we are taking immediate and decisive remedial action."

Spencer grimaces. "That won't be my pleasure but, there again, in accountancy, what is?"

"You didn't become an accountant for the fun then, Spencer?"

"Simply for the money, Jim. I get my kicks watching Sonic the Hedgehog with my two boys."

"OK, guys, off we go. Spencer, we'll miss you."

"You had better hurry. William is marching up the corridor now."

❀   ❀   ❀

Yasemin clicks the door open. "Hi!"

"Yasemin! Where have you been?"

"Doing stuff."

"Doing what stuff?"

She smiles sweetly at me.

I run up to her and hug her. "I am so pleased to see you. You really must have been mad at me!"

She pushes me back to inspect me. "Mad? No, I wasn't mad. I had things to do."

"Why didn't you say so?"

"Sorry, Adam. They were really important things. I had to concentrate on them. They were life or death situations."

"That's dramatic. Did you save them?"

"Yes, I saved them, one way or another."

"How did you save them?"

"Adam, I think that you are prying. It is not the time to tell you. I promise that the time will come, and then you will know everything. For the moment, it is best that you do not know. It would distract you, and stop you achieving your own goals, and that would be really serious, not only for you."

I look at her hard. She returns my stare unflinchingly. "In that case, I had better get you some coffee."

"That would be nice."

"Pain au chocolat?"

"Please." She raises her arms. "It is so good to be home."

I decide that work can wait a couple of hours. I phone up the office to say that I will be working from home this morning, and will be in this afternoon. To be honest, there is not a lot for me to do there until the agency presents the new ad storyboard to us tomorrow. I already know the basics. The ad will have the girl on a bar stool (and yes, the same girl is available for a shoot next week) dressed up as Father Christmas, naked beneath the red fur-lined coat. Simple and direct. It will save our bacon. Mark has been talking to the major retail chains to inform them that we are launching a new ad within two weeks, and most of them have agreed to give us extra facings.

You see, how retail marketing really works is that you spend several million pounds advertising to about ten people—the buyers from the major retail chains. They believe that your ad will generate more demand for your product, so they allocate you extra facings. The punters come into the shop with a repertoire from which to choose—Petrovsk, Absolut, Smirnoff, Vladivar, and maybe some niche ones that they rather fancy as an outside bet. They see all the niche ones huddled together in the corner for warmth, some significant presence from the other major brands with their promotions and, in pride of place, with the largest number of facings, us, introduced by a cardboard cut-out girl naked except for a Father Christmas coat. They have seen the advertising, the shop is clearly giving us preferential treatment over the other brands, so they buy us. Obviously not in every case, but that is the mass psychology; more facings lead to more sales.

Yasemin has climbed into bed. Spookily, given that I have told her nothing about the new ad, she is wearing nothing but a mock-fur coat and a welcoming smile. Our ad will certainly work, my body is telling me. I strip off and leap in.

"I wish I could put my finger on you, Yasemin."

"Adam, I think you are doing."

"I am trying so hard to understand you."

"That is a very good thing in a man, but it is imperative for the woman that he never finds out."

"Finds out what?"

"Finds out what he thinks he doesn't know."

"In your case, I know full well that I know virtually nothing. You were born in Kurdistan, you say, a country that does not exist officially . . . ."

Yasemin's eyes flash. "It most certainly exists. It is a body divided into three, but it is still a body."

"You say you have five brothers and two sisters, and that you are the youngest."

"True."

"And they are all in Turkey, Iraq and Iran."

"Back in Kurdistan, yes."

"I have never met your friends."

"Most of my friends are over there too. I have not really made friends here. There are plenty of people I like, but they are not my friends."

"With your looks, that amazes me."

"That is how it is."

"You don't tell me about previous boyfriends . . . ."

"You really want to learn about them? They have nothing to do with us."

"And you keep disappearing and reappearing without explanation."

"Yes, that's it. That's me."

"And this body does not belong to me." I stroke it gently.

"It does not belong to me, either. How could I therefore give it to you?"

"Somebody must own it."

"The universe owns it, Adam. Why shoot smaller than that? Anyway, what have you been up to?"

"The usual. Gazing ten years into the future as part of a long-term planning exercise, and rushing about like crazed lunatics to boost our sales next month."

"Long-term planning? Ten years? That's impressive."

"Well, it is probably too far out, but it gives the team permission to be more creative."

"So, long-term in your business world is nearer to five years, then?"

"At the moment, it could be February. Even a week is a long time during the pre-Christmas season. Still, in ten years' time, it will be infinitely worse. We are all going to end up as day-traders hunched over screens, scrutinising rows of numbers telling us what we are selling by the minute in each store, and inviting us to change the electronic pricing on the shelf instantaneously, or to get that ad up on the plasma screens in the main aisle by lunchtime, or to fire in a promotion. In ten years' time, with all the technology that is being developed at the moment, marketing is going to get punishingly fast."

"Fascinating."

"I bet you are not the least bit fascinated. I must bore you silly, talking about the irrelevant universe of vodka in such tedious detail."

"It captivates you. I appreciate it for that. As long as you don't ask me any questions to test if I have been listening. Now, should I take my coat off, or should I leave it on?"

❋　　❋　　❋

There are few things I like less than applying for jobs, although the build up to this one has been good. Yasemin has pampered me. She served me afternoon tea in bed (I took another day off). She chose all my clothes and got them ready for me. She gave me a big encouraging, loving kiss as we left the house to get into my company BMW 525xi.

At least this application is for something more significant than to be the branding supremo for some multinational conglomerate's chocolate countline range, like the interview I had last week. This one is the vote to decide whether I should be endorsed as a potential Labour Councillor for Reading Council. My local branch colleagues tell me that I should walk it. People with my communications expertise are very much favoured in this new age of Labour. It will be a killer time-wise if I get the endorsement yet, if I want to be an MP in a few years' time, this move is critical. I must also start networking the national Labour Party. I'll see if our Reading Central MP, Joy Mapling, can introduce me to some people. "Top down and bottom up", that is the rule of politics. "Push and pull", that is the rule of brand marketing. Go at it from as many angles as there are. Yasemin has set me a timetable: to be an MP within the next 5 years, to be a Minister by the age of 40, and to be PM by 50. She says that if I go for it, I will get it. Oh, and give up vodka, and work instead for a not-for-profit organisation. Super-smart, super-caring, committed socialist and professional business man. That will get me to the top.

I have not experienced a not-for-profit interview yet, but the chocolate one last week was dire. They were so breathtakingly risk-averse. It was my second interview. I faced a panel of five judges to explain every dot and comma of my experience. The thing that worried them was that I had not worked in "chocolate" before. Once upon a time, you could have a degree in Philosophy, bum around the world, and still land a marketing job in a leading FMCG company. Now, you not only have to persuade the selection committee that you have the skills, the drive, and the ambition of a Jack Welsh or a Rupert Murdoch, but you must also have been conspicuously immersed in the relevant industry for a lifetime (at the age of 28). All marketing jobs, and maybe all other jobs besides, are deserving only of super-heroes. In reality, they are jobs like any other, yet both sides have to play the game. They tell you how extraordinarily engrossing the job is, and how it offers you a route to the stars. In return, you inform them that you are the most talented individual they will ever meet. Bullshit meets bullshit, but we all still get sucked into it just the same.

This crew wanted a "chocolate man" through and through, or perhaps a chocolate bar with high-level brand management credentials. It was obvious which way things were heading by the increasingly desperate angles they were exploring in an attempt to anoint me with at least a sliver of chocolate marketing.

Halfway through, I got up and thanked them for their time, announcing that I would not be wasting any more of it. They looked surprised. I was disrupting their due process.

Yasemin is on my right arm as we enter the Labour Party offices where the votes are being counted. Not so long ago, marching into a room clutching an exotic dusky maiden would have got you expelled from the list of potential Labour candidates faster than you could say "Joe Gormley". The socialist members liked their champions to be sensibly ballasted by old trouts with bosoms like armchairs, working class accents, down-to-earth decency and no ambition to interfere with the male process of running the party. Nowadays, the party has run up quotas to encourage non-white, non-male candidates, and is delighted if they happen to be stunningly beautiful and naturally telegenic. Yasemin should be the candidate, not me, but having Yasemin, and all she symbolises, at my side is the next best thing.

Yasemin is in deep conversation with Hilary somebody-or-other I have seen once or twice. She is one of the party faithful who go around stuffing letter boxes with our pointless, if earnest, leaflets, ensure that the reluctant and downright dubious electors get down to the polling station to vote for you, and generally arrange things.

Yasemin has a gentle, seductive demeanour which encourages everyone to spill out everything to her. Usually, this is a big plus for me. People whom I need to influence are enchanted by her, and invite us out to learn more about her.

I have not been listening to their conversation particularly as I have been discussing the finer points of the presence of gypsies in the Reading area with Janet Scope, but I suddenly hear Yasemin exclaim "Oh my God, you have? How dreadful for you. To have to kill a living creature. You must feel terrible about it."

"I would guess that Hilary has just told your young lady about her planned abortion of a few weeks ago. She has told everybody else."

Hilary turns on Yasemin. "You prig!"

Yasemin is standing there silently, slightly whiter than usual, whether in shock or anger I am not sure.

"I am totally horrified that they let people with your views anywhere near a Labour Party office. If you want to evangelise your pro-lifer principles, you should bugger off to the Tories. Who are you to judge me?" There may have been a very non-PC hint in there that she, Hilary, is a middle-class, white and British, and that Yasemin is some sort of cultural throwback from one of the morally murkier parts of the Middle East.

"I wasn't judging you," Yasemin ripostes in a level tone. "I was empathising with you. Abortions are traumatic. I was hoping to help you."

"They are not as traumatic as unwanted babies!"

"You never wanted the baby?"

"No, I bloody didn't."

The whole room is listening spellbound. Normally, Geoff, the head of the selection committee, or Joy, the MP, would intervene, but instead they stand there twirling plastic coffee cups. I do not think to move either.

"I suppose," Hilary challenges Yasemin, "that you will tell me next that abortions are against the will of God, or Allah, or whatever." The insinuation is surfacing.

Yasemin stands her ground with total serenity. "Well, yes, of course they are. All life is sacred. Not even God takes it away."

"You could have fooled me. How comes we all die, then?"

"Because it is our time."

"God doesn't clasp us to his bosom then, young and old?"

"Yes, he does, but that is after you have died."

"So, will God be clasping me to his bosom as a common murderer, in your elevated opinion? Shall I be forgiven, or shall I be one of the damned, condemned to hell fire and brimstone."

"God forgives everyone."

"So, you know this God personally, do you, Jasemine, or whatever your name is?"

"Yes."

Hilary turns fiercely sarcastic, and still no-one moves. Yasemin remains composed and unflinching. "And I suppose He is a man, with views like that."

"No."

"A woman then, aspiring to be a man?"

"No."

"What is He then?"

"A force for life and for good. He is absolute energy, absolute intelligence."

"And I suppose He doesn't believe in short skirts either. He wants us all gliding around in burkas."

"God invented the body. I don't think he invented the burka."

"So, to recap, you are on intimate terms with God . . . ."

"We are all on intimate terms with God, whether we choose to be or not. You are on intimate terms with God . . . ."

"Not me. I am an atheist."

"It makes no difference."

"Anyway, we are getting side-tracked. You say you are on intimate terms with God, and God abhors abortions, and the taking of any life, in fact. However, He doesn't object to us all prancing around stark naked as much as we like. Is that a fair resumé?"

"Yes, that is fair."

"Yasemine, or whoever you are, you are blooming barmy, and a walking liability to your young man here, I might add. The Labour Party doesn't take kindly to raving religious nutters with delusions of intimacy with God."

"In my experience," Yasemin proclaims with surprising authority given the intensity of onslaught on her, "it never does any harm to have God on your side. Even your Labour Party would be wise not to mock him entirely, although, being a great God, he will let it pass with his usual compassion."

Hilary hunches her hands onto her hips, and appeals to the room. "Should this woman get out of here, or will it be me?"

Finally, I step forward, and motion Hilary towards the door, being careful not to touch her. "Hilary, I am afraid that it is you. People are entitled to whatever opinions they wish to hold around here, whether you approve of them or not."

"Well, that's it," huffs Hilary, folding her coat over her arm. "I wish you well in your short political career, Adam, and don't expect any help from me other than to shorten it further. If I were you, I would ditch that girl sharpish. She is a menace."

"She is an angel," I reply, hugging Yasemin at the waist in a gesture of solidarity.

Hilary slams the door.

Yasemin shakes her head. "She is a soul in great pain. She thinks that she has come to terms with what she has done, but she hasn't. I wish I could help her out of her torment."

"I don't think she is listening, Yasemin," I admonish. "Let her be."

"Of course." Yasemin smiles beatifically at the room. "Sorry about that. Should I go too?"

Joy Mapling is the first to respond. "No, you can stay young woman. We need a few people around here with forthright opinions, even if they are somewhat unexpected. Are you any good at stuffing letter boxes with leaflets? I think we have a vacancy."

The room laughs uneasily, then gradually returns to its business of finalising the counting of the votes.

❋   ❋   ❋

I am past the post. I have the official go-ahead to stand as a Labour candidate for Reading Council. Until now, I have not really thought about it, but I suddenly find myself feeling rather chuffed.

Yasemin reaches up to kiss me on the lips. "Well done, Adam. You are on your way."

"Was God on my side?"

"He definitely was." She grins.

"Yasemin, you are very convincing as an angel. Can you reassure me that you are not, and that you are only a normal human being with secretive and inspirational ways?"

"No, Adam. I am afraid that I really am an angel." She grins again.

I give her an enormous bear-hug. "You are teasing me."

"If that is what you wish to believe."

I frown in mock perplexion. "I thought that all angels were male."

"We aren't anything. We are hermaphrodite. It is just that in ancient times men couldn't believe that anything as important as delivering God's messages and doing God's will could be entrusted to anyone other than a man."

I squeeze her breasts gently under her dress. "You seem pretty feminine to me."

"We are what we want to be. We are mission-specific. Now, Councillor, let's get home. Why are people so uncomfortable discussing God in public places? What has become of the world?"

"It causes too much trouble." I turn up the air conditioning to clear the windows of condensation, blowing warm air into our faces. With the BMW, you don't even get dust. "Everyone evokes God to be on their side. Mind you, you are one of the first I have met to claim that you actually know him. People normally draw the line at claiming to know what he thinks."

"That is a lot further than I would go. I cannot imagine knowing God's mind. That is ridiculous."

"How do you know him?"

"Because I am an angel."

"Be serious, Yasemin."

"I am being serious, and honest, and truthful. You will realise it one day, when the thought stops freaking you out."

"OK, I'll leave you to your fantasy, then. Please don't tell the press."

"Of course I shall tell the press. It is part of my mission."

"Oh my God," I sigh wearily. "Does he mind blasphemy, by the way? Taking his name in vain?"

"Not at all. Everyone's at it. Besides, you have to stop assuming that He is some sort of crazed dictator, like Joseph Stalin or Mao Tse Tung. He is God. He is all-loving and all-forgiving. He doesn't take offence, and he doesn't fire off thunderbolts. What would be the point of a God who behaved as badly as Adolf Hitler, or even as you?"

"Thanks for putting Adolf and me in the same breath."

"I mean it. Rulers have created God in their own image, as a celestial super-ruler who empowers rulers on earth to behave as they wish, as the Lord's anointed. The divinity of kings. God is not like that at all. He is everything. He is love, and power, and comfort. Don't expect him to become vengeful, or angry, or even disappointed. He is all-knowing, and all-wise, and all-loving. Trust Him. He needs you, and you need Him."

"Yasemin, you frighten me. I fear that I may be in the presence of a religious fanatic straight out of al-Qa'eda, or something."

"Al-Qa'eda kills people. That is not a true religion. There is no righteousness in killing, only shame."

"I am glad that is settled then. And I am delighted to hear the news that God loves a naked body."

"He does. He is very controversial, you know." Yasemin winks.

✳   ✳   ✳

I am dreaming. At least, I think I am dreaming. I am bathed in an intensely beautiful glow of light. It is whirling in front of me like a tornado. I am in the eye of the storm, it is calm, except the flapping of wings around me, wafting cool, refreshing air into my face. There is no dust here either, I am thinking.

I am still, quiet in the face of the light, which has a presence which I cannot clearly define. It is a gentle presence, all-powerful.

"Come, Adam," calls a mellifluous, echoing voice. "It is time. Come to me. Surrender up this life. You have done your duty. You have done everything expected of you. We are most grateful."

"So why am I so hated?" I demand, angry, petulant.

"They do not understand my will, as you have done. They know not what they do."

"Did I have to end up so reviled, so despised, damned for eternity, a by-word for all that is treacherous and loathsome?"

"Yes, it was your path, and you stuck to it. Thank you."

"Couldn't I have been loved instead?"

"You are loved, Adam."

"But not by the world."

"Not by your world. Yet everyone dies, and then they will understand. It is only a matter of time."

"But why was I singled out to be a Judas?"

"Someone had to betray me, otherwise the lesson could not have been learnt. The earth had to be saved. You have behaved with great courage and great honour. You are much loved. Now, come to me, and cease resisting. It is your time."

The wings flap louder, almost threateningly, as if to blow me into the next world. The light sucks me toward it in a siren's beckoning. I can still choose to live, yet it will be more complete to die. It is my time.

I release my body into the miasma. I am floating, floating, reeled in.

I wake with a start, perspiration dripping from me. I look down at Yasemin, breathing gently. She looks up at me.

"If you dream you are dead, are you dead?"

"Are you dead?"

"I don't think so."

"Then you may have to wait a while. A lifetime, in fact. Back to sleep."

"I don't want to experience another dream like that." I wipe my forehead. Sweat has infiltrated my eye-brows and the tips of my eye-lashes.

"It wasn't a dream. It was a premonition. It won't be repeated until it becomes a reality. It wasn't so bad, was it?"

"It was horrific." I stare at Yasemin. "What will I have to do to become so hated? How will I betray God?"

"You should ask a different question. How does he have so much trust in you that he tells you so much now? That is extraordinary. Adam, I love you."

We hug tight, a refuge from a permeating feeling of desolation on my part.

"Now sleep, Adam. All will be well. All will be as it should be. Be brave. Be true."

Chapter 6

It is time to be true to Petrol, the brand. It is literally a defining moment. The team is all assembled to flesh it out.

The new ad for Petrovsk went out last night. We had a party to celebrate, just us, no partners. We went to L'Ortolan and blew a piece of our anticipated profit growth. We scrutinised each others' plates, debated them, mocked them reverentially, and grandiosely selected a different premier cru label wine with every course. It was too posh an event for New World wines and, after all, we were celebrating big brands.

The waiter brought us a vodka-based apéritif which he explained in respectful, fastidious detail. All we wanted to discover was which brand of vodka he had used. It turned out to be Petrovsk Premier. We held up our glasses in a salute. "Busman's holiday," we declared. The waiter looked puzzled, hovered, smiled and left.

"What's that in French, then, Jim?" I asked.

"I don't think it translates," he replied. "Not into anything short and pithy, anyway."

"Your good health, everyone," I toasted. "Long live the team bus."

I am now referred to as "the Councillor", although "The Ad Part 2" would do. Sales have accelerated like a BMW already running at 110 mph—smoothly, decisively. We are back on our roll. Corporate knives have been sheathed for the moment. When I asked him for the budget to fund the production of the new ad (we already have the slots), William simply said "If you take the money, you had better deliver. OK?"

We are ready to design the new leviathan, Petrol, king of the petrol stations. Hallelujah!

Ralph from Corporate, is back facilitating. "Morning, Ralph," we all cry gleefully.

"You lot are a rowdy bunch this morning. Everything going well then, is it?"

"Perfectly," pronounces Jilly triumphantly. "Couldn't be better."

"So you are all set up to define the new world-beater."

"We surely are."

"Okey-dokey. Usual rules. £5 penalties for interruptions; maximum referring."

"You have been rehearsing that, haven't you, Ralph?"

"£5 pounds to my Christmas benevolent fund for taking the mick."

"You didn't mention that rule, Ralph" protests a mockingly aggrieved Jim.

"Didn't I mention that I, too, used to work in insurance? It's all in the small print. Sorry. All right, once again, let's start. What are the hard, pencil-sell benefits of Petrol?"

"Over to Tasha and Mark . . . ." I steer.

"OK, Tasha and Mark, what is your plan?"

"We see Petrol as being marginally cheaper than Petrovsk, on a par with the leading competitors. It has brasher, fruitier flavours, reminding people in their mid-twenties that they are still young and alive."

"Unless they are really good customers," sniggers Spencer.

"That is an emotional benefit," declares Ralph, second to the punch. "Eternal youth, or at least delayed middle-age."

"Why are the flavours fruitier?" I ask.

"Because it is the only place to go. Flavours can get darker or fruitier. We see Petrol as a brand that sings off the shelf, bright imagery, clean lines, wholesome, young, tasty."

"Enough about you, Tasha," Jim breaks in.

"Actually, that was Mark" counters Tasha.

"Ohhhhh. Really?"

Mark and Tasha blush together.

Ralph moves us on. "What other hard benefits?"

"Good margins for the retailers. Product flying off the shelves. Non-supermarket exclusive."

"How can we keep it out of supermarkets? What about the supermarkets that own or franchise forecourt shops?"

"Can't we simply say that it is not available to supermarkets?"

"a. the supermarkets will crucify you, and b. it is illegal."

"What about cutting the margin to supermarkets?"

"Ditto."

"We can always cap the discount to the level of sales of a big forecourt retailer," Spencer suggests. "That's legal. It will make it less attractive to the supermarkets, and keep the gross margin up for us."

"Yeah, we can do that, but it is only a question of time."

"That's enough on hard benefits," Ralph cuts in. "We only need a few ideas as a bridge to the rest of the definition. What about soft benefits?"

"Eternal youth, fun, fizz, permission to celebrate."

"Any other thoughts?"

"Let's follow Mark and Tasha," I suggest.

"Taste, dress, appearance, symbolism?"

"Colourful, primary colours, perhaps Toulouse-Lautrec, Parisian . . . ."

"A French vodka. There's something!"

"Well, the Russian court did speak French, didn't it?" Spencer observes.

"Any mock-ups?" I ask.

"Funny you should mention them, Adam," replies Mark, teetering with excitement. We have had Blane, Peters design a few concepts for us. What do you think?"

Mark and Tasha stand up, and start to unroll some visualisation posters. Tasha takes the lead. "We have Toulouse-Lautrec over here . . . ."

There is an approving hum.

Tasha pins the next poster to the wall. "Renoir . . . ."

"Don't think so," Jim comments decisively. "Pretty-pretty. No balls."

Ralph holds up his hand. "Another £5 penalty, Jim. No pre-emptive strikes. You get to vote later."

"Mondrian . . . ."

"That's certainly clean."

"Picasso . . . ."

"How much money do you have for the artwork?"

"It's not a real Picasso; only in his style."

"And finally, Modigliani . . . ."

"Italian vodka. Even better."

"Looks good, though, doesn't it?" Mark prompts.

"I am not saying a word," says Jim, holding up both hands. "My pay packet has suffered enough."

"Before we vote, what does everyone think? Do we have enough to go with, or does anyone have any other ideas?"

"What about Chagall?" Lucy suggests.

"I don't know much about Chagall," I reply.

"Sophisticated, colourful, a bit off the wall. It would be a breath of fresh air, and still Russian. Spencer, if you could fire up the projector, I'll show you what I mean."

Mark and Tasha are looking uncertain, defensive.

"Mark, Tasha," I declare, "you have been doing an excellent job, and you are sparking off even more ideas. Great."

They remain watchful, but their expressions change when Lucy brings up the Chagall pictures from the Internet.

"I see what you mean," Tasha concedes. "That would be neat."

"I can see that "Adam and Eve" on a bottle. We could make the bottle like a tree."

"Gaudi?"

"Now you have lost me again."

"Lucy, could you get up some Gaudi?"

"Label by Chagall. Bottle by Gaudi. Wow! What a concept!" Jim's eyes are actually lighting up.

"That's it. Print." I order. "Tasha, Mark, can you get the designers going on that idea?"

"What about a vote?" Ralph asks.

I look around the room. "I think we are all decided, aren't we?"

Everyone assents.

"Right, Ralph, values."

"So what values will Petrol have?" inquires Ralph of the team, recovering.

"This is always a killer for us, isn't it?" observes Jilly. "What values can a vodka have?"

"Purity, fun, celebration . . . ."

"Those are the same as the emotional benefits."

"Purity is new."

"Purity is generic. It comes with the word vodka."

"It doesn't mean we can't own it."

"Yeah, yeah," groans Jim. "I think we have been through this loop a million times."

"Passion?" proposes Lucy.

"Passion from a lawyer?" Jim queries. "What do you think, Spencer?"

"Yeah, I like passion."

"There you are then, an accountant and a lawyer united in passion. Can you imagine it?"

"What does passion look like?" Ralph challenges, pleased to get back into the game.

"Well, Ralph . . . ."

"Ralph raises a very important question," I interject. "How would passion go with vodka?"

"Chagall is passionate. Gaudi is passionate. It would come off the artwork."

"I like passion intuitively," I comment, "but I don't quite know what to do with it. Mark, Tasha, perhaps you could work up some passion while you are at it."

I grin maliciously. They blush yet again.

"Oooooooh!" coos the room.

"Is that it for values?" asks Ralph.

"For the time-being."

"Personality? If Petrol were an animal, what animal would it be?"

"A tiger."

"A lynx."

"An eagle."

"A hippopotamus."

"A hippopotamus?"

"I think Jim is indicating that the animal analogy is a flawed technique."

"You have to get into the explanations behind the animal. Then it works," defends Ralph. "Why a tiger, Spencer?"

"Lithe, live, springing, sleek, graceful."

"Your lynx, Jilly?"

"Same idea, but slightly fiercer. I have this image of a lynx hissing with its teeth clenched."

"Adam, your eagle."

"No, on second thoughts, I prefer the cats. It was that predatory element, though."

"Jim, any advances on a hippopotamus?"

"No, I like the image of a big cat hissing. Could it be hiding in the top of the tree, sticking its head out from among the branches? That would be really vibrant, in your face."

Jim snarls, ending up in a hiss.

"Go to it, tiger!"

"I prefer a lynx. Lighter and more agile. More Russian. If you had a tiger, you would be forever wanting to chill the bottle."

"Jim's snarling lynx idea, peeping out from between the branches, would go perfectly with a Gaudi-design bottle," opines Lucy. "You could have physical branches built into the glass, and a little lynx head snarling out at you. Really 3-D."

"Yeah, you're right, Lucy," Jim responds. "Smart lawyers we have around here. You can take my job, and I'll take yours."

Lucy inclines her head with dignity to the compliment.

"Does the concept of a lynx clash with Petrol?" Ralph asks the team.

"It does a bit," Jilly replies. "We need a story about how the sacred lynx guards Russia's petroleum deposits in Siberia, or something."

"We could call it Lynx," suggests Ralph.

"No," I reply. "I like the tension between a feral cat and Petrol. High energy, fire water . . . ."

"Cat's piss," Jim interposes.

"There is that risk. Keep the flavours tangy. Avoid yellow."

"Slogan?" Ralph moves us on.

"The fire within. Something like that."

I draw a time-out gesture with my hands. "Time for a kidney break, then we'll summarise where we are and discuss next steps."

❋   ❋   ❋

Back after a forty-five minute toilet, e-mail, refreshment and snatched conversation break, we steel ourselves for the moment of truth.

Jim rises reluctantly to his feet and pins the Petrovsk and competitive brand definitions to the wall. The new Petrol definition has been cleaned up by Ralph during the break, and is being beamed onto the screen from his computer.

What we are looking for is differentiation, and therefore the repetition of any similar concepts between Petrol and the other brands. The rule is simple. If the same word appears in both the Petrol definition and that of another brand, we discuss how strongly it is owned by that other brand. If we decide that it will be hard to seize that concept for ourselves, we remove the word from the Petrol brand definition.

So "permission to celebrate" goes, and is replaced by sofa-celebration. You go to the garage, you pick up a bottle of Petrol, and you return to the sofa to celebrate your passion for your partner, while the children of Damocles hover over you with the eternal threat of their stirring.

"That's it then," I conclude. "We are home and dry. All the work, and praise for their inspirational efforts go to Tasha and Mark. You guys need to get onto the packaging designers, Blane, Peters, MDH, R&D for flavours, logistics for stock, and generally follow the NPI process. I will arrange for us to present the plan to William next week. And we don't let him out of the room until he says "Yes." OK?"

"What is NPI?" asks Tasha.

"Sorry, Tasha. The New Product Introduction Process. Mark knows how to access it. You just need to arrange a login for Tasha, Mark."

"Will do."

"So you guys work, and the rest of us wind down for Christmas. Thank you."

"Oh, yeah," Spender counters. "That will be the day. Will you be winding down, Adam?"

"No, I'll be concentrating on my political career. Yasemin tells me I have to become Prime Minister."

"Stranger things . . . ." says Jim.

❋   ❋   ❋

William calls me into his office, a very large corner office with knee-high carpet, steeped in ecclesiastical silence. That is why UV has four Marketing Directors—four corners.

Ricky Brabant, our MD, is there, perched on the desk. He rises to greet me. "Hello, Adam. Good to see you."

William motions me to a seat. This looks rehearsed.

"How are the figures, Adam? Do you think you will hold up for the duration, 13.3% topline growth, 12.6% contribution income?"

"Well, there can be a few-point variation either way, but performance is solid week-on-week. Indeed, Jim has come up with a Cosk-o-gram concept for the party season. If it is for a bloke, the girl turns up clad in only a Father Christmas coat. If it is for a woman, she gets to wear the coat, and the man doesn't wear anything at all. A bit of guerrilla experiential marketing. We think it might raise us another point."

Ricky and William exchange glances, whether because they find the idea tacky, or because they are confused to be asked to listen to the detail of a marketing programme, I'm not quite sure.

Ricky coughs. William leans forward. "Adam, the reason you are here is not to discuss your sales figures. It is that Ricky and I are agreed that you have done enough over the last two years to merit being groomed for higher office within the company. What do you think about that?"

My first reaction is "Who is going?", although, obviously, I don't ask the question. A marketing director job would be welcome. Yasemin will not be pleased though. She will think that I have been lured into the warm sticky honey of corporate contentment, sidetracking me from the high office I should be focusing the entirety of my being on.

William continues. "When you reach the level of top management, you need to broaden your experience within the company. You are a truly talented brand manager, but you need to understand at first hand how the company works . . . ."

I draw up the face of Eleanor Barrett. She had a stint in HR and Logistics. Seamus? Yes, he did Logistics and IT. George? Straight marketing, ditto William. Oh no, William did training for a while. He was lucky to get fished back out of that one.

"And . . . . ?"

"Well, Adam, we recommend that you accept the position of Corporate Logistics Manager. Needless to say, it is a job of critical importance. If we cannot get products in through the door and out again, we cannot sell anything . . . ."

Logistics Manager? Not even Director? I am being shafted. I grow the division exponentially, I deliver on all my numbers, I develop a tight and motivated management team, I am in short a high performance brand manager, and I get sidelined into Logistics! Great! Well that sorts my future out for me, that's for sure. Yasemin can relax.

I smile politically. "I think it is a fantastic opportunity, William. Thank you. Thank you to you too, Ricky. When do I start? Can I inform my team straightaway?"

"Sure, Adam. Well done, you have made the right choice. It may appear something of a sideways move to you at the moment, but you are obviously wise enough to realise that it is one step sideways, maybe two, in readiness for a future seat on the Board."

They are all smiles, too. They have conned me, they think. Just you wait for my rabbit, boyos! It is not-for-profit for me, then MP of some place I will have to look up on the map.

"We thought that we could not let you start before Christmas, Adam, as that would be to really throw you in at the deep end. How about January 1st. You can deal with all the returns."

❋　　❋　　❋

"I think that my career in UV ended today," I announce to Yasemin when I get home.

"Excellent," she replies. "They got to you in the end, did they?"

"They made me Logistics Manager."

"Wow! They really know how to reward strong business performance."

"That is what I thought."

Yasemin gives me a consolation shoulder hug, and a kiss. "Poor thing, but there again, who cares? It makes your path to greatness that much clearer. The world works like that sometimes."

"I have been looking at vacancies. There is an interesting Chief Fundraising Manager job going at Assert who specialise in enabling disadvantaged children to become more confident, apparently. I had never heard of them until today."

"Go for it."

"But if even a chocolate manufacturer demands a lifetime of chocolate immersion before they will consider me, what will a charity say when it hears that I have never even considered cause-related marketing campaigns, never mind actually done any charity work."

"I wouldn't worry. Charities need the money. If they judge that you will deliver the goods, that's enough. Obviously, proven charity fundraising will help, but you are also a prospective Labour Councillor, and maybe MP. That will really interest them."

"I doubt they are going to believe that I will make it to being an MP. Even I don't believe that yet."

"Oh, they will. It is in your vibes and your aura."

"That is job seeker counselling you don't get every day. Polish up your aura, and get your vibes spinning."

"You should."

"And how was your day? Been saving the world again?"

Yasemin looks at me hard, an expression I have already encountered once today, from William. Now what?

"Adam . . . ."

"What is it, Yasemin."

Yasemin takes my hands—a very bad sign.

"I need to return home."

"What? When?"

"Immediately. Tomorrow."

"You can't!"

"I have no choice. Higher orders and a higher calling."

"Is it your family?"

"In a way. There is someone who needs me to be there for him, to clear his path too."

"Can't he do it himself?"

"He is not someone you refuse. And when your time comes, you will not refuse him either."

"Who is he?

"You will soon know."

"I may give him a punch on the nose if I meet him, for stealing you off me."

Yasemin hugs me tight. "Adam, you know that I love you. I have adored our time together, but it is now time to let me go. We both have our callings and our destinies. We must obey them. We will get together again one day, that I promise you, although it will be in several years."

"Several years!"

"There needs to be a voice crying out in the wilderness, and the most experienced campaigner is no longer available, for want of his head."

"Are you deliberately talking in riddles?"

"It is how we angels talk. You talk in acronyms. We talk in riddles. It saves time, and confuses the hell out of everyone else." Her eyes light up. "Now let's have ourselves a wild last evening! We can have all-out fun in the sure knowledge that we are about to help save the world."

❄   ❄   ❄

Yasemin left at 7:30 a.m.

She hugged me tight, and kissed me, her tears etching cold wet down my cheek. She said her last words. "Adam, go well. I love you."

She picked up her one suitcase and her rucksack and her handbag. I opened the door for her. It is a sombre, cold, misty morning.

She walked down to the car as I remained in the doorway. She arranged her bags in the boot, and slammed the tailgate shut. She circled round to the driver's door, and noticed something lying in the street near her front wheel. She picked it up, momentarily turning back towards the house to dispose of it. She changed her mind and decided to take it with her. She eased herself into the car. She attached her belt. She did something else by way of preparation I couldn't see or understand. The car started. She pulled out into the road. She drove off in a puff of smoke.

A huge, dark voodoo creature hurled himself up to me, locked one arm round my back and, with his rough, pagan shovel carved a deep, jagged hollow in my soul.

I closed the door.

I wept.

Never such resentment again.

❋　　❋　　❋

I call a meeting of the team when I get to the office.

"Now what?" demands Jim. "Don't you have any work to do?"

"Funnily enough, Jim, that is what I was going to talk about."

"Always like to talk about work," Jim retorts.

Spencer, Tasha, Mark and Jim are there.

"I am afraid that I am leaving you," I announce.

They look surprised and definitely shocked.

"You've got yourself a new job?" asks Jim.

"Sort of," I reply. "William has moved me into Logistics." I don't think I managed to disguise the repugnance I suddenly felt as I said it.

"Logistics?" Spencer repeats.

"Yup."

"What on earth do you want to do in Logistics?"

"Grooming me for better things, apparently."

Jim snorts. Mark shuffles. Tasha watches me with uncertain, expectant eyes.

"So who will be our new boss then, Adam? Break it to us."

"I haven't a clue. I haven't been told."

"Jay Simmonds," Mark announces authoratively.

"How on earth do you know that?" asks Spencer.

"Smoking room."

"Jay? But he is a complete wanker! What on earth good is he going to do here."

In my new trajectory of prospective Board member, I should reassure them that Jay is a good chap who will do an excellent job, look after them, and be no trouble. I cannot be bothered. Jay is a crap marketer and a crap manager.

"Whatever you do, team, make sure that you split up to manage the Petrovsk and the Petrol brands completely separately. Mark and Tasha, I suggest you manage the Petrol brand. Jim you continue with Petrovsk. And you fight like cat and dog."

Already my counsel is irrelevant.

"Boss," says Jim. "There is no need to talk about work now."

"And Yasemin has left me."

That really does shock them. They all jolt forward and upward in their seats.

"You're joking."

"No forwarding address?" inquires Jim.

"Actually not, Jim. We will get back together in a few years, supposedly."

There is silence.

"When did this happen?"

"This morning. She has to return to Kurdistan for family business."

"Will you see her again?"

"Yes, I think I will. Think. Not for many years, though, and who knows what will happen in that time."

Jim looks the saddest of all. Genuinely hurt.

More silence.

"OK, Adam, with all this depressing news, there is only one solution. We all go out tonight, and treat you to a Cosk-o-gram special. Whatever any of you are doing, cancel it. This is Adam's evening."

Which is why I find myself in a bar in Reading, confronted by a naked girl in a Father Christmas suit, offering me an open bottle of Petrovsk vodka. And I get to take her home.

Desolate consolation.

❋   ❋   ❋

I have been for the preliminary interview with Assert. It went very much better than I could possibly have imagined. Our vibes and our aura were humming just right. It was a one-on-one with the CEO. As Yasemin had predicted, he didn't touch on previous charity work, or cause-related marketing, or whether I had children, or whether I even cared a toss about children. He mostly talked about Petrovsk and how impressed he was with the way it had been marketed.

"If you can do that for us, Adam, we will be more than happy," he said.

"Yes, I can do that," I replied. "It's a formula."

"You don't think charities are a little different?"

"Well, the irony with charities is that you cannot be as opportunistic with the values as you can with a product that doesn't really matter, like vodka where you can be outrageous and get away with it. In Assert, you have real values, so you are a stuck with those. We can hype them up a bit, give them some pizzazz, but your values are still your values. They are about getting a poor, lonely, vulnerable child to feel better about him or herself. Not much scope for irreverent humour there without irretrievably damaging the brand."

"So what are your thoughts?"

"I would have to go over your research, William, and then perhaps conduct some more."

"I am afraid that we do not have Petrovsk's budgets."

I smiled reassuringly "Nor did Petrovsk at the time."

William leant back in his chair. "Let's cut to the chase? Will you join us?"

Decision time. No hesitation. "Yes, William, I will join you."

"Are you on three months' notice with Petrovsk?"

"Yes, but they might let me go earlier as I would have been starting a new job about which I have no pre-existing knowledge whatsoever except shouting at them asking where my goods are."

"Please don't do too much shouting here, Adam. Assert is a very quiet place."

"I would like to change that. You cannot build a fizzing, burning team in silence. That is what I do best."

William stood up. "Then, unless there is anything else, Adam, I very much look forward to the fizzing and burning." He laughed and shook his head perplexedly. "I can't imagine it, but good luck to you."

I am walking down Victoria Street dancing on the high of a great interview, nervous as to whether I have made the right (instant) decision, and wondering why my boss has to be called William again. Not even "Bill" or "Will".

It is lunchtime, so the street is relatively busy with ambling shoppers and rushing office workers out for a bite and a hurried errand. Walking past Books etc., I consider whether I should actually buy a book for once in my life. I will have some free time now, and I cannot spend it all with Petrovsk girls. Some of my mates took me out for a forget-everything evening last night, and I bagged another Cosk-o-gram beauty, although she wouldn't come back with me. Her boyfriend was waiting at the door of the bar.

Across the street a movement catches my eye. My immediate reaction is "Yasemin!". A girl is struggling up the oncoming tide of pedestrians, desperately trying to get to somewhere. A bus? A shop? Someone?

I am drawn to her for her resemblance to Yasemin, and I shadow her from the opposite side of the street where there are far fewer people. Just by the Roman Catholic cathedral the crowd thins out, and she slows down. There is a man standing there, seemingly considering which way his life will take him next. He is carrying a heavy briefcase, and looks important somehow.

The girl rushes up to him, and then stands back. He stands back too. The expression on his face is one of totally astonished delight. He pulls a "I cannot believe it" pratfall face. He does it again, and a third time. The girl puts her arms around him. A couple of passers-by glance at them. One stares hard, as if he recognises the man.

I recognise the man. The man is me. And, although I have still not managed a clear sight of her, I am pretty sure that the girl is Yasemin.

I am wearing a marriage band on my right hand, I notice. Uh-oh! Now what?

❉   ❉   ❉

Part II

The Minister

Chapter 7

There is nothing to winning a general election, except a huge amount of grim hand-to-hand street fighting around the fifty marginal seats that make the difference. We are all struggling to seize the centre ground.

That is how political marketing works. You aim firmly for the centre ground where the most warm bodies reside, and you brand the personalities. Forget the policies. Make sure that they are all typed up in some interminable document with lots of text and no pictures, and bury them deep. When you think of all those earnest rank-and-file campaigners arguing over every word in endless resolutions at conferences, permanently aggrieved but hopeful, your mind inevitably turns to the concept of duality. What appears to be the issue is never the essential.

If you are in a company, as I was in my early career, you would imagine that the trick is to deliver groundbreaking results that enhance the growth of the company. And then you wonder at all the corporate politicians who seem to be completely clueless about getting anything done, and at best semi-detached from the process of doing so. Later on, you marvel all the more as you watch these people being promoted ahead of you. The answer is, of course, that it is all politics, all whom you know. If you are a great achiever, but otherwise remote, you are a worker somewhere out there on the commercial frontier, not one of us embedded in our mutually supportive relationships. We promote the people we know and trust, as people, as colleagues, almost as friends, in a business setting at least.

Then you go into charities, and you are at it again. Now it is more overtly political, because charities unavoidably operate in the public policy space but, yet again, this is the sideshow. The trick is networking, charity-hopping, being seen to be significant, to be on the up.

This is my third career—real, dirty politics. I am not going to make the same mistakes again. From now on I shake hands with everyone, remember their names, "engage" with them for the few minutes, or sometimes hours, where it is necessary, crony with the whips, hail all my colleagues on both sides of the house, and take every opportunity to spend as much meaningful time as I can with the P.M., Geoffrey Christian. Funny guy. He made me the Minister for the Arts and Charities, but he still doesn't seem to quite know who I am. I always remind him when I introduce myself. I cannot judge whether each time he thinks "Why is Adam always telling me his name, funny chappy?" or whether he is grateful for the prompt.

As I was one of the key members of the Election Strategy Committee, it is all the more surprising to me that Geoffrey simply cannot seem to connect with me. Having said that, I am not sure he connects with anyone. He is some sort of throwback to Edward Heath, a "confirmed bachelor", remote, charmless and alone. He does know exactly how to be in the right place at the right time, though, and he has superlative political intuition. His immediate instinct is always right. If you propose something to him in the usual compressed, can-I-just-fit-this-in style you need to have as a non-Cabinet minister, and he hesitates, you realise immediately that you have to rework your proposition. He may not pay you any personal attention, but he is listening intently. He doesn't grace you with any advice either. All you get is a Delphic Oracle "yeoww, er . . . ." or "Good. Keep me informed."

I have a great team around me in the Alternative Ministry of Worthy Causes, as I nickname it. Our ministry has nothing to do with the ordinary run of political business. It is a complete aberration from the main event of power, deals, the economy and foreign diplomacy. We are the equivalent in government to cause-related marketing. Our clientèle, the good guys, need some of our power to influence, and a lot of our money. In turn, we like to share their aura of beneficence. To be honest, we could probably cut them all dead, leave all the financial side of things to Lotto, and still get re-elected. The public knows that the government is not a charity, except to cater to its several needs and self-interest. It is the economy that sets you up there, and boredom that knocks you down again. Governments do not lose elections. Time simply defeats you. The grains of sand pile up relentlessly on top of you until you are buried, and the next desert-dwellers are ushered in with joyous celebration.

Tessa and the boys have been absolutely wonderful. Luckily we don't have to play happy families. We actually are. And maybe we wouldn't have to play it anyway. Happy families are a bit like the arts and charities. They seem to be a good thing, and maybe it is better to have them than not, just to be on the safe side, but do they really matter for electoral purposes? There are enough singletons, serial divorcees, gays, sociopaths and down-and-outs who are nevertheless MPs to suggest that it makes not a scrap of difference.

What really matters is whether you are willing to be herded when the dogs of the Whips' Office come barking. For most of us, not including me as

I represent a razor's edge marginal, it doesn't matter a damn what even the electorate thinks of us. It doesn't know us anyway, except for a couple of news items in the local rag—"Local MP opens sweet shop" and "Frank says clean up your rubbish." That's it. After that you are either Labour, Conservative or LibDem, and the label gets the vote. You never get a Conservative MP in the heart of a Northern ex-industrial conurbation, and you never get a Labour MP in rural Shropshire.

I keep relations cordial with the whips, and even seek them out for what they can do for me, but they are by nature rottweilers. They like to savage you, to serve you, then to savage you again. They listen intently to any gossip, true or false, although they have a nose for the authentic scent. They hold a scroll of potential favours they could do you, posts they can edge you towards, suffering and penalties they could inflict on you. I keep things pretty clean, yet they are forever sniffing around my non-execs, trying to detect the whiff of conflict of interest. They could not care a less morally or ethically what minor iniquities I perpetrate; it is all about bargaining counters. The whips are the most opportunistic people I have ever met. One slip and they are in there, extracting favours or stirring the discomfort. It doesn't matter which party you are from, the same rules apply.

You can always tell a whip, not that you don't always know who they are anyway. They greet you with a recital of all the favours they have done you, and they leave you with an unspoken reference to your vulnerabilities. They may have been the role models for J. K. Rowling's Dementors who suck the soul out of you if you attract their attention.

The man our whips hate the most in this world is Con Savage, MP for Dewsbury South. They say to Con "We would like you to do this", and he says "Sure thing", and ten minutes later he has gone off and done exactly the opposite. They try their best, but there is nothing they can pin on him, he is not seeking higher office, and he is very popular in his constituency, and in the country as a whole, as an individualistically principled eccentric. He is the slippery slope which all promises of favours, and menaces of doom, slide down with equal indifference.

Tessa and I met when I was already out five nights a week politicking either for Assert or as a Labour Councillor, so she never expects me to be home during her waking hours, except occasionally at weekends. It is a miracle that we had the time to develop a relationship at all, and even more so that we can retain it despite being virtual strangers. Tessa concerns herself with her PR job, the boys and the household. I work, work, work.

I am haunted by the Harry Chapin song about the father and son, where the son is forever asking his father to do something with him, and his father is always too busy. Then, when his father eases up and has time, his son is too busy in his turn. "You are just like me, son. You are just like me."

Sandy and Ben are sweet boys still, at ten and eight respectively. They give me warm hugs, and even kisses, and hang off everything I say. Those are measures of how distant we are, and of how close we would all like us to be.

Tessa has her own PR consultancy, and she has been managing some massive promotional events round-the-clock in her own right. She has been following the sun for weeks, it seems—San Francisco, London, Paris, Moscow, Tokyo, New York, Berlin, Bombay, Sydney. After all these years, she still gets her times confused, so we receive calls at 2:00 and 3:00 in the morning, as much as midday and 9:00 p.m., which is the nice one as I actually have the time to speak to her then, at least from the office. We set up twin phone numbers a few years ago which can track us to landlines and mobile phones wherever we are in the world.

As you can imagine, we are pretty reliant on our nanny, Erika, a German girl in her twenties. Sandy and Ben absolutely refuse to have her referred to as a nanny. "She is not a goat, and nor are we," they say in unison. "She is our bodyguard."

So, at least two members of the family already have bodyguards. Even I was allocated them once in the last few weeks when some idiot artist decided to provoke Muslim outrage, and bring a fatwa down on both him and me. Mine lasted about three days. Thankfully, Erika has been with us for coming up to five years. We are a bit worried though, as there appears to be a serious boyfriend lurking. For her sake we wish her all happiness, and for our sake a devastating heartbreak which puts her off romance for at least five more years, without being so traumatic as to persuade to return to Germany to recover, or to ruin her life forever.

When I first turned up in the Ministry, propelled by that fateful phone call from the Prime Minister's Office, although not from Geoffrey himself, the initial emotion was one of complete panic in the face of chaos. Civil servants are lined up to escort you around the building, but no-one gives you any informal counsel. The advice, when it comes, arrives in formal briefings inside bright red boxes, nuanced down to the order the documents are presented to you. My one bit of fun over the first few days was to start my box in the middle, a tactic that almost sent Sir William, my Permanent, into apoplexy.

"You should really start at the top, Minister, if I might say so."

"Yes, but they are all boring at the top, and I don't understand a word of them. The end ones are trivial. Only the middle ones are even midway entertaining."

I could see that Sir William was not pleased to be lumbered with another joker.

"The top ones are still the critical ones to master, Minister."

"I am sure that any policy that has already been mastered by your staff does not need any of my help."

"You still have to endorse it, Sir."

"Thanks, Sir William, but I am going to focus on something else: the strategy of the Department. Without a strategy, we do not know what to focus on, and what to leave out, however excellent a cause it may be."

"We have been running several strategy workshops, Minister. Would you like to read the minutes?"

"Yes, Sir William. Even more I would like to view the summary slides."

"They are in minute form at the moment, Sir. We are still at the exploratory stage."

"Who are you using as your consultants?"

"E&Y, Sir. They may have some slides for you. I'll call them. They can e-mail them over."

"Great. Now if you put those at the top of my file, I will promise to read them first."

❋ ❋ ❋

Much to Sir William's horror, I have decided to run a few strategy sessions myself, E&Y or not. E&Y are certainly not happy about it, and keep phoning me to try to arrange a meeting to explain their strategic process.

"Tell them I know their strategic path already," I say to my secretary. "They start by being briefed, and they end up with lots of money. The section in the middle is mostly irrelevant to all of us, but chews up thousands of valuable man hours anyway."

I have told William that I want three mixed teams of enthusiastic people to work with. It will be an excellent way of getting to know the brightest minds in the building.

To be fair, the Ministry policy documents are superb, excruciatingly detailed, word-perfectly precise and concise, truly professional, distilled nectar. What I am missing is the Ministry flair. What does it stand for, what does it hate, whom does it love, what will get it noticed? These are not the thoughts of any government ministry where every moment is impassioned by the single-minded requirement for disinterest and even-handedness. I want to be PM. That is not on their agenda.

My first meeting with a selection of ministry guinea-pigs kicks off nervously. Sir William Singleton is there as the Permanent Secretary, as is Livia Arnold, a senior civil servant who has been leading the strategy development project with E&Y, and my own special advisor, Susan Welsh. The other eight people in the room are painfully aware that they are in the firing line of a tussle for power between the Minister and "his" Permanent Secretary. Apparently this happens whenever a minister is appointed who has not been a minister before. The civil service usually wins through sheer weight of numbers and information. There is a tension even between seasoned ministers and their ministries, but it is rarely the open struggle for power that us greenhorns tend to get ourselves into on the momentary exuberance of receiving a job in the government.

I am tempted to kick Sir William out of the meeting once he has introduced the exercise so as to endorse it. I have been debating this with myself all week, and garnering advice from colleagues. The unanimous view, except from Con Savage, is that it is virtually suicidal to antagonise your Permanent Secretary. There is always a way they can get you back, and you simply cannot operate without them.

Still, with his dominance over the table, it is going to be hard to get a genuine discussion going.

"OK," I announce, "before we start, we will run two laps round the table."

That certainly startles Sir William, and bemuses everyone else, except Susan who has had a glimpse of my tactics already. So we are up on our feet first, gently shooing on the rest into a moment of spell-breaking physical exertion. Nobody actually runs, but they do all stand up, and start moving. It is then that I notice the guy in the wheelchair.

"I am sorry," I say to him. "I do not know your name yet."

"Michael Sanderton, Sir."

"Michael, will you please wheel yourself round, if you can. I think you could probably set the pace."

And off he goes, extremely agile on his wheels, and threatening to run everyone else over.

"Two laps!"

And we sit down again.

"After that ice-breaker, Sir William, could you please introduce the session?"

"Certainly, Minister. Ladies, gentlemen, the Minister has asked me to initiate some additional strategy sessions to help embed E&Y's work into the ministry. He feels, and I agree, that without widespread participation within the ministry in a matter of this importance, only limited change will occur, or change will only occur slowly, or both. We all want the E&Y project to succeed, and to ensure that this ministry plays at the top of its game in a way that we can all be proud of. The minister has asked me to ensure that you have all been briefed on the outcomes of the E&Y work to date, so I hope that you are all up to speed . . . ."

He inquisitions each person at a time.

"Yes, Sir."

"Good. Unusually, the Minister himself will be leading these sessions, firstly as a token of the importance he accords to this initiative, and secondly because he has a deep experience of running strategic planning processes over many years. There will be three teams of people working with us on this aspect of the project, of which you are obviously one. We hope that you find it to be an enjoyable and insightful experience."

Sir William gestures to me magnanimously. "Over to you, Minister."

"Thank you, Sir William, and good morning."

"Good morning."

"I think that we should get to know each other first, so can each of us spend two minutes detailing who we are, and what our biggest passion is outside work? I will start. My name is Adam Melton. I am the new Minister of the Arts and Charities, and I am delighted to be here. I have worked for a charity for several years, so I clearly honour their efforts in trying to make the world a better place. My passion outside work, apart from my wife, Tessa, and my two boys, Sandy and Ben, is vodka."

Everyone laughs politely.

"That is a throwback to the days when I used to be the brand manager for Petrovsk vodka, which is still the number one vodka brand in the UK, I believe. Sir William, I think we can spare you your introduction, but what is your extra-curricular passion?"

"Sailing, actually, Minister."

"Where do you sail?"

"In the Solent mostly."

"Are you the captain?"

Sir William smiles politely. "No, I merely crew. Being captain of one ship is enough for me. I sail to relax, and to watch someone else being in charge."

Sir William has an endearing smile. There is a hint of a blush, and of a real sense of humour when he is not required to be ponderous.

"Susan, you do need to introduce yourself."

"Hello, everyone. May I say firstly how pleased I am to have the opportunity to meet you all in this more informal setting? Knowing the Minister, it will be very informal, and equally incisive."

She nods at me.

"My name is Susan Welsh, which I am not . . . . In my various careers, I have been a civil servant in MAAF and the Home Office, a journalist and a lobbyist for a PR firm. I am employed by the Minister to give him third party advice, not being either a civil servant now, or a politician. I am his confidential sounding board, if you wish."

"And your passion, Susan?"

"I rather hesitate to say, Minister."

"I think you have to."

"Well, actually, it is breeding pet snakes."

"Now that is something I didn't know about you. You are no lover of mice, then."

"I have nothing against mice, but a snake has to eat."

"Livia?"

"Good morning, Minister. My name is Livia Arnold. I have been in the civil service for seventeen years. I have worked in several ministries, including the Home Office, the Foreign Office, and the DSS. I started my career in Customs

& Excise. I am now, among other things, chairing the strategy development committee, and my passion is eating."

"Anything?"

"No, Minister, I am very particular in what I eat and where I eat it."

The other eight people in the room proceed to take their turn. Passions include football, films, trekking across India and extreme sports.

"Right, well thank you for all that, and for your honesty, which is enormously important. I don't know what your usual ministry rules are for meetings, but my rules in these sessions are that you must feel free to say anything you like, however controversial or silly, without, of course, giving any undue offence to anyone else. Whatever you say here stays within these walls in terms of attribution. And I promise you, there will be times when I demand that you say the most absurd and/or heretical things you can think of. OK?"

Probably not. They are waiting and seeing.

"The discussion for today is our stakeholders, and what they really want from us. We will cover off what we want to give them in return at another time. Livia, you must have a list of stakeholders."

"Indeed, Minister. Here it is."

"Has everyone seen this list?"

They all claim to have done so.

"There are 138 categories of stakeholder here, which is 135 more than we can cope with today. So, I am afraid I am going to take the unilateral decision that we focus on only three of them—the Treasury, the general public and the press. What I need you to do now is to brainstorm onto Post-it Notes what you think the Treasury wants from us. Now, I know this exercise has been done formally already, but I would like to see some suggestions that do not appear in the formal list. I want you to think the thoughts no-one else dares say, and to jot them down. When you have written down each suggestion on a separate note, you place it in the middle, and I will shuffle them up, so you will only by chance ever be forced to read out your own. And then we will destroy them, so that no-one can check your handwriting. OK?"

"Yes."

There is the usual reaction. The guy in the wheelchair, Michael, rattles off about ten thoughts in ten seconds. The pretty girl opposite me, Julie, sucks on her pen earnestly, and completes only two ideas, and on the same Post-it Note.

"OK. Time up. What have we got? John you start."

"It says here, and I repeat, it says here . . . ."

Hesitant conspiratorial laughter, indicating that the room is warming to the task. Phew!

". . . . that the Treasury wishes that we were 100% in the private sector."

"Thanks, John. What do you think that means anyone?"

"They don't want to pay for us."

"Good. Next? Cilla? And are you from Liverpool?"

"Close, Minister. Birkenhead."

"Just a river crossing away. What do you have?"

"I have the same, more or less. They wish that we did not exist."

"George?"

"Yes, mine is identical. Close down the department."

"Does anyone have anything different?"

"I have that they wish we would move to a tax haven."

Laughter.

"Michael, what have you got?"

"The suggestion here is that the charities should be taxed on their revenues, thus funding the arts."

"That is a bit more radical. Anyone got anything else?"

Paul holds up a note. "It says here that medical charities should be the responsibility of the Department of Health, and be incentivised to develop preventative solutions to cut the health budget."

"That is really good. I like that. Daring. OK. Let's do the same trick again, this time for the general public."

This time, the completing of the Post-it Notes is much more flowing and spontaneous.

"Oh, I forgot, could you give all the old suggestions to me, and I'll tear them up while you write the next lot. Thanks, Paul. Thanks, Julie."

Four minutes, and the pens are stilled.

"Jason?"

"Fund art that people want to see. No stuffed sheep in glass cases."

"Yeah, I have that, except that it says here no stuffed bishops."

"Bishops?"

"It's what it says."

"I love it," I declare. "We are getting past the reverential stage."

Julie quivers. "Mine says use taxpayers' money to fund lapdance clubs for the over 60s."

Sir William frowns.

I grin. It is so important to welcome people taking risks. All eyes are on my reaction. "Now that is daring," I beam. "And I am only twenty years away. What with my free bus pass as well . . . ."

The room is with me, even Sir William and Livia.

"Michael?"

"Put a cap on how much of the revenue can be spent on administration—10% max?"

"Good. Excellent. Any more like that?"

"Nearly. Tax charities in full if admin costs rise above the approved threshold."

"Are these thoughts based on any research by any chance?"

"Yes," Livia answers. "We did some market research last year, and this was one of the key themes, along with removing charitable status from politically motivated charities."

"Did your research tell you which are people's favourite charities?"

"Well, there are about 250,000 of them altogether, and the ones that get the most money are medical research charities, children's charities, disability charities, poverty-relief charities, old age relief, individual protection charities, like the NSPCC, Children in Need, the Red Cross (although these tend to overlap with other categories) . . . ."

"I can see that. I can see that a lot of categories overlap; old age with medical, disability with medical, disability with old age . . . ."

". . . . Quite right, Minister, then you have education, the arts, the environment and religion. I am ignoring all the straight financial charities, or perhaps not so straight ones."

"Taking the point made earlier, by Paul was it? Yes, Paul, about medical charities being the appropriate responsibility of the Department of Health, could we theoretically farm off other categories onto other ministries? Let's see, what do we have? Could I have the list again, Livia?" I know that I am cutting across the process and taking over, which is dangerous, but I want to reinforce the notion that there is no unthinkable idea.

"Medical, children, disability, protection/rights, education, arts, the environment and religion."

"So, the arts are definitively ours. Disabilities could also go across to the Department of Health, arguably, although, cynically, I would argue that there is good mileage in them. Rights should really be the Home Office. Education is the Department of Education. Environment heads for Environment and, frankly, in this country, religion—who cares? I am sorry if I offend anyone with that statement."

Everyone shakes their head.

"So what if we focused on children, old age, and possibly disabilities, and then the arts, although I think they are on another level. They are unavoidably part of our brief, on a different plane. So you could term them the three disabilities—physical, childhood and old age. Sorry, four: physical, mental, childhood and old age. That would be hard to argue with, don't you think? Less controversial than gay Marxists, or whatever. Roll over, Ken Livingstone."

"Except, Minister," cuts in Sir William, "that it is our duty to be scrupulously impartial."

"Sure, Sir William, I understand that. I am not talking about public policy here. I am talking about how we promote ourselves. I want our ministry to be viewed universally as a very good thing, and I cannot see that anyone is going to quibble with those, except from an angle of self-interest, which we can deal with relatively easily. In reality, we must do what is required of us, but it does no harm in a high spending, philanthropic ministry that cannot make a business case, to be able to tug relentlessly at the heart strings. Cause-related, highly emotional, experiential marketing. Values on your sleeves for all to see. We can do a lot with that, and it puts our friends in the Treasury on the spot. Does anyone have any Post-its to support that?"

"Support the charities people care about."

"Keep away from controversial charities."

"That would be another good reason to pass medical research charities onto Health. Stem cell research is a subject I don't want to deal with. Rights charities are also a bit iffy, too. Amnesty International, NCCB, Liberty, or whatever. Any suggestions against?"

Silence.

"Livia, could you remind me that we need to quickly explore general trends before we finish today? Thanks. Right, let's turn to the Street of Shame, to quote Private Eye. What is the press looking for?"

It is fluid now. Woomph!

"Scandal," Michael announces, reading out his own.

"Hold on there, Michael. Great suggestion, but people have not finished writing yet."

"I am sorry, Minister. I got carried away there for a moment."

"No need to feel the least bit sorry, Michael. Whilst I remember, and I don't know if I can ask you this or not, but when I was talking about the emotional appeal of disabilities, did you feel insulted?"

"No, not at all, Minister. I would be only too pleased if this ministry focused people's attention on the difficulties people face with physical and mental disabilities. That would make me really proud to be working here."

"Thank you, Michael, for that. Interesting. So it could even make the people who work in this building feel good about themselves?"

"Definitely, I would think."

Many murmurs of approval.

"So, as we all seem to have finished, we have Michael's scandal on the table. Who thinks the press is interested in scandal."

There is a ripple of chuckling, and everyone's hand goes up sharpish, with Sir William and Livia bringing up the rear, participating nevertheless.

"Scandal about what?"

"The scandal of people's money being wasted," Jason suggests, "and the scandal of the issue in the first place. Here are all these vulnerable people, and not enough is being done."

"Which takes us back to the administration fees?"

"Yes." Emphatically.

"We can explore solutions around that another day. Good. What other than scandals?"

"It is sort of related," volunteers Paula for the first time, "but any story that tugs at the heart strings."

"Great. Anything else?"

"Crucifying the government. It is a disgrace!"

"That they wish to crucify the government? I couldn't agree more."

"No, that the government is acting disgracefully. Stopping good things happening mindlessly, pulling fast ones, running off with people's donations, not keeping its side of the bargain, that sort of thing."

"Surely not," I comment with ham irony.

"I am afraid so, Minister," counters Sir William, playing the straight guy. We could work up a comedy duo yet. Good deeds and humour. Wow!

"Sex," Julie shouts, a little over-enthusiastically. The group dynamic is roller coastering.

I nearly respond with "Anything you say, Julie," but that could be to get a cheap laugh now, and to be forced to repent for all time. I go half the way by simply raising my eyebrows. Julie giggles nervously. She waves her post-it at me.

"Um. If we say that we are focusing on disabilities, childhood and old age, I suppose you have several good news stories, and one horrific one, paedophilia."

They nod gravely.

"So, if I may summarise, the Treasury wants to wipe us off the planet, although I would suggest not the government as a whole. We go for the four disabilities—physical, mental, childhood and old age—and the press will lap up stories about heart-rending situations put right, and some sort of curb on administration costs. Is that where we are?"

"That sounds fair to me, Minister," Sir William concludes. General agreement.

"Livia—trends. Thank you for reminding me."

Livia colours up. "You have beaten me to it, Minister."

"Never mind. You will be faster next time. Are there any macro trends that support or undermine our proposition today?"

"Well, the main ones, Minister, are the demographic shift towards the elderly, and the break up of the nuclear family, necessitating support for the children who are victims of the tragedy."

"That works then."

"That works, Minister."

"Any trends that work against us?"

"Not that I am aware of."

"In that case, I think I can stop getting between you and your lunches, and conclude by saying that I found it a most enjoyable and educational session, and I very much look forward to the next one. Thank you."

Research has observed that good group interactions norm, storm and finally mourn. There is an atmosphere of "Oh, is it over?" which is gratifying.

"On behalf of us all," Sir William interposes, "I would like to thank you too, Minister. I think that I can speak for us all in saying that was a most inspirational session, and a wonderfully informal way to get to know you as our new minister."

"Thank you, Sir William."

"One more of these sessions, and I will be shortening my name to just Bill. Only joking."

"Well, you can't shorten my first name much, although I have been called Ad a few times before now. However, I think I will stick to Minister. It has novelty value for the time being, and I am not quite ready for the 'just call me Tony' bit, yet."

"Very well understood, Minister. And thank you again."

"Prime Minister, Adam Melton at Charities & the Arts."

I grab the momentary opportunity to present our initial musings to Geoffrey Christian.

"Good. Keep me informed. Good for the government. Good for the Party."

Chapter 8

I very rarely get the chance to talk to my ministerial colleagues in the major Departments: Roger Danby, the Chancellor of the Exchequer, Janice O'Sullivan at the Home Office, Robert Salstice, Foreign Secretary, and Lucy Twining, Minister for Health. I am more on the level of a Junior Minister in those Departments.

Therefore, I regularly make the rounds of the Junior Ministers, to air my views. Along the way, I get the more than strong impression that they view me as a bit of an aberration, the Minister for Wacky Thoughts, who just happens to be qualified for the job he is in, by virtue of his previous high office in the not-for-profit sector, but who would be an utter deadbeat and a liability anywhere else; that I am one reshuffle away from the backbenches.

I am evangelising the merits of branding the government. "Branding as a discipline is not a nice add-on to what we do; it is an essential part of our survival."

They don't get it. It is so much less important than wrestling between their civil servants and their Secretary for State over taxation policies, or immigration, or the terrorist threat. For them, no doubt, branding equates to PR, and they do plenty of that as it is, briefing lobby journalists weekly on their departmental initiatives, and briefing against every other department on the QT, all to purloin a larger slice of Budget Pie.

Anyway, Tessa is home again after her whistle-stop double tour of the globe. Everything has gone excellently well, and she is hyped up for the next adventure in two months' time. I am also getting home by seven most days of the week, so the boys, Sandy and Ben, are bemused, perplexed and, I have to say, marginally threatened, by finding themselves in the clutches of a nuclear family for about the first time in their lives. They keep watching us to gauge whether they would rather be with us, or in prison, or with the Foreign Legion. Facing two parents laying down rules in determined concert after so many years of "Erika, Mother says . . . ." or "Mother, Father says we must eat chocolate, it is good for us," is proving to be spiritually and physically restricting. They inquire regularly, and with ever more hope in defiance of recent experience, whether my work won't pick up again soon.

"Your father is only the Minister of Charities & the Arts. It is a very boutique operation, the C&A, you know. Now that he has got it sorted in his own mind, and probably in everybody else's, he can relax for the first time in years. He is a very clever man, you know, your father. Anyway, I am pleased to see him for a change."

I often speculate as to what happens to Tessa on her world tours, or in lonely hotels in Kilmarnock or somewhere when she is managing a sales launch for the national sales reps of a Scottish brewery. Does she ever flirt with her clients? Of course, she does. That is only good business. Does she ever stray further, a kiss, maybe the occasional one-night adultery? She is an extraordinarily sexy lady, 32, long blonde hair that flows down her head like vanilla ice cream, and tiara eyes. Am I jealous? That would be peevish, wouldn't it? After all, I am not much of a husband, and even less of a father.

For my part, I have never even as much as consciously flirted with any other woman since I met Tessa in the offices of Assert, when we hired her firm to manage some publicity for us. Sure, I recognise the attraction of all the pretty young things around me, and as I get older they seem to get prettier, the more mature ones too. The thought of sex with them might even flit for a millisecond into my mind and out again, but I am really not that interested. I don't have that sort of ego any more. In my younger days, I picked my fair share of the crop when I chose to enter the field. Today, it is extremely good sex with Tessa about once a month, and a fortnightly ministerial masturbation in the cool, boxy upstairs toilet at home, with the door locked, after watching Playboy TV for about ten minutes. I am not locking the door against Tessa. She has no objection to my watching the sex channels, indeed she joins me sometimes, which accounts for somewhere like 50% of our amorous conjunctions, but you don't want your ten year old son to walk in on his father tapping the rubber tree, do you?

The big gambit for inflated budgets at both the Home and the Foreign Office is "the Terrorist Threat" (capital Ts), as has been reliably the case for a few years now. There are apparently over 3,000 trained operatives prowling around the United Kingdom, all armed with nuclear bomblets and smoking flasks of bacterial catastrophe, their numbers and their menace are growing by the day as their cells replicate like crazed chromosomes, and THEY MUST BE STOPPED, ho ho!

What is extraordinary is that anyone believes this guff, but even the Opposition does not dare to so much as insinuate a moment's distrust of these wholesome gruesome prognostications.

Who are they kidding? Everyone apparently. 3,000 al-Qa'eda operatives in Britain? Don't be fucking ridiculous. Has no-one ever run a volunteer group?

You get 50 people who like to be kept informed, of which 15 turn up to meetings ever, 5 regularly, and two or three who actually do something on a committed basis. Why should al-Qa'eda, or the IRA or the Sendera Luminosa, or whoever else be any different? They reckoned that at the height of the IRA threat, there was an absolute maximum of one hundred active members, and most of those were probably tied up in administration. When the Sandinistas first threatened to topple the Samoza fiefs and thieves in Nicaragua in the mid-1970s, they comprised Daniel Ortega and two mates hiding out in the mountains making growling noises, and his two co-conspirators were both poets, for Christ's sake. It was enough, just the same, to provoke the Ford regime in the US to set up and finance those venomous psychopaths, the Contras, who gloried in raping and mutilating men, women and children with gleeful regularity (pregnant women and nuns a specialty, from memory, or was that El Salvador?), thereby fuelling and fanning the Sandinista fire until the government really was overthrown. So, I give al-Qa'eda a 99% discount at worst—30 very nasty people who would undoubtedly blow up you and me for sport, given the chance, but that is it. If there were really 3,000 of them in the UK, how much would that be worldwide—50,000 plus? And what have they done over the last ten years? 18 of them have blown up the Twin Towers. Seven have blown up London on a couple of occasions. Three or four operatives in Spain. Rather more in the Far East. I count fifty tops. The other 49,950 must be right lazy buggers. But, hell, it pays the rent for designated Secretaries of State, their Junior Ministers, their civil servants, the armed forces, the police, the shadowy miasma of spooks, the press, security firms, and the list expands and expands. After all, what do you say to the nation? There is a very serious threat in this country. 12 nasty Middle-Easterners really want to kill us, plus a pair of sad white Caucasians who think they are Muslims? You can't tell your minister that if you are hoping for some decent funding, the nation would laugh its socks off. Wrongly, as it would turn out, because even twelve committed terrorists can create one hell of a mess of thousands of people's lives. Nevertheless that is what would happen.

And where do all these al-Qa'eda terrorists stash all their weapons-grade plutonium or uranium which they use to manufacture their nuclear bombs in industrial quantities? In their wardrobes? Behind the skirting board? In the bath? If this were really the case, then why have the security forces never found any of this stuff when they do their early wee hour kick down the door raids on unsuspecting foreigners shoe-horned into their clandestine cells in residential Neasden? Radioactive substances are not exactly hard to detect. They are marginally easier than national airports. One Geiger counter and you are there. Indeed, a handful of Geiger counters and you have closed down every operational al-Qa'eda unit in Britain overnight. I really don't think so.

Now the real trick with terrorists, in my far from humble opinion, is not to glorify and magnify their achievements, as we are inadvertently doing at the moment, by making a stage army out of a handful of lunatics who thereby look like the rivals to the efficiency and ruthlessness of Mossad. It is to play down their achievements and to frustrate the hell out of them in their every breath. What you have to understand about these grim activists is that they don't have blood, they have bile. They hate. They hate their mothers, they hate their fathers for abandoning or brutalising them, they hate their brothers and sisters, they hate all the people around them, and they hate the authorities they believe should have made everything all right for them in the first place. However, the person they hate the most is themselves. They loathe themselves, they despise themselves, they think that they are good for nothing. All the rest is displacement. They hate others to displace the unbearable pain of hating themselves. Watch any teenager, and you will recognise traces of this syndrome, which is why terrorists are mostly recruited in their teenage years.

From there, they become determined to prove that they are worth something, indeed that they are better than anyone else. So they go off on a crusade, using their displaced hatred to fixate on a genuine grievance. When it comes to the "Muslim threat", that grievance is the way Western powers have interfered in the Middle East, establishing the State of Israel, and supporting barbaric, despotic regimes like the Saudis in their greed for oil. You can trace most of al-Qa'eda's origins to Saudi Arabia. So they hate, and then they kill in a righteous crusade. Seeing that there have been 1,000 years of war between "Christian" Europe and "Muslim" Arabia, why would it be that surprising that they should enlist in the continuing armed struggle? You had the Christian crusaders invading Arabia from the eleventh century, the Arabian invasion of most of Southern and Eastern Europe until the late fifteenth century, an armed stand-off for a few hundred years while the Western powers concentrated on beating up each other, then the wholesale invasion of the North African states by the Western European powers in the nineteenth century. These terrorists may be angry, but they are also traditionalists, radical fundamentalists in a political, as well as a religious, sense.

All of which may explain them, but doesn't suggest what to do with them. For me, the most effective gambit is to treat them like bags of different acids. If you keep them under hermetic restraint, they will end up leaking all over each other rather than corroding the rest of the world. If you frustrate these bags of homicidal fury long enough and consistently enough, they will eventually turn their blind hatred to a more attainable target, which is invariably each other. It is the battery hens principle. They live in appalling conditions, they cannot take out their truly justified revenge on the farmer because it is physically impossible for them to do so, so they scratch and peck each other to death instead. If you contain and frustrate terrorists, they factionalise. There may only have been 27 of them to begin with, but split into three rival factions of nine each, they begin to hate the other factions far more than they hate their original common enemy. Their displaced hatred is reallocated to more attainable targets. Simmer and stir occasionally.

Anyway, I am tired, I have drunk several glasses of whisky too many, and I will now stop ranting and go to bed. I can tell Tessa all about it in the morning, but like all politicians' stories, they are so oft-repeated, that she can probably recount them more word-perfectly than I can nowadays.

✻　　✻　　✻

I have been running my next planning session with another group of enquiring minds within the ministry, and it is a disaster. Sir William is there again, as are Livia and Susan, there are another eight assorted folks around the table in the same room. We kicked off the session with the same speeches and the same jokes, the topic is the same (stakeholder analysis), and yet they are as resolutely unresponsive as corpses. I cannot get a contribution, never mind a creative thought, out of them.

I have been running through my repertoire of creative springboards, designed to provoke new and original ideas. I tried the "heroes" game: "What would Bill Gates of Microsoft want from us if he were the Chancellor of the Exchequer? What would Richard Branson of Virgin want?" They exchanged glances with each other. Why would Bill Gates be running the Treasury, when he is already running the world?

"I don't want you to take this literally," I explained.

Nothing. Anomie.

I tried the "Why? Why? Why?" game. From a Treasury perspective, why do we exist? Why do they think that, then why do they think that, and so on. It is called Laddering. You start with a basic premise. For instance, why do people buy petrol (of the petroleum kind this time, not UV's vodka)? To put in their cars. Why do they want to put petrol in their cars? So that they work. Why do they want their cars to work? To get them from A to B. Why do they go from A to B by car, rather than by any other form of transport? Lots of answers, including convenience, it is easier and it saves time. Why do they want to save time? Because they have busy lives. Why do they have busy lives? Because they feel more worthwhile and important if they are constantly busy. Why do they want to feel worthwhile? Because it is a basic human need, and it has not been satisfied for them (back to the terrorists really). So the real reason why people fill up their cars with petrol is to lead satisfying lives. That is where you build your brand, or your policy.

Not this lot. They cannot think of one reason why we should exist from a Treasury perspective. Maybe they are simply telling me the truth.

So then I gave Kipling's seven trusty men a go: what, why, when, how, who, where, how much? Not reliable in this case.

In a final act of desperation, I went for "Ridiculous", my favourite game, the one that never lets you down. "Look, old Roger Danby has been involved in an all-night boozing session at the House of Commons. At two in the morning, he turns to his Treasury Minister, Ellie Battle, sways alarmingly, and boasts what he is going to do with the Department of Charities & the Arts. What does he boast? Please write down the wildest idea you can think of."

Eight people reluctantly wrote down their answers. Seven of them said "Close it down." The eighth said "Sack the Minister." Praise be to the Lord. A sign of life!

"OK," I decide. "I think we can forget stakeholder analysis for the moment. I admit defeat. As we have some time left, I briefly want to ask you about the arts . . . ."

"Believe in them. Promote them. Make them important." Billie is almost shaking in his high octane Scottish accent across the table from me.

"You mean that we don't, Billie?"

"Do we ever? I hope I am not being too forthright, Minister . . . ."

"Fire away, Billie. I have been hoping for this for the whole of this session. Thank you."

"What do we do for the arts? We hand out a few quid to the amateurs and the crackpots . . . ."

The group is watching Billie intently.

". . . . In most people's minds, the arts break down into Entertainment, the stuff that people actually want to pay good money to experience, and Tracy Emin's bed. You remember the exhibition where they found everyone assembled around a fire extinguisher, agonising over whether it was an exhibit or not. A very good point for the contemporary art movement, but irritating to the public. That is the sort of thing we fund. Street acrobats, the thirty minute play in Fulham performed entirely in the dark in complete silence, the worthy 150 piece classical orchestra playing Harold Truscott in my native city of Glasgow. We fund it because no other bugger is going to pay for it, not even the rich culture-vultures who actually go and see it, and can well afford to pay top wack. When have you ever seen a Minister of the Arts juggling balls on the tele with a red nose and floppy shoes . . . . ?"

Uproarious laughter.

"Well I have seen many a minister do more or less that, metaphorically speaking."

"Well, yeah, there are a few clowns . . . ."

"Billie!" Sir William interjects.

"Billie is all right, Sir William," I respond. "He is saving my bacon. He can do and say anything he likes at this moment. Continue, Billie. You are firmly categorised as entertainment at this precise moment. I'll definitely pay to hear more."

Billie rummages around his papers. "I have got my contract around here somewhere. Seriously, when has the Ministry ever run or sponsored an awards ceremony. Most Adventurous Classical Concert outside London, Most Admired Street Performance, Most Original Play, Most Biting Political Satire, Most Incomprehensible Artistic Exhibit, The Artist Most Ahead of His Time?"

"We are not allowed to do that sort of thing," pronounces Sir William.

"Oh come on, Sir William . . . ." Sir William bristles at the familiarity. Billie should not mistake him for me in the euphoria of the diatribe. ". . . . we could persuade the BBC to set that sort of thing up as a Ministry initiative within minutes. We wouldn't have to do a thing, or even pay a penny more. John Humphreys could front it. Joan Bakewell could make all the decisions. The only corner you would have to cut is to pretend that five million people had cast a vote."

"Why not?" I said. "Obviously, we are not going to lie, but as the Ministry of the Arts we are entitled to be very creative with the truth."

"I'll look into it immediately," Sir William volunteered. "Livia, perhaps you . . . ."

"Can I make a suggestion?" I interrupted. "How about Billie working on this one? I rather suspect he is going to come up with something distinctly challenging."

"I'll do it, Minister. Can I be taken off my normal duties? Frankly, they are boring the butt off me."

"As to that, Billie, I cannot say. However, as a piece of advice, if you come up with something outstanding for us to do with the arts, I won't care either."

And suddenly the whole room was talking over each other, trying to insinuate itself onto Billie's committee.

※　　※　　※

Four months later, Sir William and I are at the Barbican as part of our new campaign. We are addressing a plenary session on the contemporary arts, "Deconstruct or Reconstruct?".

I have been asked to give a keynote speech, and somewhat to their surprise, I have agreed enthusiastically. I have even cleared my diary to do it.

My address is entitled: "The arts are the foundations of the future. No government policy is so essential to the well-being of society." Sir William was doubtful about the hyperbole of the proclamation. He might get some fall-out from the other permanent secretaries. "Forget it, Sir William. That is the beauty of inhabiting the murky depths of the oceans. No-one will hear us. And, if they do, it was all my initiative."

Sir William winces. "That would get me into even more trouble. When a rabid dog gets on the loose, it is his handler who faces prosecution." His eyes regard me beadily to see how I respond. I wait for a moment or two for a token apology for the brute inelegance of the thought. He says nothing.

I hold out my hand. No weapons. "Sir William, I do believe you are lightening up. But do remember the way back for when you have to deal with your next minister."

"I'll have no problems returning to the path of relentless self-restraint, Minister. I have trodden it for years."

"In that case, Sir William. Where do we find the girls?"

Sir William's jaw hits the floor with a deeply satisfying accompanying bulge to the eyeballs.

"I am just checking that I can still shock you."

"You can certainly do that, Sir." That little pink, boyish smile of his.

I give the speech my all to a gratifyingly packed audience. Here we are late morning, and it is standing room only. The press is there, encamped across several rows. Too late for caution now. I am committed.

I deliver the speech entirely as Billie has written it. I even deliver it much as he would have said it, Scottish accent removed. There is complete silence in the hall. I attack the previous government's obsession with monetarism (which everyone knows is ours as well). I declare that the true, authentic arts, are not safe in the hands of the commercial entertainment companies (Geoffrey Christian will be receiving a frenzied, ebullient call from Rupert Murdoch in about forty-five minutes). I rave that our smug, bourgeois, complacent values must be challenged ferociously, otherwise we will become too self-contented to survive. I give them soundbite after soundbite, enough to be dismembered by the P.M.'s office a thousand times over.

There is silence when I finish as well. More silence. Stunned silence. Then rapturous applause, and the scurrying of the little media rats as they rush to spread the disease.

I spend a further hour taking questions. Was I really delineating approved government policy? What did the Cabinet think? Would they be seeing Geoffrey Christian in Covent Garden market, rather than at the Covent Garden Opera?

As we return to the ministerial car, Sir William turns to me and says "I thought that was excellent too, Minister."

It is at that moment that I am suddenly confronted with my younger self, of about the time when I was at UV, a few steps ahead of me, turning round to see who I am.

"Hello, again, I greet him."

"We have met before?" my other self asks.

"Many times," I reassure him, "but you don't know it yet. You will get used to it, Adam, and learn to accept it. What were you doing today? Ah yes, the retail conference. Good wasn't it?" I lean over and whisper into my ear "I enjoyed that one, although we have done many even better ones since."

"Sir William," I say, introducing the Permanent Secretary, "this is my younger self, also called Adam, naturally."

"Named after you, Sir? I thought I could see a family resemblance. An absolutely remarkable resemblance, in fact. Are you in politics, Adam?"

"Only local stuff," he replies.

"That will change," I reassure him. "You are in for a meteoric rise, I can assure you. Enjoy your good fortune."

"Yes, sir," he replies.

I hold out my hand. "The next time will be easier, Adam. Must move on, I am afraid." We walk briskly off in front of me. I am suddenly reminded of how I am feeling on my first encounter with the supernatural, and my legs jolt for a nanosecond.

❋   ❋   ❋

The phone goes, and apathy competes not to answer it. Ben sometimes gets the urge, if only to discover who is at the other end, but he has learnt by now that phone calls are much more often a burden than a benefit. He is not even interested in talking to his grandparents. He sees them so rarely that he hardly registers who they are. Old people who phone asking for Mummy or Daddy, and who turn up with presents (hurrah!) and the pall of extended afternoon visits.

Sandy is curled up in front of Cardcaptors.

I have been conversing with people all day, and want some peace and quiet.

Tessa could physically leave it to ring through to the answerphone, but invariably intercepts at the last minute. It could be work, and in her business crises and opportunities blow up in seconds. A couple of weeks ago it was Max Clifford wanting £1 million not to go to the press, and she and her client had to scramble into action like a World War II spitfire squadron.

"Tessa Melton . . . . Oh, hello, Tim."

Is that my father, or another Tim, Tim Bell, perhaps?

"Oh, yes, he is certainly here. I'll call him over." Tessa waves the cordless phone at me in semaphore, and pulls a concerned expression. "It's your father. He has to speak to you personally."

She goal hangs.

"Hello, Dad. How are things?"

"Not good at all, I am afraid, Adam."

"I am sorry to hear that. Is it mum?"

"Mum is dead, Adam."

This is the last announcement in the world I am expecting, and it shocks me numb. What are the chances of a reprieve, of having misheard him? "Sorry, Dad, could you repeat that?"

"Your mother died this afternoon, Adam. She was run over by a car."

"Oh my God!" My exclamation is enough to make Sandy look up from the TV to gauge the turn of events. Despite my horror which is beginning to manifest itself in a cold trembling, I am pleasantly relieved to know that I am still capable of spontaneity, of reacting like a human being after so many years in the trenches.

"How? Where?"

"It was absolutely the stupidest of things. It was seconds. Stupid thoughtlessness, and then she was lying dead in the road . . . ."

"Carry on, Dad. Take your time . . . ."

"We had just been to the post office together. We came out onto the street. Your mother was going to the supermarket. She decided not to take the car because Waitrose is only a couple of minutes away at the most, as you know, and she only wanted some butter and some Branston Pickle for me. I said I would go and see if there were any bargains in Oddbins. Waitrose wines are so expensive. Your mother said she would meet me at the car. I set off for Oddbins, your mother turned and must have tripped on the curb. The next second there was a gasp and a clunk, and the screeching of brakes, and people running, and your mother lying in the road covered in blood. Her head was a mass of blood, pouring out onto the road. The driver was terribly shocked. He stood there saying that he hadn't seen her, he just hadn't seen her, he couldn't have seen her. I went and knelt down by your mother, but it was obvious she was dead. Her eyes were open. She was totally still. I didn't need to take her pulse. No-one bothered me. They kept a respectful distance. The police arrived very quickly and took over. They were very courteous, and concerned and professional. They must get a lot of training in how to handle this sort of thing, and maybe a lot of practice, too, I suppose. I accompanied her to the hospital in the ambulance. They didn't try to hook her up to anything or anything. They knew she was dead at a glance. An ambulance person stayed with me in the back, holding my hand. She was very kind. Everyone was very kind. They escorted me everywhere. They got me hot coffee, and gave me some counselling, I suppose, and asked lots of questions like how old was she, how long had we been married, where do we live, did she have any children. I told them that you were a government minister. That impressed them. They set a private room aside for us, and left me there with her. There doesn't seem to be the pressure on beds that there used to be a few years ago when your mother went in to have her back operation. I think I could have stayed there all afternoon, and all tonight, if I had wished. I asked if I could take her home with me, and they said that regretfully there were some medical formalities to complete with the police, so that would not be possible. Would there be a post-mortem, I asked. They said they doubted it. It had all the showings of a tragic split-second accident, but they had to wait for the police say-so before they could release the body. I may be able to get her back here tomorrow. I miss her so terribly, Adam, you cannot imagine. Even dead, it would still be a great comfort for me to have her here now. I cannot bear to spend the night alone. Is there anything you can do to help me, Adam? Are there any strings you can pull? I must have my Joyce here at home with me. And to think that I will have this loneliness with me now for the rest of my life. Even when she gets here, I cannot keep her here forever, can I, as a corpse in the deep-freeze. I have to let her go, but, please God, not yet. Not tonight."

"Dad, so you are at home now?"

"Yes, I am at home now, Adam."

"I am running for the car as I speak. I'll be up with you in three hours. I will try and get things sorted with mum along the way. The police are usually fairly amenable in this situation. Do you have the name of the police officer?"

"Yes, his name is Sergeant Paul Blessington. He is at the local police station here."

"I'll call him. Hold on, Dad. Have a drink or two. It cannot hurt tonight. I don't need to see you sober. So long as you are capable of letting me in when I get there."

"I shan't be drinking, Adam. I have not sunk as low as that yet. Give me time, and I am sure I will, but tonight I will stick to tea and my private thoughts. I'll be conducting my own memorial service. I am not quite sure how I killed her. Was it my need for alcohol, or my selfish demand for a cheese pickle sandwich, or my reluctance to waste money on petrol, or my inattention in not making sure that your mother crossed the road safely? She was so independent, you know. She hated a fuss. If any of those things had been missing, she would be sitting here beside me watching TV. Avoiding any one of those things could have saved her. It happened so fast. How could it happen so fast, Adam? Why did it happen so fast? Why did it happen? What shall I do?"

"Sit tight, Dad. I will be with you as soon as I can."

"Have you been drinking?"

"No, Dad, I haven't been drinking."

"Are you fit to drive? You must be constantly worn out with that job of yours. I've seen you. You look exhausted half the time."

"Dad, I will be there."

"I couldn't bear to lose you too, Adam."

"You will not be losing me any time soon, Dad. God loves the arts, and he has a soft spot for charities too, and I may be the only chance he has got to save both of them. Hang on in there, Dad. I am on my way."

"I'll be waiting for you, Adam. I won't have a drink before you arrive. I promise."

"Dad, you are entitled to a drink. Have one."

"No, I'll wait. Alcohol has done quite enough damage for one day."

"Had the driver been drinking?"

"No, I don't think so. Anyway, there is not a thing you can do if a pedestrian hurls herself head first into your bonnet, is there? You cannot do anything to mitigate that."

"I'll see you when I see you, Dad. I love you."

"I love you too, Adam. I so wish your mother were here now. Oh Joyce, I miss you."

"OK, Dad. I'll be in the car in a second."

"Don't forget to phone the police and to do what you can. They must listen to you. It will be such a relief to have your mother here at home with me. You cannot imagine what it will mean to me. Just tonight. That is all I am asking for. Just tonight."

"I will do everything I can, Dad."

Click.

I turn and the tears are running down my face. Tessa walks slowly up to me and puts her arms around me, burying her head into my shoulder. "I have to go to Dad."

"What happened?"

I explain.

"God can be so unnecessarily cruel sometimes. What could Joyce have ever done to him?"

"It is the way things happen. You cannot blame God."

"I want to blame God. I want you to blame God too. It will help get you there safely. I am worried about you driving. Should I come up with you?"

"Could you?"

"Of course I can, if you want me there. If I won't be intruding on your private grief."

"Tessa, it would mean more to me than anything if you could come."

"I'll just brief Erika, then, and throw some clothes into a suitcase. You go and talk to the boys. Are you sure your father won't mind?"

"Of course he won't mind. He adores you. He will be honoured that you have decided to come at a moment's notice. He knows how busy you are."

"See you in a second then."

How to break it to the boys? They have never seemed that bothered about their grandparents, but who knows how they will react in the face of sudden death? This is the age when death becomes a bit of an obsession.

"Sandy, could you turn off the TV, please." I ready myself to be forceful, but he switches it off immediately. "Ben, come here." I put my arms around both of them, one each side.

"Sandy?"

"Yes."

"Ben?"

"Yes."

"I am afraid that I have something very sad to say to you. Granny Joyce died in a car accident this afternoon."

They look down at the ground and remain silent.

"Do you understand?"

They both nod their heads.

She has gone to a safe place. Nothing can harm her now.

"Will she always be dead?" Ben asks.

"Yes, Ben. I am afraid so."

"Forever?"

"Forever."

"We will never see her again?"

"No, she will be buried or cremated in a few days, I don't know which."

"What is cremated?"

Idiot. Why did I decide to go into such unnecessary detail?

Sandy turns on Ben scornfully. "Burnt, stupid. Everyone knows that, Ben who doesn't know anything."

"How should I know?"

"Everyone knows."

"Why do they know?"

Sandy is silent. "You are stupid. Really stupid."

"I am not!" Ben makes to slap him over the head.

I grab them closer to restrain them. "OK. OK. Shush! It's OK. It's OK to be upset."

"Ben is so stupid, Daddy. He doesn't know anything."

"I am not stupid!" roars Ben at the top of his voice. "you are the one who is stupid."

"Why am I stupid?"

"You just are."

"Hey, hey, hey. What's all this? Adam?" Tessa sweeps into the room.

Sandy sleepwalks blindly over to Tessa, his eyes closed. "Ben is so stupid. Stupid!"

Tessa cuddles him. "Sandy, that is not a nice thing to say. You know that we don't call people stupid, do we?"

"But he is!"

"No, I'm not!"

"No, Ben you are most definitely not. You are the cleverest boy in your class. Come here. Daddy, could you put the case in the car?"

"Straightaway." I get up, relieved momentarily of the additional emotional burden of calming two distraught children. Tessa is so much better at that sort of thing.

Erika intercepts me before I reach the door. "I am so sorry, Mr Melton."

"Thank you, Erika." She gives me a brave smile. She has been crying too.

We do not talk much as we drive up to Huntingdon. I am replaying many thoughts in my mind, most of them related to neglect. I have so rarely seen my parents since I left home. We used to be so close once, before I started going out at night. It must be terrible looking at your children at the age of eleven or twelve, realising that in five years' time you will have lost all intimacy, all human touch with them. You can cuddle them, but only for a few seconds, and they will be stiff, embarrassed, doing it out of duty and for old times' sake. I wonder if my mother had that presentiment. I see my own children, Sandy and Ben, in my mind's eye, and mourn their death from us.

"You are so brave, Adam. When you get to Huntingdon, you must collapse. You must let your father see exactly what you feel. It is very important for both of you. Will you promise me you will do that?"

"We'll see. I cannot do it on cue. I am not an actor."

"Will you promise me, Adam?" She is willing me to say yes, staring me hard and challengingly in the face.

"I will do what I can."

"Tonight you have the power to make a miserable old man a little happier, to lift his sorrow a fraction. Please take this opportunity."

"I was thinking more about Sandy and Ben."

"They took it very hard, harder than I expected."

"They are probably afraid they will get fewer toys in the future. They must sense that grandfathers are much less reliable than grandmothers."

"Adam, that is grossly unfair. They were genuinely upset. Grandparents mean a huge amount to small children, even if they have only seen them from time to time. Grandparents remind you of your parents at their nicest, when they are all relaxed and indulgent."

"Yes, I was being very unfair. Sorry."

"So you were surprised by the boys' reaction too?"

"To be honest, that is not what I was thinking. I was reminding myself how little time we have left to us with the boys. One blink and they will be gone. And I have spent so little time with them too. Not enough time with them, not enough time with my parents. Not enough time with you."

"You have done what you could."

"It isn't enough."

"It is never enough. I feel as guilty as you do, and I see my parents and our children much more often than you do. You cannot run a business or be a government minister and be at home all the time. It is a fact. Either your home life or you work life has to give. You cannot have it all. And things are much better now than they used to be. We have seen you three nights this week. The boys are beginning to get used to it. Don't mislead them, Adam. Don't start what you cannot continue. They have suffered enough.

They were used to your not being there. Don't raise false hopes. That would be too cruel."

"I should be all right for the moment. I have got the Ministry more or less under control, and you do not get many crises in charities or the arts. You get massive disasters, but the charities are well-practiced in coping with those. All I need to do is to posture, and to try to say how terrible it is in words that are different from the ones I used last time."

"And now we have our own disaster."

"And I don't really have any words for that at all. Only disturbed emotions."

"Just try to share them with Tim, Adam. Be close to him. This is your first chance for twenty-five years. Don't miss out on it. Remember Sandy and Ben and how pleased you will be when they are forty and they hug you when I am dead."

"I hope to God not."

"Probably not, but think of it anyhow. It will be your guide."

Part III

Secretary of State

Chapter 9

"Adam. Geoffrey here. The Prime Minister."

Is this retaliation, or is this why I always announce myself to him?

"You know that a reshuffle is in the wind . . . ."

I'm a gonna, except that if I were, he wouldn't be phoning me personally.

"Yes, Prime Minister."

"We have decided that you have been making yourself far too popular in the C&A. You are making us all look bad. So we have decided to fix you."

"Thank you, Prime Minister."

"So I am offering you the Home Office. Try climbing your way out of that one smelling of roses."

"Thank you, Prime Minister. It is rather unsuspected. I had better phone my wife."

"Can you reach her within an hour?"

"Yes, I think so."

"Do so. We have to make an announcement by the 6:00 p.m. news. Make sure that you have communicated your acceptance to Peter by 5:30."

And with that Clement Atleeism, I am promoted to one of the most important posts in the land, well in line to be Prime Minister.

"Holy fucking shit!" I exclaim.

Tessa, who was in the sitting room, appears in the doorway with an irritated shushing face. "What on earth has got into you, Adam."

I draw myself up very straight and become stern. Tessa watches me quizzically.

"Firstly, may I inform you that I did not use the word stupid, so you have nothing with which to reproach me, however many swear words I chose to use. Swear words are accepted in this household."

"In limited doses given that we have two boys on the verge of their teenage years, who hear a great deal more than you give them credit for, especially things you do not want to hear."

"Secondly, my good woman . . . ." Ben has poked his nose into the hallway too to appraise himself of the situation. ". . . . from now on you, and the boys, and you Ben in particular . . . ." Ben's eyes widen. ". . . . will refer to me as Mr. Secretary of State for the Home Office."

Tessa gives an almighty whoop, and leaps in the air. "Holy fucking shit," Ben exclaims. "Wait till Sandy hears this."

Erika finds the whole family dancing around the salon in inebriated celebration, without so much as a drop of alcohol having passed our lips. She joins in too, joyfully, without asking why.

"That must be worth something," calculates Sandy. "I wonder . . . ." He is an astute child, almost too intelligent for his own good.

❋   ❋   ❋

I recall a few years ago looking up the Home Office structure on its website, which proclaimed at the time: "Home Office structure: Find out how the organisation is structured and run."

I think there was a comma missing. It should have read "Find out how the organisation is structured, and run."

It is enormous. It is responsible for law & order, passports and immigration, drugs, race relations, the police, prisons, and the science and research facilities related to all of the above. A few years ago they chopped the Department in two, prevention and detection on one side, and prosecution and punishment on the other, but they were soon glued back together again.

To be honest, it is not its vast scope which is the problem (at least it is relatively cohesive), it is its vast capacity for crisis. If you are the Home Secretary, the last place you are to be found is at home.

Except in my case. I have decided to follow the doctrine according to Ronald Reagan as President of the US., and as Governor of California before that. Get up at 9:00. Have a light breakfast and read the funnies. Get to the office by ten. Knock off any issues immediately requiring my attention by 12:00. Play a round of golf. Take a siesta between 2:00 and 4:00. Finish off the day's business. Snuggle up with Nancy, and a nice cup of Ovaltine or, in my case, Tessa.

Tessa has made me promise never to disappoint the boys by becoming an absent father again. I dare not disappoint Tessa anyway, so that takes care of the boys too.

I have my first meeting with Sir Edwin Palmer, my new Permanent Secretary. Just before this, I have my last official meeting with Sir William at the C&A. I remind him to watch his Ps & Qs from now on.

Susan Welsh transfers with me, and sits in on the meeting.

"Good morning, Sir Edwin."

"Good morning, Mr. Secretary of State." He regards me expectantly. He suspects me off secreting some rubber shoes and a stick-on red nose about my person. He is a totally different character from Sir William. He has the boyish face, the coldness and the ambition reminiscent of Paul McCartney, at least if you are a John Lennon fan. So, in my turn, I ready myself for a spirited rendition of Mull of Kintyre. Imagine the shame of it. You have spent fifty years penning musical masterpieces, and all that people remember you for is Mull of Kintyre. What a tragic end to a life.

So we are standing there, both guarding ourselves against fits of giggles.

"Anything up, then, Sir Edwin?" I inquire casually.

"This is the Home Office, Sir. Never a quiet moment."

"So what are you going to entertain me with?" I restrain myself from bursting into Mull of Kintyre.

"Well, Sir, for your delectation for today, we have, in no specific order of importance, the outcry over Martin Spasbury who was let out on remand last Thursday, and promptly proceeded to rape and murder two old age pensioners in the nearby park yesterday. There is the shock and outrage over the crack-heads being fed free crack and the heroine addicts being fed free heroine, as part of their programme of rehabilitation, again. There is the dismay that sixteen Sun journalists disguised as illegal immigrants managed to get into Britain by bus—of course, having authentic British passports might have helped. There is the guy who tried to set fire to himself in Oracle's headquarters in your old haunt of Reading as a protest against globalisation, and losing his job. There is the ongoing identity card crisis, the ongoing detention of immigrants crisis, the ongoing al-Qa'eda crisis. Need I go on?"

"So, everything is under control then, Sir Edwin. No decisions for me to make."

"Well, if you could weave the same sort of magic as you did over at the C&A by waving a magic wand, that would help."

"I am none too sure I want to do that again. Expectations are too high, and this Department is far too complicated for quick fixes. What should I concentrate on immediately?"

"For my money, Mr. Secretary, I would focus on al-Qa'eda. Something is brewing. Sir Julian, my counterpart over at the Foreign Office and I have been swapping notes over the last few weeks. Something is definitely about to happen."

"Do the security services agree with you?"

"They always agree with you if you think there is a threat. They are paranoid. I realise, Mr. Secretary, that you are on record as saying that we talk up these types of threat to national security in order to aggrandise and enrich ourselves, and, off the record, I would have to confess that I have a tendency to agree with you. We are all in politics with a big P or a small one after all. However, this is something different."

"What makes you say that?"

"I cannot tell you exactly. This Youssouf character, possibly. He seems to be of a different pedigree from your off-the-shelf, off-the-wall identikit Muslim agitator, haranguing the West for its iniquities."

"For a start, he isn't a Muslim, is he?" I am pleased I have picked up a few essential details about him in my travels.

"No. He claims to be a Christian Muslim ecumenical, except that I don't believe he uses the word 'ecumenical'. He is all for Christians and Muslims joining forces, and purging undue Western influence, and Russian influence for that matter, from the Middle East."

"Where is his power base?"

"Geographically or organisationally?"

"Both."

"His geographical power base is on the Kurd borders of Iraq, Iran and Turkey. His structural power is in that he is loosely tied into al-Qa'eda. We cannot prove it yet, but we know it to be true. He spends far too much time denouncing the Saudi royal family to be other than in al-Qa'eda's pocket."

"And his implications for us?"

"None specifically. It is simply that the Middle East is heating up, we have too many radical Muslims living here ready and willing to prove themselves in a Holy Jihad, there is the possibility of hard core dissident cells having gained enough knowledge of biological and nuclear technology through two defections from the Iranian development programme to consider WMD manufacture, and Youssouf wants to make a high profile visit to the UK to explain his doctrines, and the sainted Mayor of London wants to invite him. Finally, it is Prime Minister's question time in the House this afternoon, as you know, and you are required to give answers to three questions, for which we will brief you in a few minutes, if that is all right with you."

"I think I am already nostalgic for the cosy calm backwater of the C&A, although I am relishing the challenge."

"We have survived so far this morning. We merely have to keep up the good work for another five years."

"Susan, is there anything you would like to say?"

"Not for the moment, Mr. Secretary. I am taking it all in. Soaking it all up like a sponge."

"Be careful, Susan," counsels Sir Edwin. "People tend to get squeezed around here. The pressure to judge things exactly right is intense, and the deadlines are deadly."

"I have known Susan for many years now, Sir Edwin. She is of the type of sponge that soaks up water but does not release it again."

"An invaluable skill, Sir."

"Susan is indeed invaluable."

❉   ❉   ❉

"Susan, I need to free myself up. Can you take up some of the slack? Actually, I mean a great deal of it."

"Certainly, Adam. What are you planning to do?"

"I am planning to avoid being sucked down the vacuum cleaner hose. You cannot judge where you are once you are in the bag."

Susan exudes extremely quiet confidence. Silence mostly. She only passes on a few observations during any given week, yet they are all ruthlessly insightful.

"You take over here. I am going home to read my boxes. Please send over the additional boxes as they arrive."

"And if Sir Edwin wishes to speak to you personally?"

"He may do, but I am not coming in, and he is not invited over to my house, short of Youssouf landing on Pevensey beach with a squadron of ships and a battalion of archers."

"He will do his best."

"I know. Use my permanently engaged private line. I hope Sir William has not tipped him off about that."

"I doubt it very much. He and Sir Edwin are mortal enemies. They were both up for this job."

"Ah."

"The other thing I would like you to do for me is to find out how popular or unpopular I am."

"You are very popular, Adam, both here in the Home Office, where everyone has high hopes for you, and in the country at large. You are the most popular government minister."

"Yes, I have seen the papers, but I would like chapter and verse, and for the fundamentals to be tracked each week. I am talking about the general public. What makes me popular with the electorate, and how can I leverage that? I have an instinct that we are going to have to make some pretty hard decisions, and I want to be on as high ground as possible when we do."

"How should that be funded, Adam?"

"Have a word with Sir Edwin. Wrap it inside a thorough measurement and tracking of the reputation of the whole department. That can come from departmental funds."

"They will have rules, no doubt."

"Susan, I want to know exactly where I and the department stand. Understood?"

"Yes, Adam. Talking of the which, your old colleague Tasha from UV called to speak to you yesterday, to congratulate you on your new position."

"Really? Now, if you could get her on the payroll . . . ."

"Presumably we could as a contractor. It would take a little too much time to get her recruited and selected by the civil service."

"Find out what she wants. Thanks."

"Do you realise, Adam, that your sentences are getting shorter, and your pronunciation more clipped?"

"A sign of leadership, Susan. Leadership. And I look people straight in the eye."

"Have a good day, Adam. I will be in your office if you need me."

✳   ✳   ✳

"Adam, what are you doing?"

"Reading the papers and having my breakfast."

"Shouldn't you be in the office?"

"That is the last place I should be."

"I am confused. What exactly are you doing here?"

"Working."

"Reading the papers? Not even your official papers?"

"Exactly."

"And then?"

"And then I go out and meet people, or attend Cabinet meetings of whatever for the rest of the day."

"It looks a great life if you can get it."

"Tessa, you made me promise that I would be at home to see the boys."

"But they are at school, and I am at work. How does this help?"

"I take the boys to school. I see them every morning, they know I am in the house half the day at their beck and call if they want to contact me on their mobiles, and I catch up with them, and you, at least two evenings a week."

"What does the Prime Minister think of all this? And Sir Edwin?"

"Not my concern, really. What are they going to do about it?"

"Geoffrey could sack you."

"Then he can go right ahead, but he isn't going to sack his most popular minister in a hurry, unless I become too popular and threaten the rest of the Cabinet."

"Are you the most popular minister?"

"That is what I am finding out at the moment but, either way, I will be."

"Well, it is certainly different."

"Look, Tessa. You wanted me at home. I am at home, indubitably. What exactly are you complaining about?"

"I am worried that you are making a fool of yourself. That you are acting arrogantly, which will lead to your downfall."

"a. I am not going to fall, and b. what if I do?"

"Then you will be out of a job."

"I have worked solidly for over twenty years, I have my non-execs which bring in a living wage, you have your own source of income. Why worry?"

Tessa scratches her head. "I suppose I am confused by the sudden change of attitude. I am frightened, perhaps even guilty, that I have insisted on something which will only damage us all in the end."

"Sit down, please, Tessa."

Tessa consults her watch anxiously. "I have meetings with clients to prepare for. I must be going."

"When are you meeting your clients?"

"One this afternoon. One tomorrow."

"Where is this afternoon's client?"

"Here in London."

"You have ten minutes."

Tessa pulls out a chair reluctantly, and assembles herself awkwardly at the other end of the table. "What do you want to tell me?"

"I want to explain my thinking. We spend so little time doing that with each other. When I have finished, I think that you will be as calm and relaxed about the whole thing as I am."

"OK."

"Tessa, am I a strategist?"

"Yes, Adam, you are definitely a strategist."

"Did I put Petrovsk vodka on the map?"

"Yes, you did."

"Did I put Assert on the map?"

"Yes, you did."

"Did I help put the Labour Party in government?"

"Yes, you did."

"Did I put the C&A on the map?"

"Yes, you did."

"What is the capital of China?"

"Yes, you did." Tessa smiles sheepishly.

"Do I need to put the Home Office on the map?"

"No, I would think that it is pretty much there already."

"Do you think that the Home Office can run itself, without much interference from me?"

"I should think that they would even prefer it that way."

"What are the two things Sir Edwin cannot do temperamentally, despite all his other virtues?"

"Be a politician?"

"Exactly, he cannot be a star, and he cannot make judgments on the basis of their popular appeal in direct contradiction to their merits. That is where

I can help him, but only if I am a star, and only if I know what the people, and the tribunes of the people, the media, want. That is what I am very, very good at. I have no interest in running a department on a minute-by-minute, or minutiae-by-minutiae basis. Luckily, there are tens of thousands of people attached to the Home Office who love doing exactly that. What they cannot do is what I am good at. They cannot work with the big picture. Only a few people are gifted in that way, and I am pleased to say that I have proven over the years that I am one of them. So that is my strategy. I let the department run itself. I let Sir Edwin make all the decisions he has always wanted to make, and where he has previously felt total resentment against dimwit ministers interfering. Now he can lord it over the junior ministers instead, with my blessing. My job is to ensure that whatever decisions he makes coincide with what the country, or at least that part of it that votes, or could vote, Labour wants over the medium term. I am not interested in what will benefit people in thirty years time. I shall not be a politician in thirty years time. Equally, I am not interested in Chinese meal policies, deeply pleasurable for an hour or two, but leaving you dissatisfied thereafter. What I am looking for are policies that will deliver when I need them to deliver, partly now, partly in about three to four years time, when Geoffrey steps down and I make my bid for his job. I can only do that by having an intense understanding of, and insight into, the public mood, as it is now, and as it will be over the next five years. That is why I am commissioning research on myself and the department, and will be tracking the ebb and flow of public opinion on a weekly basis. That is why I have hired Tasha, because she is good, and because I can trust her. We must invite Mark and her over here, by the way, along with Susan and Tony. That is also why I scrutinise the newspapers for at least two hours every day, to really know what questions people are asking, rather than sitting there like a goose having arcane facts pummelled down my throat because a bunch of civil servants think that is what I should know. I will be the judge of what I should know, not them. And when I need specific information, for instance in response to a Prime Minister's question, they can tell me. In the meantime, I sign all the papers, scrumple them up a bit, scan them for anything that might catch my eye, and put them back. And to keep Sir Edwin on his toes, I give him five questions a day I want answers to, without my having to go to the effort of looking for them. And I make sure that one of those questions is a complete nightmare to answer, based on my research of the newspapers. That keeps them all occupied, embarrassed because they cannot deliver exactly the answer I want, and out of my hair. For the rest of the time, I go out and smile at people and make nice, listen to people's concerns, grab photo opportunities, show empathy with the TV cameras. People don't want ministers to make decisions. They want us to make them feel more important, to listen to them, to agree with them, to be able to say to their friends that they had a chat with me personally last week, and that I listened to everything they said, and agreed with them at the end. 'What is he like?' their friends will ask. 'Oh, he is a very nice guy, very approachable, very human. I feel I could have had a beer with him. No side.' Getting it right is easy, really. Just stroke people's egos, make a bunch of popular decisions then, a couple of times a year make some really tough ones so that people don't ever get the impression that you are a wimp."

"What are your popular decisions for today then?"

"Leave prisoners with a history of violence in prison. Find another way of handling the identity card issue. Have something that people actually want to have, perhaps work with the credit card companies. Praise the police for managing an impossible job with dedicated professionalism, and try to persuade them to sort out their embedded racialism once and for all. Avoid any discussion of immigration and illegal immigrants. Leave that to the courts. I can try to stamp out racialism in the police, but I don't stand a chance with the public at large. I cannot really have an impact on the rate of immigration because it is all governed by European and international law, and it is one of those issues that whenever you open up the box, you are never going to win, however Draconian or liberal you are. So, don't open up the box, stupid. People have an absolute right to be concerned about the racial harmony of our country. We are working night and day to promote an appropriate level of integration within the communities, everything else is subject to a commission, in the courts, and subject to multilateral treaty negotiation. Period. That is my conclusion."

"You are still going to face some horrible crises sooner or later."

"Sure, but I am going to approach them fresh. The whole of the Home Office is trained on a daily basis to deal with crises. They can handle the crisis. I will handle the PR, in an affable and approachable manner."

"I just hope it all works."

"So do I. I have been assured by a very much higher source that it will."

"Not the angel again."

"Well, she contacted me. I didn't contact her."

"Then she walked out on you and broke your heart."

"She obviously decided that her job had been done, and that she didn't care about my heart. Easy come, easy go, that's angels for you. I think I'll aim for an archangel next time. More bottom."

❋   ❋   ❋

"Well, what have I got?"

Tasha introduces me to Sylvia Lawless from Research International who has been overseeing the market research.

Sylvia pushes herself forward.

"Pleased to meet you, Mr. Home Secretary."

"Tell it how it is, Sylvia. I prefer honesty, although I have to say it is disconcerting being my own product for a change."

"You have very little to worry about, Mr. Home Secretary. The results for both your department and yourself are exceptionally good."

We settle down. Sylvia sits next to me, intimately placing her printed presentation between us. I can feel her breath on my face. By the same token, she is probably experiencing mine. I hope I am not smelly. If I am, Sylvia is controlling her natural reactions dutifully.

"What do you want to address first, your department or your own personal image?"

"Have you ever met a politician who is not an out-and-out egotist?"

"I do not know many politicians in that depth."

"Put it this way, does the research describe me as an egotist?"

"Not in the least."

"So how does it describe me."

"May I explain the methodology briefly?"

"By all means."

"We ran six focus groups according to the profiles Tasha Wolf submitted to us. Tasha and Susan watched four of the groups." Tasha and Susan nod in confirmation.

"The outputs of these groups provided the variables as input to the quantified study we ran against a nationally representative sample of 2,000 people."

"Understood."

"We used mostly closed questions in the quantitative study, with five open ones to make the interview run more smoothly, and to capture some spontaneous mentions, which have a value in their own right, separate from, and over-and-above, the quantitative analyses."

"Understood."

"For instance, one of the open questions was 'Which member of the government do you think is mostly likely to listen to the Arctic Monkeys?'"

Tasha and Susan giggle conspiratorially.

"And the answer?"

"Well, the real answer is that no-one in the government is very likely to listen to them. However, if anyone were to, it would be you. You were about the only mention, 3% of the total sample, 85% of all mentions."

"Is that good, do you think?"

"It was not a quantitative question, so we could not correlate the results to the overarching measures. My guess is that it suggests that you are at least still alive."

"A useful attribute in a minister, I suppose. What next?"

Sylvia hesitates.

"OK, Sylvia. In one breath, one, two, three, go!"

"Intelligent, slightly rebellious, courageous, young in attitude, a bit smug, a likely contender to be the next Prime Minister."

I try to bury my smug emotional reaction. Keeping as straight a face as I can, I observe "I can settle for that. And the department?"

"Concerned for the security of the country, a little autocratic and nanny-state-ish, competent, patriotic, reliable."

"Excellent. What is our present rating, out of 100?"

"73%."

"And mine?"

"64%."

"Oh. Room for improvement then."

"We ran your results against our normative database for politicians. You are well within the top 10%."

"So, how do we improve?"

"Overall, you need to show greater humility, both you and the department, but it is not a big issue. If you are both a bit dominant and yet clearly know what you are doing, that is perfectly satisfactory. In these dangerous times, the people are looking for a firm lead and flawless competence from the Home Office and from yourself as the Home Secretary."

I lean back in my chair. "So, we are in the gravitas business are we?"

"Gravitas, yes, but also a new way. Finding some solution to the impending threat. Intelligence and questioning are key attributes as well."

"A tall order."

"Tough times."

❋   ❋   ❋

We enter the Cabinet Room and head for the seats where the attendant blotters proclaim our function. There are twenty-one of us today, and we pat each others' egos in passing conversation as we edge towards our places.

Geoffrey Christian joins us last, and proceeds towards his traditional chair at the head of the table, in front of the fireplace in this elegantly chandeliered mid-Victorian shrine to civilisation.

As with most British institutions, a Cabinet meeting is a denoter of hierarchical status. The Prime Minister is, inevitably, top dog. The Chancellor of the Exchequer and the Secretary of State for the Foreign Office are in pole position and I, as a newcomer to the Cabinet, yet as Secretary of State for the Home Office, am straight in there at number 5.

However, the hierarchy acknowledged by the Cabinet Room is not the hierarchy of the Party, and even less the hierarchy of life. That requires a much more complex calculation than this attestation to appearances. To work out your true hierarchy score, use the formula current position x trend (over 100% for upward mobility, less than 100% for declining years) x bookies odds for Prime Minister (scored again in percentage terms) x obsession with obtaining the top job x underlying state of health. On that basis, I am coming up fast on Roger Danby as Chancellor for the Exchequer, several points ahead of Robert Salstice in the Foreign Office who has repeatedly seen his decisions being overriden by the PM, and watchful of Nathan Ketts, the Secretary of State for the Environment who is the star burning brightest in the media at this precise second.

In short, I am surrounded by colleagues who are also foes, which is safer than being the Prime Minister who is surrounded entirely by either those wishing him dead, or fair-weather friends who will remain so as long as he remains useful. In this respect, Geoffrey is a role model to be emulated. He is a master at balancing his favours, and at leaving the succession wide open. Once it closes down to a couple of identifiable successors the media can rally behind, he is gone. There again, after three terms he will be gone anyway, although one thing you can definitely say about the Labour Party is that it is far less ruthless than the Conservatives, and surprisingly tolerant of failure. If you are the Conservative leader, and it looks doubtful that you will win the next election, you go down under a threshing of knives. The Labour Party will at least stand back and let you lose.

My guess is that we are talking two to three years before Geoffrey is replaced. That might suit him too. He is looking increasingly strained and isolated. The real problem is imagining what he will do after retirement. Politics seem to be his only life, which might induce him to hang on for a period beyond his natural term. He will probably continue in parliament after his demise as a lordly father of the party until he is no longer able to stand or speak. Given his dour personality, it is safe to assume that he will cause very few problems for his successor.

The Middle-East is near the top of the agenda today, as it often is. Geoffrey wants to exchange intelligence, with both a capital I and a diminutive one, which is not the same thing as diminutive intelligence, except in Robert's case (sorry, I could not resist that cheap joke).

Robert is playing the Middle-East safe. Recognise the maximum level of threat, and tread cautiously. Geoffrey senses that the country has an appetite for action, for us to be seen to be in charge of events, which we manifestly cannot be in reality. What do I think?

"Well, Prime Minister, my advice is that we should exercise restraint, underplay the threat while still acknowledging it, and come to a judgment as to whether Youssouf is a potentially useful ally or an outright menace."

"Is that your advice to us, of your department's advice to you?"

"That is my working hypothesis which is broadly in line with the advice I am being given."

Robert and Roger both raise their eyebrows at me.

"You are saying, therefore, that we should consider building bridges with this Youssouf, despite the fact that US intelligence has classified him as a firebrand with indelible al-Qa'eda connections?"

Geoffrey is of the school of British Prime Ministers who believe that we should never stray from the side of the US president on anything beyond whether US embassy officials should pay the congestion charge in London or not.

The two Rs are shaking their heads in dismay. The rest of the room is watching me with rapt attention. Will I stumble at the first fence? Am I staking out political ground that I will sink straight down into?

"My personal feeling, Prime Minister, after careful analysis of his speeches, and with the able assistance of several Middle-East experts, is that Youssouf is forging an increasingly independent path, backed by a groundswell of opinion, where he is beholden to no-one. He appears to be, in fact, a genuine radical."

"Continue."

"For instance, he is calling for Muslims and Christians to recognise the common origins of their beliefs and to work together towards a peaceful solution. That is some way away from our understanding of al-Qa'eda's doctrine, and indeed from that of most other movers and shakers in the Middle-East. He is also sharply critical of China's genocide, as he terms it, in Tibet. I have never heard of al-Qa'eda attempting to make common cause with Tibetan monks. Chinese politics are entirely off their radar screen, beyond a certain desire to cadge some money off the Chinese government, and therefore an extreme reluctance to criticise it in any way. You then have his proclamations that God does not abhor the female figure, and does not require that it be hidden from the gaze of men any more than that the male figure should be disguised from women. That runs completely in the face of the fundamental beliefs of the Iranian government, the Taliban, al-Qa'eda, Hamas, you name them. In fact, it is extraordinary that he is still alive. Someone up there must be looking after him."

"And you think that perhaps we should too?"

"Perhaps. I only raise it as something that should be explored and not ruled out until we have gained a clearer picture."

"No way," Robert interjects. "If the Home Secretary is right in saying that Youssouf has a tendency to rub al-Qa'eda up the wrong way, he is not likely to be around for long, so why would we compromise our position supporting a soon to be non-existent loser. If, on the other hand, he is distancing himself from his historic allies all the better to support them, we would be dupes to fall for his game. Either way, we should stand well back, in my opinion."

"Agreed," Roger declares.

"What does anyone else think?" Apparently not too much. It is dangerous ground on which to venture an opinion when it is not required.

"In that case, for the present, I recommend that we simply watch and wait, and keep in step with the Americans. They do not have any plans of which I am aware to take him out of the frame, and certainly no plans to befriend him." He sweeps the room for confirmation or disapprobation. "Let's move on, then."

After the session, Robert comes up to me. "We must make absolutely sure that we speak as one on this one. Any hint of a disagreement, and the press will have us for breakfast, lunch and supper. Youssouf is an incendiary issue, mark my words, and he will sink us all before he is done if we are not extremely careful."

"I will not do anything which diverges from what was agreed today in Cabinet session, I assure you, Robert. I concur entirely that this is not a topic for frank and open debate between ministers on Newsnight or the Today programme. We must proceed with excessive caution. All I am saying is that I have an emerging suspicion that the Americans may have got him wrong, at least with regard to his links with al-Qa'eda. Of course, he is absolutely not a friend of the US foreign policy for the region, and is utterly damning of the Saudi royal family, so there are other reasons why the US may wish to see him neutralised before he foments endless trouble, or sets off a domino effect. Equally, if they are seen as condoning his attacks on China, that could threaten global stability. It is a difficult one. There again, the Middle-East is a real twister, as you know better than I. I only have to worry about the ripple effect over here."

"That is plenty to worry about, Adam."

"Yes, indeed it is."

❈　　❈　　❈

Round the bend in the road, we emerge under the walls of Wandsworth Prison, and turn through the gates. Julian Fleming, my Home Office minister, is with me. A select posse of warders awaits us, fronted by the Prison Governor, John Ward.

"Good afternoon, Mr. Home Secretary. Good afternoon, Minister."

"Pleased to meet you, Governor."

"Another day under the grey Wandsworth skies."

"That is probably what your guests think."

"They live under Wandsworth Prison neon. That is even more unchanging, and maybe as depressing. Please follow me, gentlemen, and I will show you around."

This is my first prison visit. I am not quite sure, even, why Sir Edwin and Susan set us up with this one, except that it is within twenty minutes of the Home Office, and it is one of the largest prisons in Europe. No doubt the next one will be in Scotland, and bristling with serial killers, violent gangsters, and mother and father rapists. Wandsworth contains a regular class of prisoner, in comparison, and offers them relatively civilised conditions following its refurbishment of a few years ago.

I would still not want to live or work here on either side of the locked door.

We are escorted along a row of cells while Ward chats away to us in practiced commentary. I ruminate on the fact that this prison was built at about the same time as the Cabinet Room was made operational, in the 1850s. Worlds apart, except that both environments are overly bright. There is a definite absence of chandeliers here in Wandsworth, though. As we pass the seventh or eight cell on our route, I glance inside and gain a fleeting impression of a middle-aged man sitting there with his head in his hands, looking frail. I stop in our tracks, and take the few steps back, bumping into a couple of our entourage in the process. They both apologise to me immediately. I peer into the cell. It is unoccupied.

"Was there anything you specifically wanted to see?" Ward asks me accommodatingly. That one is empty, so we could look inside if you wish, not that you cannot inspect even the occupied ones with the permission of the inmates."

"We need their permission?" Julian questions him.

"No, not absolutely, but it pays to ask. We will be entering their homes, so to speak."

"Understood."

We move on, and spend about two hours in the prison altogether, during which time we are offered the formal opportunity to invite a group of prisoners to opine on the conditions here, and to raise complaints if they wish.

From what I think I saw in that empty cell back there, it will be very much in my interests to address any issues they raise, which they don't, beyond the quality of the food. I think the emaciated prisoner I observed back there was a ghost of the future, of my future indeed.

Chapter 10

Tessa is worried that I may be visibly shirking my responsibilities. There are so many issues circulating around the Home Office, and so much public concern, yet I am hiding out in our house in Barnes.

Susan and Sir Edwin have suggested much the same thing, and now the tracking results are indicating some statistically significant declines in popularity and respect for both myself and the department.

Time to take myself out on a media roadshow.

With Susan's help, I make myself available to be interviewed by almost any broadcaster who will have me. Let us see what happens, and whether my initiative helps or hinders our overall reputation.

It is a morning, noon and night operation. By the time I have finished, millions of people around the country will be exclaiming "Not that man again! Is he ever off our screens? Hasn't he got anything better to do, like run the country?", throwing their slippers at the set, if anyone wears slippers nowadays. I can then retreat to Barnes, confident of having taken Project Overkill to its limits.

I may not be there, but at least the boys can still see me at night, although their grasp of politics is shockingly under-developed.

I decide to go into my campaign to answer questions on the "Muslim threat" head on. Susan and I have worked out my angle. There really is a Muslim threat. There have been a thousand years of Muslim threat which, in Arab countries, is known as the Christian threat. Yes, there are indeed some very nasty people out there who would like to kill us at any opportunity they can carve out for themselves, however to use this fact as a basis for discriminating against all British Muslims is not only outrageously unfair, it is also irresponsibly dangerous. To play up the real danger is to act as a recruiting officer for the terrorists. Young British Muslims will start to think it is their duty to sign up for active service because everyone else is doing so. Yes, we could go even further and stamp down hard on anyone who gives off any hint that he or she might be related to al-Qa'eda, but that would be to bring the sky down on our heads when the problem at the moment is that there appears to be an ominous crack in the ceiling. Our best defence against terrorism is hope, tolerance and prosperity—traditional British virtues. How many people do you know living the good life, with partners, children and a promising career who want to strap explosives to themselves and rocket themselves off to Paradise from Wigan, Barnsley or Stoke-on-Trent town centres? Terrorism thrives on poverty, low self-esteem and hopelessness. That is what we really have to combat. Nearly every Muslim you meet in Britain is your friend. One in 20,000 perhaps is not.

And what about Youssouf ben Abdul? Well, the political scene in the Middle-East is notoriously tricky. Those whom you believe to be your friends turn out to be either your enemies or futile liabilities. Those you believe to be most hostile to the West can prove to be invaluable allies. Watch and wait, and do not leap to conclusions either way.

Before making any real appearances, I go into a recording studio to run a dummy interview with the retired broadcaster, Trevor McDonald. His instructions are to press me as hard as he can. He does an excellent job. I walk out of the test virtually suicidal, until Trevor says "Excellent performance, Home Secretary. Very tight. I couldn't gain a foothold anywhere." The film is then shown to twelve focus groups around the country to gauge their reaction. They prove very positive to the message. Contrary to the rantings of our more outspokenly chauvinist press, most people do not want the roller-coaster of a racial witch hunt, however exciting that might end up being. Indeed, they don't want any excitement at all. All they crave is to be allowed to carry on shopping in peace, and without interruption, in the certain expectation that they will get to return home with lots of bags and no shrapnel wounds.

My first joust is on Newsnight against the Shadow Home Secretary, Malcolm Brown. He is packed with more explosives than the average terrorist. He tries to out gung-ho me, and hoists himself magnificently on his own irascibility. In French, a pétard is a fart more than a mine. He makes himself look like a right stupid fart. I don't encounter him again during these three weeks of interviews. After a couple of appearances, the Conservatives start tossing me Liberals instead. We just sit there agreeing. The punters turn off in their droves. "I think you had better publish a book," John Humphrys tells me after Today has gone off the air. "There is no mileage left in the Muslim threat unless something dramatic happens." The security spooks keep telling me that a bombing is inevitable within the next three months. We watch and we wait.

In the meantime, the only things to explode are our ratings. Sylvia and Tasha report the results as if they were for the World Cup finals. The department and I are both skyrocketing. Whether I like it or not, we are co-extensive. Our reputations rely on each other's successes. Sir Edwin walks round with a little, sly smile on his face. For the moment all is well.

❋   ❋   ❋

Which it shockingly isn't at home. It was Tessa who noticed it initially. Sandy seemed to find it hard to focus. His mind raced and rambled. He fixated for long periods on static objects, like the privet hedge outside the kitchen window, or the kitchen counter. He is convinced that the driveway used to be longer, and that the flower bed used to be shorter. It becomes increasingly difficult to persuade him to recall anything accurately.

"I am lost in my head, Dad," he explains. "Leave me alone. I am happy to wander around in here."

"I think you need to do your home work, Sandy."

"Home work? No, I don't have any home work."

"Sandy, it is sitting here."

"Oh, that. I can't be bothered with that. It is pointless. Let me rest for a bit."

Sandy sleeps a lot. Most teenagers sleep exorbitantly, but he is barely a teenager. He is only just fourteen. He loved his birthday, and thanked everyone wildly for their presents, however I found him several times during his party sitting alone.

As a parent, you do not want your children to be ill. As a busy parent, you cannot really afford it. As a Cabinet Minister, a son in mental distress can open up some menacing chinks of vulnerability in your carefully constructed armour. I would like to think that this is not a consideration, but truthfully it is.

Ben, two years younger than Sandy, watches the developments in his brother cagily. Until recently, they have been very close. Now, Sandy is pushing Ben away, and Ben is pushing back, albeit reluctantly, resentfully. I can see that he is profoundly disturbed by his brother's behaviour, more so than any of us, but he is internalising it. I sense that he tortures himself with shadows of guilt, the suspicion that some of his unkind words may have snuck in and turned his brother's soul.

I am watching Sandy slouching opposite me on the sofa. He is staring at the shifting pictures of the TV, without engaging with them. I ask him if he would like some coffee. He transfers his gaze to me, without replying.

"Would you like some coffee, Sandy?"

He is still staring at me.

"Sandy?" I urge more forcefully. "Coffee?"

He smiles sweetly. "Sorry, Dad. I just can't get my brain together at the moment. Don't worry. It will catch up with me eventually."

I sit with Sandy in his bedroom. We are holding each other.

"Do people ever tell you things, Dad?"

"All the time, Sandy. I mostly ignore them."

"What if they are decent, trustworthy people?"

"Those are exactly the ones who give you misguided advice. The people who want the world to be better than it is are no guide to the world as it is, I am sorry to say. I learnt many years ago that the world does not work from first principles. Nothing is a should be. Everything is as it is. It works, it doesn't work. That is the only test. We can spin our theories about how things work, and how things can work better, but the people who actually make things work, and actually make things work better, do not follow those theories. They work from instinct, and from precise intelligence that targets their actions. They are invariably pessimists, not nice people at all. They recognise the world at its worst when everyone else is wishing it better, and grab everything for themselves while the rest of us are distracted in wishful thinking. Successful people do not dream, they plan, and they plan on the weaknesses and the dreams of others. They give to people what they think they want, and they take what they actually want. Do not listen to kind people, Sandy. They are not worth it. In fact, do not listen to people at all. The bad ones will get you into even more trouble than the good ones, unless you are already in their camp, and I don't think that you are. I know that you aren't in fact."

I hold Sandy and remember the boy he used to be, so loving, and trusting, and believing, and so wanting me to be there to play with him when I often could not. How will this illness change him? Is he hearing voices? Is that what he is alluding to?

Sandy kisses my cheek. "The decent people say that I should love you Dad, with all my heart. You badly need all the love I can give you on the path you are following. What do they mean, Dad?"

"I don't know, Sandy. Who are these people?"

"They say they are angels, Dad, and that they have come to guide us all. They say that you already have an angel who is returning to you. Trust her. Obey her, wherever it takes you. She has a mission you must not ignore."

❋   ❋   ❋

The nice people are advising Tessa, and I suppose me, to check Sandy out as a possible schizophrenic. Tessa is all over the place with worry, and is consulting every source of information possible.

She pulls down a list of symptoms of schizophrenia from the Internet, and ascribes, reluctantly, the vast majority of them to Sandy.

"Adam, they say that if it is schizophrenia, it must be treated early. The earlier it is treated, the more effective the treatment. We need to get him to a specialist now."

I have been reading up on schizophrenia too. The fascinating thing about it is that its symptoms cover pages, and overlap with the symptoms of a thousand other illnesses. In fact, schizophrenia is mostly defined by what it is not. If it isn't drug-induced, if there isn't a temporal lobe tumour, if it isn't syphilis or AIDS, if it isn't Alzheimer's disease, if it isn't Wilson's disease, if it isn't Fabry's disease or Fahr's or Hallevorden-Spatz disease, if it isn't heavy metal poisoning, if it isn't Creuzfeldt-Jacob disease, if it isn't Huntingdon's disease, if it isn't Wernicke-Korsakoff syndrome, and if it isn't about a hundred other things, it must be something, so let's call it schizophrenia. It is getting more and more like autism as every minute passes. If someone picks up a telephone directory and starts to read it, and he doesn't hear you announcing lunch, hell he's got it, God darn it.

"We have to act fast, Adam."

"Why?"

"Haven't you been listening? Because the sooner this thing is addressed the better."

"So he'll be put on Risperdal, or something."

"Probably, but it will be better than his suffering from hallucinations. It is such a vulnerable time for him, during puberty. Children don't understand. They'll tease him to death. He will get worse and worse. If we can bring the symptoms under control, he can live an ordinary life."

"I am not convinced he is suffering from schizophrenia, Tessa."

"Adam, you are in denial. You don't think there is much of a Muslim threat either."

"I don't think one should over-react, and I don't think quick fix solutions, like drugs and fascism, solve many problems either."

"I really think that we should at least consult this specialist."

"And, if he diagnoses Sandy as being definitely schizophrenic, we believe him?"

"Are you an expert on schizophrenia, Adam?"

"If I read any more articles on the subject, I will be. Or rather, by reading all those articles I know that no-one is an expert. A diagnosis of schizophrenia is merely a point of view. Anyway, what does Sandy think?"

"He is willing to try it, Adam. He is scared. He is very scared." Tessa bursts into tears. I move to hug her, but she shrugs me away. When she has recovered her breath she says "I can't help thinking that you are making things more difficult than they need be here, Adam. I know you do not want your son to be ill. I promise that I don't either. Yet, if he is, we must do everything we can to help him. That is what he is begging us to do. He thinks he is going mad."

"He doesn't sound that frantic about it to me."

"Since when have you ever really talked to him about it? You haven't the time, understandably. I am his mother. I can still feel what he feels, even if he is fourteen years old now."

"OK, Tessa. We'll consult the specialist, but resist being the eager pupil, I beg of you."

"Let us hear what he has to say, and keep an open mind."

It sounds like my Middle-East policy . . . .

❋   ❋   ❋

. . . . which is in shatters as of ten-thirteen this morning. A huge bomb has gone off in the Trafford Centre, outside Manchester, killing four people, and injuring forty-three. The police are pouring over CCTV footage to identify the culprits. They believe that at least one of the victims was a bomber.

I am cavalcaded into the Home Office at great speed, sirens whizzing and lights flashing, and convene an emergency meeting with Sir Edwin, Julian and eight key departmental staff who are experts on security issues. My flight up to Manchester Airport is booked for 13:40. It is imperative that I am on site in time for the evening news. My security experts warn that there is an outside chance that there will be a second attack on the most likely flight for me to take, which is the BA flight I am actually taking, or at the airport. I decide that I have to take that chance.

The press wants to know if I have changed my mind about the severity of the Muslim threat. I declare emphatically that what I said before still stands. There are a few people out there ready and willing to perpetrate the most appalling atrocities, but there are not many of them. Unfortunately, you cannot guard everywhere around the clock, and the security forces cannot be expected to pick up on every possible incident before it happens. I pray for the victims and their families in their grief and suffering.

The press plays down my response, and focuses on the fact that I was warned that something like this might happen a few months ago. It also speculates whether I am really up to the job of being Home Secretary, and whether I devote the amount of hours to it that it truly requires. Somewhere in there I detect the hidden tongue of a Roger Danby or a Robert Salstice spokesperson, although I cannot pin them down. Malcolm Brown gets to Manchester before me, and mocks me for being so slow to get there, and for failing to prevent this terrible tragedy from happening. His party would, naturally, have invested a great deal more money in this very real threat, and acted on any intelligence far more quickly and effectively.

At the next Cabinet meeting, the Cabinet votes to increase the anti-terrorism budget, and afterwards Geoffrey Christian himself announces that I will be introducing new legislation to crack down on terrorism.

I am losing out on all sides. Mr. Sunwady, the specialist, detects "without a shadow of a doubt" that Sandy is suffering from the early stages of the onset of schizophrenia and prescribes a short, sharp dose of Risperdal.

"What are the potential side-effects of Risperdal, Mr. Sunwady?" I enquire.

"Side-effects in a patient as young as Sandy are most unusual, Mr. Home Secretary."

"And in other, more vulnerable, people?"

"Well, to give you a full list, they can include blood clots and haemorrhaging, vomiting, constipation or diahorrea, aggression, anxiety, chest pains, impotence, dizziness and respiratory infection."

Tessa frowns.

❋ ❋ ❋

"The Manchester bombing has certainly dented your ratings, Adam," Tasha announces. "You don't want too many of those."

"I never did, ratings or no ratings."

"The research suggests that your best bet is to make a statement denouncing Youssouf ben Abdul as being potentially personally behind the attack."

"We have any evidence for this?"

"That is not my department, Adam. I am just telling you what the research says."

"Hum."

"And you might be advised to embark on another round of the TV studios, preferably denouncing Youssouf ben Abdul. That would maximise your recovery potential."

"Tasha, I am going to take some of Sandy's Risperdal, and drown out your evil suggestions."

"Adam, as you always say, say it as it is."

"Indeed, Tasha. I am grateful, really. Do you fancy a spot of lunch?"

"Why not?"

"Well one why not would be if a paparazzi caught us on camera. Home Secretary dallies while Manchester burns. Never mind, we cannot live our lives in permanent fear of media terrorists. Let's go."

Seated at a discreet table far into the interior of Belgo's, I catch up on the careers and lives of the Petrovsk crowd. George Grice died of lung cancer a year ago. William Cranwell is now the MD. Ricky Brabant has gone to Diageo, Jim has split up from his wife of thirty-seven years and is living on his own, Spencer now has three children, Lucy has retired to the country with her rich banker husband, Gerry is living in the Welsh mountains playing keyboards, and Jilly is still there, albeit now in my old job of Brand Manager.

"How about you and Mark?"

"We've been going through a difficult time. Mark is working all hours at Britvic, and living in a flat in Chelmsford four days a week. He seems to be building his circle of friends out there, and seeing less and less of our old friends around Reading. He is drinking too much, too. We had a huge row last weekend. Mark wanted to bring some people down from Chelmsford, and I said no way; I never see him as it is. I am a bit suspicious. The person he keeps wanting to introduce me to is a woman called Ginny. He talks about her quite a lot. Perhaps I should get him to bring her along so that I can get a good look at her. And you Adam, now that you have heard my woes?"

"Well, the big worry at the moment is Sandy. He has been diagnosed as a mild schizophrenic, as you know. He is on an increasing cocktail of drugs, the one to offset the side-effects of the other, and he seems to me as if he is going downhill rapidly. He won't talk to me at all, or to anyone else as far as I can tell. The drugs seem to be isolating him, which is not a good thing."

"How is Tessa coping?"

"Much the same as me, extremely nervous. We are having quite a few fights of our own too, truth to tell." I flick my head round in a scan of the room to ensure that nobody is over-hearing us.

"Oh dear. It used to be so much more simple in the UV days."

"That is because you had only just started work, and you were getting off with Mark."

"We were even talking about having children then, before I found out that I couldn't."

"Did you go for IV or anything?"

"No. To be honest, our relationship has always been a bit rocky. I sometimes wonder whether I haven't conceived because I thought we might never last."

"How long is it now, the best part of twenty years?"

"Almost exactly, come to think of it."

"I am surprised that you ever got it together. You used to fight like cat and dog."

"Nothing much has changed there then. I think it has been a mistake really. Too late now. By the way, have you ever seen that Turkish woman again who walked out on you?"

"No. Never again."

"So how did you meet up with Tessa?"

"She came to Assert's offices, and she sold herself to me. I think she was drawn to my charitable side."

"How does she cope with your political side, then?"

"She is an excellent wife. No complaints. Being in PR, she does and says all the right things, looks good, and even gives me timely advice, although she is somewhat peeved that I did not act more decisively, as she sees it, in relation to our omnipresent friend Youssouf ben Abdul."

"Oh well. Somebody will assassinate him sooner or later. He seems to be making plenty of enemies, especially among the religious fundamentalists."

"Yes, I think they are having rather a hard time with him. Not as hard as the US and China though, not to mention Saudi Arabia. I think the verb is to fulminate. He fulminates against them at every opportunity. The Russians like him. He can always go and live in Moscow if the Middle-East gets too hot for him, if he can afford it, that is. As far as I can tell, he is one of the few of that lot who are not stashing the cash into foreign bank accounts. He may just have to stand there with his back to the wall and take it. Interesting character. You cannot help admiring him really. He has some integrity in amongst all that noise. I hope I am still off the record when I say that."

"Your secrets are always safe with me, Adam."

"Where are you off to now, then?"

"Home. I think I'll go and collapse in front of a film. Giving you all that bad news this morning has exhausted me. And you?"

"Back to the office. It is more relaxing than home at the moment."

❋   ❋   ❋

"How about a weekly blog?"

Tasha laughs down the other end of the phone and affects a seductive voice. "Is that an indecent proposition, Mr. Home Secretary?"

"I suspect that Sir Edwin will view it that way, and probably the Prime Minister and several of my Cabinet colleagues as well. It had better be a good one to make it worth my while."

Tasha laughs again. "I specialise in good blogs, Mr. Home Secretary."

"Do you really?"

"Actually, yes, I ghost write three of them at the moment, two corporate ones and one technical one. It is a cheap, easy, immediate and engaging way of communicating with your target audience, as you well know. What does Susan think about it?"

"I haven't mentioned it to her yet. It is an idea I only had during the early hours of the morning, when I was awake worrying about Sandy. I went to his room notionally to guard over him. He seems to be regressing. He had Lego pieces all over the floor. I think he is trying to assemble all the smallest pieces into a complex model of his own design as a metaphor for what is happening in his own mind, and how he can pull all that together too."

"I am really, really sorry, Adam. It must be heartbreaking."

"It would be if I didn't have so much faith in him. Something tells me that he is going to be OK, and that he would be infinitely better if we took him off his medication. He is already grappling with a very elusive, and destructive foe, without befuddling his mind further with anti-hallucinogenic drugs. They seem to clamp him into his mental casing, rather than letting him breathe the air of chaotic freedom. I have been thinking of taking him along to a cranial osteopath, to literally help his mind to breathe."

"And Tessa?"

"Tessa is fully signed up as the guard on the runaway pharmaceutical gravy train. There is no reasoning with her. I keep saying that I want Sandy off these mind-bending drugs, and the next thing I know she is cracking open Mr. Sunwady's latest chemical present."

"How does Sandy react?"

"I think he would trust me enough to follow my lead, but he loves his mother, and wants to take her pain away."

"How are you and Tessa holding up?"

"I don't think we are. We are developing our own little Middle-East, Christian against Muslim divide. I appear to be on the side of the Muslims, the medical infidels, radically opposed to scientific progress, the free market and democracy."

"That may not surprise too many people, Adam."

"So how do I get this thing kicked off? Will you write it for me, together with Susan? You can cover off the marketing angle, Susan the political one."

"If she is game, I am. It will distract me from Mark's affairs, anyway."

"He is definitely having them now, is he?"

"I don't have any evidence for it, but my woman's intuition tells me definitely yes. He is behaving towards me physically very strangely, long periods of distracted distance punctuated by aggressive demands for sudden intimacy. I don't think he is going to leave me as yet, but he is certainly grappling with things, and almost certainly with someone, I would guess this Ginny woman. Maybe I am wrong. Maybe it is a man."

"Mark? I don't think so."

"You could tell?"

"Yes, men can usually sense if another man is gay, as women will probably recognise a lesbian."

"I am not sure that I could."

"Anyway, I must move on. There is total mayhem here. The security spooks are expecting another bombing within the next couple of weeks. They think that the terrorists will want to prove that they can strike on a repeated basis. I fear they may be right. I am about to authorise a high profile raid on the usual suspects, lots of kicking down doors and men in blankets being forcibly ducked into unmarked police cars. Our hope is that the public will find it all very reassuring, and that it will scare the shits out of any cells as they prepare for their strike. If we can make them anxious enough, they may either decide to put their plans on ice for a while, or get panicked into making a mistake."

"And in the middle of all this you are thinking of setting up a blog?"

"It just struck me that the public might be more reassured if they felt that they had a direct line to my inner-most thoughts. It would also be a great way of explaining on a regular basis what we are doing. We have to get those ratings back up there somehow."

"Well, if you discuss it with Susan, and she agrees, I am ready when you are. Here's to your being the greatest thing since sex."

"I thought it should be sliced bread."

"I don't know how quickly people identify a new brand of sliced bread, but they say that a sex site is discovered on average within 30 minutes of launch. It is one thing to publish a blog, but another to get it read. I think we need to get a couple of articles written about it in the Sunday newspapers. Should a Secretary of State have the right to publish his own blog? Pros: that Police Chief Constables are already doing it, and it is a fundamental human right to be able to express yourself, plus the public gains a greater and more informed insight into the day-to-day workings of government. Cons: collective Cabinet responsibility, the Official Secrets Act, rampant ministerial egotism. That should kick things off nicely."

"I will have a word with Susan straightaway, and come back to you Tasha. Thank you. I am most grateful. How long will it take, do you think, to get this thing off the ground?"

"When we have the content, about three to four hours. If you are confident that you are going ahead, I will set up the site now. You can buy the software for around £100. Site hosting with robust bandwidth, assuming tens of thousands of hits a day, another £500, say. All-in-all, let's call it a £1,000 set up and then my fees on top at £2,000 a blog, as a quick estimate, assuming 1-2 days' work a week."

"That doesn't sound too unreasonable for the amount of publicity it will get, and the opportunity to build up a really trusted communications channel. Do people get the chance to comment on what I say?"

"Yes, that tends to be included as standard in most software."

"I think we should definitely encourage that."

"Then the cool thing is to unleash some of that Internet crawler software onto the content to automatically analyse it for you. Well worth £150,000 a year, I would say. I don't know what your department spends on its publicity machine, but I would bet you that £150,000 is a drop in the ocean."

"I will discuss it with Sir Edwin after I have spoken to Susan. So long as Susan is supportive of the idea, we will go ahead anyway and run it as a pilot. I will simply tell Sir Edwin that he is paying for it if he values the continuation of our cordial relationship, not to mention his job. We will have to clear a couple of hours a week together to devise each publication, and we will have to get them approved by both Susan and a civil servant nominated by Sir Edwin to ensure that they do not contravene the law or the ethics of government in any way. Is there any day of the week which is best for publishing a blog?"

"I would suggest it should be a weekday, and that we set up an automatic alert to inform people that a new blog has just been published. This should go out between 10:00 and 12:00 in the morning, or between 2:00 and 4:00 in the afternoon. If it comes in overnight, people tend to treat it as SPAM. SPAM detectors are a constant problem in this sort of game; they are real poacher-gamekeeper territory. It would therefore be best if additionally you were to publish your blog at the same time on the same day of the week so that people know to go and search for it if the alert doesn't get through. The negative to that is that you might get one million people crashing into the system at the same moment, if we are really lucky, which will have the tendency to provoke a denial of service through system overload. If we buy enough bandwidth, it shouldn't be a problem. I think I'll up it a bit."

"OK, Tasha, you go off and do your bit. I'll do mine. Exciting times, eh?"

"Indeed they are, Adam. This could be fun."

"And I'll agree some dates with you for us to meet up once I have all the clearances at this end. Where should it be do you think? Can you get to the Home Office OK?"

"For £2,000 a pop, I'll meet you anywhere."

"Let's start that way, anyway, then we'll see. Good to do business with you, Tasha. Have a good day."

"You too, Adam."

Chapter 11

Tessa has taken to her bed. I say her bed because she wants us to sleep separately a. until she is feeling better, and b. until we can agree on Sandy's treatment.

I have been trying again tonight to lay down the law and insist that Sandy be spared his drugs. I argue that we could at least see what happens. We argue endlessly.

Eventually both Sandy and Ben appear at the door of our bedroom, having woken up, anxiously concerned.

We explain what we are arguing about. Sandy stays by the door, a curious rat perched on the edge of a roomful of cats. Ben ventures in, and sits bolt upright on our bed.

In desperation, I turn on Sandy and ask "What do you think, Sandy? Do you think your medication is good for you?"

"Don't know. I would be happy to stop taking all those pills. They are getting harder and harder to swallow, and they make me feel pretty toxic. If I kissed someone, she would almost certainly die."

"You kiss me rather often, and I am still alive," Tessa counters.

"Mum, you are in bed ill. That may be why."

Tessa realises that she cannot rationalise her way round that one. "It is too great a risk."

"What is the risk?"

Tessa goes all starchy. "We need to discuss this when we are alone. It is unfair to involve the children in a topic they are not qualified to discuss, and you know it. You are employing cheap debating points. Keep that behaviour for the Commons, if you don't mind."

"None of us is qualified to discuss it, not even Mr. Sunwady, I get the distinct impression, not even the greatest living schizophreniologist. Schizophrenia is an unmapped terrain."

"There are some people, Adam, and Mr. Sunwady is one of them, who know a very great deal more about this subject than you do. No doubt, having been Home Secretary for a few months, you have been flattered by your departmental lackeys into believing that you are God almighty, and are capable of becoming an instant expert on anything and everything without the unfortunate chore of having to study the topic in any sort of depth. Some people have at least experienced case after case after case of schizophrenia, so even if they are not 100% certain about the diagnosis, they can have a damned good shot at the prognosis. And they have had a damned site more experience than you have. They believe that it is in Sandy's best interests to continue taking his medication because, if he doesn't, he may have to suffer this thing for the rest of his life. He will have to suffer it, Adam. You won't."

"Tessa, you may be absolutely right, but I would still like to try Sandy without it for a few days. I am not demanding that we take him off it forever, only that we give him a few days' holiday, and see what happens."

"The Trafford Centre happens, that is what happens. That is what always happens when you watch and wait."

"OK, Tessa, you win, and having won there is no longer any need to look so fucking miserable."

"What are you trying to do to our children, Adam?"

"What are you doing, moping around the house as if the Doomsday machine were pointing at our front door?"

"Adam, I am under a great deal of strain. I have a child who is very ill, and I still have a very demanding business to run without tens of thousands of people to help me."

"Oh, and I was under the impression that these wonder-pills were taking care of everything."

"Adam, just go away. I am ill, the boys should be in bed, and you are picking fights to relieve your own tension. Go and relieve yourself somewhere else, and come back when you can behave like a civilised human being."

"Done," I shout, and walk out of the house. I take the car which, is not that wise an idea as I am probably somewhere close to the limit. I return to the office. The security guard is pleasantly startled to see me. "Good evening, Mr. Secretary. In for a spot of overtime?"

"We have to make ends meet somehow. Children are hideously expensive to rear nowadays. £250,000 each, or something, don't they say?"

"Well, I don't think ours cost quite that, not on my £200 a week."

"Oh well, some children must cost millions and distort the average." I have lost him.

I walk along the darkened corridors to my office. I used to enjoy working late at night at Petrovsk. You felt that you owned the place. Nowadays, in a sense, I do.

The mobile goes. I do not answer it. The phone goes. I pick it up.

"Adam, come home. The boys are extremely upset. Let's not fight."

✻ ✻ ✻

Victoria Street. Lunchtime. I am wondering around really only for a spot of exercise, and perhaps a little to show off that I don't have any bodyguards. People keep looking at me, shuffling on, turning to look at me again. In a minute or two, someone is going to walk into a lamppost. I am tempted to wave at the more curious who are holding a particular adjacency to a lamppost. I could do with a good belly-laugh, although that might not appear quite seemly.

I hear footsteps rushing somewhere near me. Light footsteps, so I am only mildly alarmed. Someone accosts me head on. I try to push the person away. I wish I had a bodyguard after all. "Adam!"

I recognise the voice without being able to fully attribute it. It is a woman. It is Yasemin. I get immediately excited, which necessitates that I hold her close to me until I can work it down again. People notice every detail about a public figure.

"Adam! You are pleased to see me!"

"What on earth are you doing here?"

Somebody in a second is going to take a photograph. Now that every one of 75 million mobile phones in the UK has an integrated camera, I am surrounded by forests of the little sneaks as I stand there. Picture. Send. Instant news story round the world, with photographic evidence courtesy of our 24/7 society.

"Don't worry, Adam. I don't think I show up digitally. There will be a picture of you hugging some clothes. Freaky but not incriminating." The momentary panic has flattened my erection.

Come to think of it, I never did manage to get a photograph of Yasemin during our brief relationship, not that I tend to take many photos anyway. There was one session we did at the arboretum near Lightwater, one sunny, misty autumn weekend morning. I must have taken twenty photos of her walking towards me from the car, lounging against trees, jumping in the air, promenading around the lake, draped across several follies, and walking back towards the car. Somehow, the film had become exposed to the light. There was only a riot of red and yellow blanketed over impressionistic shadows. I wasn't left with clear shots of scenery and uninhabited clothes. I got nothing. It had never occurred to me that Yasemin was beyond unphotogenic. In the early days of our courtship (hate that word), Tessa asked to see pictures of Yasemin, and was surprised, and actually shocked, that I did not have any. She immediately made sure that I was stocked up with five or six photographs of her in tastefully blocked Habitat frames.

"So what are you doing here?"

Yasemin does not look an hour older than when I last saw her fumbling around in the front of her car twenty years ago. She might even look younger.

"You look amazing. Don't you ever look your age?"

"Several thousand years old, is that what you mean? What should that look like?"

"Is that how old you are?"

"Yes, but time passes extremely quickly when you are constantly saving the world and all the lost souls within it."

"Is that what you have been doing?"

"Invite me for a coffee and I will tell you."

We wonder into Starbucks. Standing room only. "Yasemin, it is amazing to see you."

"You too, Adam. I have been waiting a long time."

"Over several thousand years, you must have met a few men, though."

"Believe it or not, very few I have been as fond of as I am of you."

"You must be after something."

"You know I am."

"I am a married man, Yasemin."

"And not that, as you also know."

"Your boss doesn't believe in adultery, doesn't he?"

"I believe he has passed a law on the subject. No-one says you have to get married but, once you do, you should honour your commitment. In fact, two laws. I mustn't covet my neighbour's husband either."

"Have you ever met Tessa?"

"No. I was gone long before you hooked up with her."

"I thought perhaps you might have checked out the competition."

"No need to torture myself. Besides, I have been far too busy."

"So has God arrived yet?"

"Yes, for many years now."

"Do I know him? Have I heard of him? Does he use an alias?"

"He will reveal himself in his own time."

"He is a he, is he? None of this post-modern feminist she-God stuff?"

"No, he has decided to remain a he. I am not sure why. He will have his reasons."

"And you will not tell me who he is?"

"No. You can wait to receive further orders."

"Will I ever meet him?"

"Yes, you will meet him."

"Is he scary?"

"No. He is lovely."

"And he won't let us continue where we left off?"

"Yes, he will let us. How we behave is our choice. That is why he gives us free will. He would not approve, but he won't stand in our way. It is I who am standing in our way. This time, Adam, it is strictly business. I am here to ensure that you become Prime Minister. We cannot afford you making any mistakes that cannot be recovered. Of course, you will make a mistake, Adam, so I am here to clean up after you."

"What mistake will I make?"

"You already know what it will be."

"I will be too generous to the terrorists?"

"No, that you will handle exemplarily."

"I will get myself sacked for something I say in my blog?"

"No, but you are getting closer."

"I'll go down in the Night of the Long Cabinet Knives?"

"Not even that."

"What is it, then? What could be close to a faux pas in a blog?"

"A faux pas with a blogger."

I laugh mockingly. "You think I will have an affair with Tasha? You are joking. Why would she look at me?"

"She has always looked at you."

"I am hardly going to betray Sandy and Ben like that."

"You didn't mention Tessa."

"Things are somewhat strained between us at the moment. I prefer to nail my moral boundaries to my children."

"Children do not stop affairs. Consult the statistics."

"Do you want me to have this affair?"

"The issue is that you want to have this affair, and you are in the habit of getting what you want."

"And it won't cause untold misery to my children?"

"Yes, it will."

"But God will not punish me for that? It is a matter for me and my free will."

"God is about to cause untold misery to your children anyway."

"I know that. He is already doing it with Sandy."

"That has nothing to do with God. He doesn't decide who can cross thresholds, and who cannot. Sandy has a gift and a curse. In time he will learn to manage it appropriately."

"With the help of Risperdal."

"Risperdal does not benefit the process. It only makes it more bearable while Sandy learns to manage it."

"So he should continue with his medication?"

"It doesn't matter. One course leads one way, the other course leads another. Neither is significantly better than the other. Flip a coin."

"So what are you going to do now?"

"Right now?"

"Yes."

"Come with you and meet Tessa. I would like to make her acquaintance."

"She is in for quite a shock."

"Yes, she is."

❋   ❋   ❋

We enter the house. Tessa wanders into the hallway. "Hello, Adam. Home early." See spots Yasemin. "I see that you have brought some of your work home with you."

"Tessa, Yasemin; Yasemin, Tessa."

At the double mention of the name Yasemin, Tessa pays attention.

"*The* Yasemin," I answer Tessa's unspoken question.

"Hardly."

I smile, perhaps a little condescendingly. "She is."

"Only if you dated her at the age of six." She turns to Yasemin. "I am lost here."

Yasemin inclines her head. "I am very pleased to meet you Mrs. Melton. I have known Adam a long time; 20 years."

Perplexion shrouds Tessa's face. She simply stands there.

"I have aged well," Yasemin adds, with a girly shrug which does nothing to ingratiate her.

"You must think that I was born yesterday."

"Comparatively speaking," Yasemin replies.

"What is going on?"

"It is exactly what we say, Tessa. What is the problem?"

"There is no way this girl is forty,"

"No, she is not."

"So?"

"Tessa, Yasemin is an angel. Her body doesn't obey universal laws." I say it as if I had known this all along.

"Adam, you know full well that I have never swallowed all this angel rubbish."

All three of us crowd out the hallway, trying to work out what we do next. Eventually, Tessa shrugs and tosses "Come in" over her shoulder.

"Thank you."

Tessa continues conversationally "So, do you work for Adam?"

"No."

"How do you know him, then?"

"I met him in a bar."

"I thought Adam's bar frequenting days were over."

"They may well be. I met him many years ago."

Tessa turns on Yasemin. "Look, I am not falling for this. All right? If you want to shag my husband behind my back, fine, but don't pull all this supernatural nonsense down on me, OK? It demeans us both."

Yasemin retreats into an intense calm, and says nothing.

"Isn't that why you are here? To worm your way in with my husband, and maybe offer him something he will have to be grateful for, probably for the rest of his life?"

No response from Yasemin.

Tessa turns her back. "Oh, forget it." She marches upstairs.

Yasemin turns to me. "Adam, we'll speak another time." She lets herself out. I follow her through the door, but she is already out of view.

I go upstairs to try to sort things out with Tessa. She is preparing to have a bath.

"Adam, honestly, how could you?"

"How could I what?"

An object flies past my ear and lands somewhere on the landing. It looks like a pair of socks.

"Bringing your little bit of skirt here. Haven't you heard of hotels?"

"Yasemin is not a little bit of skirt. She is an angel."

"Adam, don't be completely bloody ridiculous. At least get your facts right. Angels are male. Unless that girl is a transvestite, in which case you are weirder than I think you are, she is not an angel. She is a quick screw."

"And why would I do that?"

"God alone knows, Adam. Tell me. Perhaps your wife does not understand you." As she is speaking, Tessa is peeling her clothes off in an empty striptease.

"Tessa," I almost hiss. "Yasemin is who I say she is. Believe it."

"I don't, and I won't, and I am not having you screwing your secretaries, or your interns, or whatever they are, in this house. This is my home. I could say that I demand discretion at least, but that would not be true. I demand loyalty."

She announces this, naked irritation on her face, naked bottom and upper thighs, cellulited, I suddenly notice, marching away from me towards the bathroom. "I have had enough of this. Clean up your act, or get out." She is still leaving me a loophole.

❋   ❋   ❋

I am trying to understand where Tessa is coming from. Why is she suddenly kicking up a fuss in the pretence of believing that I am a man rocketing into male menopause with a weapon of trash seduction?

It is not as if I have ever given the slightest hint of philandering. Is that the problem? Does Tessa believe that, as she cannot detect me flexing and celebrating my political power through the medium of conspicuous periodic flirting, I must be going the whole way behind her back? Has she become a paid-up member of the "all power corrupts" school of regret? Or is it merely that she is totally freaked out by Sandy's menacing condition? I am a dog, and she is possessed of a stick with the urge to relieve her intolerable anxieties. Or is the all-out war between us over the merits of Sandy's medication destroying our relationship head-on?

Because that is where I see us going. Tessa gets to keep the house in Barnes and both of my children, and I hole up in some sad one-bedroom apartment in town, where I stoke my political career and rue the death of my emotional existence, until I move into Number 10 and royally invite Sandy, Ben and their friends to stay, to sate their curiosity and revel in the resultant kudos, while I hope that Tessa is seething in resentment and humiliation.

This is ridiculous, but I cannot imagine our relationship improving. It has caved in precipitously, yet it is as if its demise has suddenly been revealed to have been inevitable for several years. Until recently, we have spent only a minimum of time together throughout our relationship, and it has become like an old hollowed-out oak, threatening the immediate environment with its imminent collapse, and insusceptible to repair.

I feel sad, very, very sad. And angry. And spiteful. And devoid of even the desire for a solution. The future is written, and the children are already being flayed by their own anticipatory grief.

I will increase my working hours again, and see if this return to the normality of our relationship will reduce the tensions between us, or raze any remaining buttresses to our marriage.

❋　　❋　　❋

Back on Newsnight. The hot topic is my new blog, whose first posting will take place immediately after this programme. Timing is all.

What the presenter, Kirsty Wark, and indeed the nation, wants to know is whether it is "a good thing", whether I am the forerunner in a trend for Cabinet ministers to project their personalities and their inner dialogues onto the Internet, and whether it is safe. Could writing a blog constitute a breach of confidentiality, a breach of collective Cabinet responsibility, or even a potential breach of security?

What I want to know is how many visits this imminent bushfire of publicity will be worth, and will the site that Tasha has set up for me cope with the demand? Will its pipes be big enough? Given a halfway-controversial interview, the topic is bound to be picked up and amplified by the leader articles of the national dailies, by other BBC news programmes, and by competitive networks. I might get in excess of one million visitors a day reading my blog and submitting considered, intemperate or entirely irrelevant comments. Great vehicle, Adam!

When I enter the Newsnight studio, I am expecting to be up against a Tory hopeful, such as my old adversary and punching bag Malcolm Brown. Instead, sitting there in Make-Up, as sprightly as a spring lamb, I discover Nathan Ketts, the dynamic, up-and-coming and highly competitive Secretary of State for the Environment, all ready, and definitely willing, to hose me woundingly with friendly fire. He is playing the caution-distortion and plum-faced gravitas card. "This sort of thing should be given a great deal of thought and be subjected to in-depth debate, before we open up the sluice gates and destroy politics as we know them. It may only look like a bit of harmless fun produced by a barely-responsible left-field maverick, but it has the potential to blow the system apart," not that he says exactly that.

Fortunately, Nathan is a technology backwoodsman, so I should have acres of space to swan around him on a subject which will resolutely evade his grasp.

"Is it appropriate," I am asked, "for a Cabinet Minister with considerable access to highly confidential documents and discussions, to share this information with people from all around the world over the Internet? After all, you cannot control who reads what you write."

"I wasn't planning to discuss state secrets," I reply. "Besides, everything I write will be vetted by officials in my department, by my personal political advisor, and by our lawyers, if necessary, prior to publication."

"Should Cabinet ministers be allowed to peddle their own policies directly to the people, over the heads of the rest of the government, and of their parliamentary party?"

"Look," I lecture as I lean forward into my theme, "when democracy was first invented in ancient Greece, you didn't have government ministers enthroned in corner offices in inaccessible and guarded buildings. The key players were out on the street, mixing it with their electorate. Over the years, government has become remote and unaccountable. Once a government is in power with a working majority, it can pretty well do what it likes, operating as an elected dictatorship. Many laws are not even voted on by parliament; they are passed into force as parliamentary orders at the discretion of the relevant Secretary of State, established under broad-brush paving legislation. This is not democracy, and it is not interesting to the electorate, which is why so few people vote at election time. They have switched off. While voter apathy can be read as a sign of voter contentment, I believe it is much healthier if issues are debated with heat and passion. We live in times saturated with contentious and very important issues—terrorism, identity cards, concerns over the leniency or otherwise of judicial sentences, immigration, to name but four.

Each medium dictates its own pattern of behaviour and of communication. Official announcements are designed to avoid provoking a response. They are therefore wordy, pedantic and anodyne. Blogs, on the other hand, naturally encourage personal cries from the heart. I would prefer us to avoid dampening down debate, even if some people go way over the top and start fomenting racist and abusive views."

Nathan is waggling his bum on the chair, itching to pitch in. "Adam, you know full well that racist and abusive views are illegal, and have been for some time. Are you amending government policy unilaterally, threatening a return to the callous politics of racial hatred, and playing straight into the hands of the BNP? Has your blog already persuaded you that you are a law unto yourself, even before you have published it?"

"No, Nathan. None of those things."

"I am not sure that the commentators will agree with you."

"Then they can say so in their blogs, and you can say so in yours."

"I wouldn't have the first idea where to start."

"You start by having something worth saying, Nathan."

"Gentlemen, gentlemen, before this turns nasty, I would like to ask you, Home Secretary, about your views on electronic referenda. It has been suggested in the press today that you are in favour of putting many more issues to popular vote."

Nathan is feigning amused disdain.

"To be honest, Kirsty, and there are a few of us left who try to remain honest, I cannot recall ever discussing this subject with journalists." I turn to Nathan. "And it isn't raised in tonight's blog either."

"Tell us what is," Nathan demands.

"No," Kirsty intervenes, "I would like the Home Secretary to have the chance to answer the question . . . ."

"I was just hoping to be able to have an open discussion with Adam, on matters he feels passionate about, in the traditional way, where I even get a chance to respond with my own point of view."

"You can reply to my blog, Nathan."

"Not only do I not know how I might do that, but I also suspect that I will not be accorded the same amount of airtime in your blog as you take unto yourself."

"You can write exactly as much as you like, Nathan, and post it in direct response to mine."

Nathan grimaces. "I suspect, Adam, that you are being somewhat disingenuous. People will visit your blog to read your comments, not mine."

"Then start your own."

"That would be to condone your behaviour, which I do not wish to do. I do not approve of government ministers blogging out their personal opinions to the detriment of their government colleagues."

"It is not . . . ."

"Home Secretary," Kirsty interrupts me, "can we move swiftly back to the question about electronic referenda?"

"As I was saying, Kirsty, I do not recall ever publicising my opinions on electronic referenda but, having said that, I certainly have a few."

Nathan sits back in his chair. "Now there is a surprise."

"My view on electronic referenda is that they should be seriously considered as a means of gauging political opinion, initially without any commitment to be bound by that opinion, although potentially in the longer term we could even run a popular democracy that way."

"You are suggesting that you could cut out parliament altogether, and have the voters decide which legislation is passed into law directly?"

"Let's hope that you are in favour of hanging, then, Adam."

"No, I am not in favour of hanging, or of capital punishment in any form, Nathan, and, as it happens, it would be against the European Human Rights Convention to bring it back in again anyway."

"Perhaps the electorate would take us out of Europe too. Very likely, in fact."

"Nathan, there is always a risk in any true democracy that the people actually decide to have things the way they want them, even at the resultant cost of regretting them later."

"Something tells me that the electorate would soon be profoundly unhappy with the powers you had granted it."

"Maybe so, but I am not advocating adopting popular electronic democracy tomorrow morning, or even ever. I am mainly saying that it is a technological possibility, and at least we could use it to gain valuable feedback on proposed legislation before it is debated in parliament."

"So you would still have a parliament, then."

"The original meaning of the word 'parliament' was to describe a talking shop. Issues clearly need to be debated in many ways, in people's homes, in pubs, in blogs, in the media, in Cabinet, and in parliament. This is a separate issue from the question of how laws are enacted, as indeed it was in former times. The landowners got to discuss, the king got to decide."

"So there is the possibility of your dispensing with parliament's legislative role . . . ." Kirsty tosses in.

"Who knows, Kirsty? I repeat, I am not advocating popular electronic democracy at this time. I am merely commenting that it is technically possible to put forward reasoned propositions, as discussed in parliament and elsewhere, for the electorate to have a chance to record its point of view. That is all. And that, if this were to happen, it would make our process of decision making in this country decidedly more truly democratic, for good or ill."

"It would ruin the economy, though. A whole nation of economic illiterates over-ruling the Chancellor of the Exchequer would be a recipe for total disaster, wouldn't it?"

"I am glad you have so much faith in your fellow country folk, Nathan. Illiterates?"

"I did not say that they were illiterates, Adam," (got him), "only that most people in this country are not qualified to draw up a Budget speech."

"Well, you can work on that when you become Chancellor of the Exchequer, if they don't make you Minister for Technology instead."

Kirsty claps her hands together, a lively section of Newsnight having been entertainingly delivered. "Gentlemen, I am afraid that is all we have time for." To camera: "If you want to read the Home Secretary's blog over the Internet, I believe that it will be posted as soon as he gets back to his computer."

"Yes, you can read it on http://www.adammelton.com, all one word."

"There you have it, but as it is not for a few hours yet, don't abandon Newsnight where we will now be discussing the latest developments in stem cell research with the eminent . . . ."

❆   ❆   ❆

We were meant to go up to Huntingdon to visit my dad. We haven't seen him for a while, which is unconsconsciably lax given his infinite distress at losing my mother. He says that he seeks her everywhere, and I believe him.

He could have come to us, but parents of his generation are reluctant to visit their children too regularly for fear of being considered to be either interfering or a burden. In fact, we have often encouraged him, and pleaded with him, to come down to Barnes, only for him to decline our invitation resolutely on each occasion. Maybe he wishes to be confined as a prisoner within the very halls of the memory of my mother.

Tessa announced last night that she would not be coming after all, nor would the children, while at the same time insisting that I proceed without them. This used to be a regular, almost allergic, reaction she had to staying in my parents' house, and I would often find myself arguing with her that it was too late to cancel the promised trip within less than a day of our being due there. She has always felt that my parents never really accepted her into the family, that she was classified as my spare rib, and no more. Maybe she was right, although my parents never shared a word, or a hint, of criticism of Tessa with me.

I offered to take the boys, all the while recognising that they would much rather stay at home. What are they to do with a late middle-aged man for two days, other than to watch TV?

Coincidentally, Yasemin phoned me, declaring that she absolutely had to see me. When I suggested that she join me in visiting my father, she jumped at the opportunity. She only saw my parents once, but it was love at first sight. I half-winced and half-grinned at what Tessa's reaction would be when she found out.

I pick up Yasemin in Swiss Cottage. "Where exactly are you staying at the moment?" I inquire.

Yasemin points over the rooftops to the north-east. "Almost exactly about there. Right, left, right, straight on, left and on your right. It's a large Victorian residence carved into flats."

"What's it like?"

"Worn carpet, narrow stairs poorly converted, cheap front door badly scratched, the smell of curry, and the crying of baby and parents from the neighbouring flat."

I resolve not to rent an apartment like that when Tessa and I split up. There again, the Home Secretary rarely lives in student quarters while still in office. I'll probably set up in the next street in Barnes, and recommence my life as a sitcom.

"Is that all you could find?"

"It'll do. I am rarely there. It won't be for long."

"Why not?"

"You'll see."

"Oh. You've become much more mysterious, and frankly irritating with it, since I last knew you. Is there anything you can tell me?"

"Yes, that you are driving more than thirty miles an hour, and fast approaching a speed camera. Too fast, in fact."

I brake abruptly, eliciting the erratic blast of a horn from the guy in the car behind me.

"Well, that was useful information, anyway."

"Wasn't it!"

"Anything else?"

"There are many things I could tell you, Adam, and many that I can. However, you are much more interested in the rest. Who is God? Why do I live where I live? Do I still love you?"

"Do you?"

"Yes, Adam, I do."

"I was never sure that you loved me before."

"Then that was due to your insecurities, and your foresight that it could not last for long given my vocation."

"Is this time any different?"

"No. Very much the same."

"So, I'll just get used to seeing you from time-to-time . . . ."

". . . . and I will be called away? Yes. And then I will be back again."

"But only for a short time, right?"

"That I don't know. I only know what I have to do up to the end of my mission. After that it may be negotiable."

"With God?"

"Why negotiate with anything less?"

"So, to paraphrase, you do love me and you may stick around in the end, d.v."

"What is d.v.?"

"Didn't they teach you Latin? I thought that was a prerequisite for membership of the heavenly choir."

"That's it. I was never a member. I always sang soprano, when I was meant to sing bass."

"d.v. means 'deo volente'—God willing."

"A very appropriate acronym, Adam, and I assume a cliché."

"Not much nowadays, except in certain London clubs, Oxbridge and the Inns of Court."

Yasemin places her hand on my knee, and my flesh tingles into my groin.

"I have missed that."

"It is where it stops, I am afraid. Unlike last time."

"Pity."

"A tragedy, really. C."

"C?"

"Credo. I believe."

I have not warned my father about Yasemin, so he is momentarily puzzled and nonplussed to be approached by us holding hands. He glances uncertainly from one to the other before a distant memory whispers in his ear. "Am I going senile?" he asks.

"I'm not sure, Dad. Are you?"

"This is Yasemin, isn't it?"

"Nice to see you again, Mr. Melton. It was such a pleasure the last time. Your wife is so sorry that she cannot be here too."

"You are still pretending to be an angel, are you, Yasemin?"

Yasemin smiles sweetly. "It's a habit, Sir."

"Mind you, if you are really Yasemin, and I am convinced that you are, I had better start listening. You haven't changed one iota in twenty years."

"So everyone keeps saying. Tessa took me for the office scrubber."

"Anybody would be extremely foolish to confuse you with a scrubber," my father replies gallantly. "I have never encountered anyone with such natural grace, not even Joyce."

Yasemin inclines her head. "Thank you, Mr. Melton."

My father peers urgently at Yasemin as we approach the house. "Is Joyce perfectly OK?"

"She misses you terribly. Such a stupid thing to do, she keeps saying. Mind you, she is surrounded by souls who have done stupid things, and who are regretting their lives' reminiscences. Not her, though."

"What will happen to her?"

Yasemin hesitates. "She'll have a rest and come back."

"As another woman?"

"Too early to say."

"Not as a cow or a sheep, I hope." My father is genuinely alarmed.

"I very much doubt it," she reassures him. "They tend to reserve that sort of stunt for tyrants, terrorists and other world class troublemakers."

"Terrorists automatically become farm animals?" I but in. "Can I put that in my blog? Bah to the terrorists!"

"You can put anything you like into your blog, Adam. Make yourself look as foolish as you wish. Make my mission twice as hard as it already is."

"I read all your blogs, Adam," Dad enthuses. "Sorry, Yasemin, did I interrupt you?"

"No, Mr. Melton. Adam and I were only exchanging non-verbal communication. He is affronted that I describe my mission with him as being so hard to pull off. It is your own fault, Adam. If you will behave like an idiot." More non-verbals ensue.

"As I was saying," my father continues, "I always read your blog, Adam. In fact, I am rather proud of the fact that I have mastered the technology."

"It is only a website on the Internet, Dad."

"It may seem that way to you, Adam, but it is quantum physics to me. I don't remember you ever writing as well as that before. English literature was not really your forte."

"I have a ghost writer who helps me—Tasha—who used to work with me at UV."

"So the thoughts are not really yours."

"Oh, the ideas are mine, all right. Tasha just tarts up the prose."

"A felicitous choice of words," Yasemin comments.

"I must say that your English is very much more fluent than I remember it being last time," observes my father.

"It comes and it goes, I suspect."

"Before I offer you a nice cold glass of wine, I'll ask Adam to escort you to your room, and then, if you don't mind, I would like five minutes in private with him."

"By all means."

The five minutes Dad wants is to understand whether Tessa and I are still together, or whether I am back with Yasemin. I assure him that Tessa and I are still together, that Yasemin is on a quick trip to the UK, Tessa couldn't come because of pressure of work, and it was a great opportunity to catch up with Yasemin for her to come along too.

"I sincerely hope Tessa sees it that way. I don't think Joyce would have done." Care lines his face with a dark cloud. "You'll never fully understand how much I miss your mother, Adam. It is a shocking thing for me to say to you, but I yearn to die. I pray for it. I would never have guessed that it would ever come to this. Contrary, perhaps, to appearances, we had a pretty stormy relationship for many years. Don't give up on yours. Being a Cabinet minister will not save you from the anguish."

❋   ❋   ❋

Tasha phones me at the office to say that she is feeling really ill, and has had to take to her bed, so she regretfully cannot make our blogging session this morning.

"Is Mark there looking after you?"

She snorts. "I wish."

"Tasha, I don't wish to be harsh, but we really need to get this blog out. If we don't, it will look like I have succumbed to pressure to cool it for a while."

"I don't see that as an issue, Adam. When you publish the next one, only a couple of days late, you will soon dispel the rumour."

"Perhaps I will try something with Susan, and then forward it to you as at least a basis from which you can work. That might gain some time, assuming that you are not knocked out for a week."

"Adam, if you really have to, you can always come here. I am not dead. I can still take notes."

Yasemin's warning and dismissive aside both toll softly in my ears. I as much savour them as heed them. "I could do that. Would you mind?"

"Not at all, so long as you don't mind catching whatever I have. Can the nation spare you for a few days if the worst happens?"

"I don't know, but it is a lovely thought. I have had a frantic and troublesome few days. An imposed rest would do me the world of good; give me back my perspective." I jot down directions to her house.

I take the train from London Waterloo to Reading, first class. Its being mid-morning, I get a block of four seats to myself. I have transferred some of my red box papers to an ordinary briefcase. I fall asleep after about ten minutes, leaving the document I have been reading splayed out in front of me. I wake up as we approach Winnersh Triangle, and am relieved to find the document still safely in my hands.

At Reading, I take a taxi to Europcar. I have decided that taking a taxi to Tasha's house would not be wise. It would be to leave alive (what else?) a potential witness to spread rumours in the press.

"I used to live around here once upon a time," I inform the Europcar desk hand. "My wife, Tessa, and I are considering a house further out of town for when we retire."

"That must be quite a few years away, yet, Sir," he replies. "You have hardly started. Your public will miss you."

"Kind of you to say so."

"My father used to vote for you when you were a Councillor here. I was too young, of course."

"And your mother?" I ask, throwing caution to the wind in case she had died during childbirth, or been kidnapped by aliens, or something, or, more likely, married someone else.

"I don't think she ever voted. 'It only encourages them', she used to say. She is dead now, I am afraid."

"I'm sorry."

"That's all right. At least you haven't lost a vote."

I discover Tasha's house easily in Three Mile Cross. It is a big house, with an extensive driveway. They have either both done exceedingly well for themselves, or one of them has inherited.

Tasha comes down to open the door for me. She is wearing a nightie, with an equally diaphanous, frilly, gown layered over the top of it.

"Sorry, Adam, I had just dosed off. Do you want me to come down to the sitting room, or can you bring yourself to work in my bedroom?"

"Oh, I reckon that after twenty years of acquaintance you are an old enough friend for me to risk mopping your fevered brow in your bedroom."

"Thank you, Adam. It would be a lot more comfortable for me. I am feeling cold and exposed down here. I think I may have a fever."

"So how are things going with Mark?" I inquire as we climb the stairs.

"From bad to worse. He didn't come home at all last weekend. He said he was overloaded and desperately needed to catch up. I reckon he was six inches deep in his work, if you know what I mean."

"Oh dear."

"I've got past caring," she declares, tossing her hair slightly. "And you and Tessa?"

"I think that we are splitting up. I am not entirely sure. I made the mistake of taking Yasemin home to meet her the other day. That did not go down well."

"So, Yasemin has turned up again after all, has she?"

"Yes, I bumped into her in Victoria the other day."

"And?"

"To be honest, she hasn't really said much. I took her home to meet Tessa, as I said, which was disastrous, and we both went up to see my father in Huntingdon last weekend."

"Really? What was his reaction to that?"

"Mildly shocked, and pleasantly surprised, I think. I am sure he rather fancied Yasemin the one time he met her, and she hasn't changed a bit."

"She must have got a little older over the last twenty years . . . ."

". . . . no, that is the whole point, she hasn't. If anything, she looks even younger, but that might be from the perspective of my own advanced age."

"She still looks in her early twenties, or whatever she was?"

"She was 26 when I last saw her. She may be 24 now, for all I know. She says that she is a few thousand years old, but I am never quite sure when she is teasing me. Anyway, Tessa thought I was sneaking home some young totty for at least a session of intensive mutual flirting. She absolutely refused to believe it was Yasemin, and I didn't get the impression that Yasemin was intending to do too much to persuade her otherwise."

"So, how is it with Yasemin? Are you hankering over lost time?"

"Well, she is extraordinary, totally untouched. It is as if she just went down the road and immediately came back again."

"Sounds ominous."

I stop to watch Tasha climbing into her bed, raising the duvet up to her chin.

"No, nothing will happen between Yasemin and me. She is on a mission, and an affair with me is not part of it."

"Do you regret that?"

"Yes, in a way, intensely. The old magic is definitely still there."

"You must be getting a tad frustrated. A wife who wants nothing to do with you, an ex-flame who has transmuted into a nun. Anyone in the office? Susan?"

"No, neither of those."

"Oh well, there is always me."

"You, Tasha? I have never had you down as one of my fans."

"You don't know the half of it, Adam. I had a real crush on you when I started working for you at UV. You were unobtainable, of course, the God of marketing, and my boss. Then you met Yasemin, and by the time she walked out on you, I had something going with Mark, which really pissed me off when you were suddenly available again. I stuck with Mark, and now we both know what an enormous mistake that was, twenty years later."

"I would never have guessed any of that."

Tasha lowers her duvet slightly. "Do you want to see what you have been missing?"

"I thought you were ill."

"I suddenly feel an awful lot better. You are doing wonders for me, Adam."

"At least I am doing them for somebody."

"If it is only me . . . ."

"That is not at all what I meant."

"To hell with it. I'll show you anyway. You can always walk out in disgust."

Tasha throws back the duvet, stands up immediately in front of me, well within touching distance, peels off her dressing gown, and removes her nightie. She holds herself exposed before me. I can smell her skin. "What do you think? Am I still a relatively well-preserved forty year old?"

"Very," I say. I haven't moved.

Tasha climbs back into bed again, this time leaving her breasts exposed.

"What are you thinking?"

"I am rather taken by surprise. Not shocked, just surprised. On the one hand I am thinking that I should not be here, on the other I am finding it very hard to move. I am transfixed here, fascinated."

"How do my boobs compare with Tessa's."

"A lot bigger. Tessa's went about that size when she was pregnant, but she is back to an A-cup now. You must be about a C, are you?"

"Ever the connoisseur." She watches me expectantly. "Aren't you going to kiss them, or shall I cover them up again?"

So I kiss them, the right one first. At the same moment I am thinking "Adam, what on earth are you doing?"

"Maybe I am fulfilling the prophecy," I reply to myself.

Tasha places her arms around my neck. "That is nice."

Parts further down tell me that things could be even nicer.

However, it is as if my entire electorate, Susan as my political advisor, Sir Edwin, Tessa, Yasemin and my mother were in the room, not criticising me as such, just observing. Where is the line here, if the press were to get hold of the story? If they had pictures, I would be done for, but if I merely had to deny an affair, without their having any hard evidence, what could I say? What would they say? When is the moment when a sexual affair starts? When does it start to be sex?

Tasha lowers the duvet to a millimetre above her pubic hair line. Her stomach is flat, and convects warmth. I kiss her belly button. Below me, another level has been exposed, what my mother would call her 'nether regions'. They have the intense, intriguing smell I picked up earlier.

Tasha places two fingers against her entrance, and slips one inside. She removes it again, and guides my right hand there. My middle finger finds its way in. Surely I have crossed the line now, although I persuade myself that I haven't. I am still at the smoking but not inhaling, cigar foreplay stage.

I can hear Sandy saying "Dad, why are you abandoning me? Why are you doing this?"

"Sandy, I am anything but abandoning you. I am having some fun for once."

"At my expense, Dad."

"More at my own expense, I suspect."

"Said like a true egotist."

"Where are you?" Tasha asks me suddenly.

"Addressing my demons," I reply.

"Well, undress them then," she ripostes.

"I am trying to work out if I should."

Tasha laughs. "The offer does not last for long. Don't look a gift horse in the snout."

I undress, to Tasha's helpful encouragement. Now that I am naked, have I crossed the line?

I commence the foreplay.

"Oh forget that, Adam," Tessa lectures me decisively. "I am good and ready already."

I climb onto her, and slide my penis inside her. I have crossed the line. Five acutely sensitive inches have transported me across the Styx to the village of the damned. I am an adulterer, a man not to be trusted, an ex-father, an ex-husband, maybe an ex-minister. Can anything that feels so exquisite as this does at this moment be so destructive of us all? We shall see, although I already sense the answer marching resolutely towards me. Tasha is well away, fearing nothing apparently as she undulates indulgently beneath me.

❋　　❋　　❋

I crunch across the driveway, and get back in the car. I switch on my mobile phone. It takes a deep breath, and then splurges a whole rapid fire of beeps at me. It then comes alive, pounding out my Arctic Monkeys' ring tone. I escape. I phone Europcar to say I will be there shortly, and could they call a taxi to take me back to the station?

"That was quick," comments the voice. "Did you find what you were looking for already?"

"I've been called back to the office. Urgent business as usual. Nothing for you to leave the country for."

At Waterloo station, the Evening Standard hoardings proclaim "Home Secretary and wife split." Now there is timing, I mutter to myself. I buy a copy. The news vendor double-takes as he recognises me. "It is my best chance of finding out what is going on in my own life," I quip. He pulls a face.

Tessa has given an extensive interview, or more likely published a detailed press release. She cites years of hardly seeing each other as we separately worked our careers, the tensions that have built up over Sandy's illness, and differences of opinion over how he should be treated, and the last straw of my bringing home a young girl from my office, and her realising that we were living a lie of convenience. "I miss Adam tremendously," she finishes, "but we can no longer live together. It is very hard for the children. That we both very much regret. We have at least agreed to arrange everything amicably for the sakes of Sandy and Ben." She has supplied the newspaper with photographs "of happier times", a shockingly younger-looking me celebrating winning my first election, and a much more recent one, the one that I really hate, where I appear tired, care-worn, maybe even clinically depressed or drunk, with my tie torn askew.

I should go back to Tasha and design a new blog, I think to myself, realising suddenly that we haven't written the last one. Perhaps I will give this one a go myself, straight from my anguished heart. There may be some good votes in it. Alternatively, I may only manage to paint myself as a sad old git, over-ripe for a return to the backbenches. What would a life be like where I did not have to calculate every angle?

Chapter 12

They have been showing the shocking event all day; what they can of it, anyway. There is no official footage, but a tourist was tracking the cavalcade as it crossed over Westminster Bridge, and within three hours he had sold user rights to the world's news corporations for an estimated £12 million. He must be about the luckiest man alive, for several reasons.

The shaky picture shows the cars coming towards the camcorder, the official car flanked by two police cars. People are stopping to watch them, trying to guess the identity of the occupant. The cars roll on. They are about to pass the cameraman, the front police car is drawing level, when there looks to be a puff of smoke from the wheel of the official car, which immediately veers wildly directly at the cameraman, who is torn between capturing monumental footage, à la Zapruda, and trying to get out of the way. His plight renders the footage even more compelling. The camera suddenly loses all sanity, and whirls around seemingly randomly. There is a loud crash, and people scream. Then one voice, a cultured Scottish voice turned panicky, shouts "The lamppost, mind the lamppost, get out of the way, get out of the way, watch out, watch out!". There is another enormous crash, and the camera shakes again, just as it was recovering its balance. Then it is steady. From very close up you can see that the lamppost has crushed the official car, flattening the cockpit entirely. People can be heard running everywhere out of shot. Then another voice can be heard shouting "It's the Prime Minister! It's the Prime Minister! Is he dead? Is he dead?"

The camera shoots forward in close up. It is very hard to make anything out. There seems to be at least some clothing resting between the front seats. The police arrive. Two of them try to open the mangled messes of two car doors. A third tries to grab the camera, which evades his grasp, and goes blank. The next sequence is taken from a distance, showing fire engines racing across the bridge, followed by three ambulances. Several police cars are also arriving. Two members of parliament are easily recognisable—John Featherstone, MP for Wakefield, and Lucien Sharp, MP for Bermondsey. The workers still cannot get into the car. The firemen are rushing forward with oxyacetylene torches to cut off the superstructure. The problem is that the car is bullet-proof, bomb-proof, gas proof, and certainly emergency-services proof.

Newscaster with grave, grey face: "News is coming in that the Prime Minister has been involved in a car accident in London. Details are still hazy at the moment. We will keep you informed as developments occur. Over to our reporter, Richard Canning, who has just arrived on Westminster Bridge. Richard . . . ."

"Good morning, Frank. We are looking at the wreck of the Prime Minister's car. At 11:32 this morning, the Prime Minister's cavalcade was crossing Westminster Bridge when his car suddenly swerved violently onto the pavement, colliding with a lamppost, and narrowly missing several pedestrians. The lamppost buckled, and fell onto the car, crushing the cabin almost flat. No-one knows why the car swerved, or whether the Prime Minister is still alive in there. The emergency services, led by the fire brigade, have been trying to gain entrance to the car but, as yet, to no avail. There are believed to be three occupants still in the car: the driver, John Preston, the Prime Minister's bodyguard, Bruce Major, and the Prime Minister, Geoffrey Christian himself. There were many witnesses to the incident, several of whom are being treated for shock as we speak. No onlookers have been directly injured. Madam, I understand that you were watching when the accident occurred . . . ."

"Yes, it was terrible. I saw three cars racing across the bridge, so I was watching them. It looked as if they were being chased. Then the middle one seemed to skid and smashed straight into the lamppost which toppled over right on top of it. They say it is the Prime Minister in there. Nobody could come out of there alive. It would be a miracle, an absolute miracle."

At 13:15, the camcorder footage is released to the BBC and ITV stations simultaneously. It is shown repeatedly from then on, often several times in a row during a single broadcast. Poor old Geoffrey must have died a thousand times at least.

I was reviewing a demonstration of some new ID equipment at a company in Slough when the news beeped through on my Blackberry. Almost simultaneously the phone rang with Sir Edwin on the line announcing that arrangements had been made to bring me back to London in all haste. I apologised to my hosts and hurried to the car. Once inside, I asked Sir Edwin the key question "Is he dead?"

"Yes, Mr. Home Secretary, he is dead. We are delaying the announcement for a few hours, but he is dead. Robert Salstice, as Deputy Prime Minister, has called an emergency Cabinet meeting for three. We need to have clear plans by then, both for that meeting and for the country. It is already being insinuated in the press that Middle-Eastern terrorists, encouraged by Youssouf ben Abdul, are behind this."

"Is that likely?"

"We have no evidence to suggest it. No evidence at all. We have no evidence for anything in fact. We are totally baffled. There has been not even the slightest intelligence hinting at an assassination attempt. All anyone says is that the Prime Minister's car suddenly swerved, skidded or whatever. We cannot get to the car to do forensic tests until we can get the Prime Minister's body out of there. We cannot start ripping the wheels off with him sitting there. It would look like we were scrapping him. Until we can get to the wheels, or possibly the steering system, we haven't a clue what happened. It is very, very awkward, and there are already dangerous developments. Muslim communities are requesting police protection, and that is to put it mildly. There are many people in Asian communities fearing mob rule, lynchings, that sort of thing. We have a lot of work to do to keep things calm. You need to make an immediate broadcast to assure the nation that everything is under control, without divulging that the Prime Minister is dead. So, when you arrive here, you will go straight into the recording studio. We are writing your speech now. We will be e-mailing you the first draft in a couple of minutes. It will be rather rough, of course, but it will give you the chance to provide early policy input. Mr Salstice has asked that you call him immediately. I will connect you now.

"Adam? Robert here. Have you been briefed?"

"Yes, Bob. It is horrendous. Do you have any idea of what happened?"

"That is for your department to work out, Adam. We need an explanation as soon as possible. We will not announce Geoffrey's death until shortly before the evening news, but it must be obvious to anyone that he is dead. Keep me informed, and I will see you at three."

Sir Edwin is back on the phone again. "Your speech is being patched through to you now. I'll phone you again in five minutes for further instructions."

My Blackberry beeps, and I scan through the e-mail. "It appears that the Prime Minister, Mr. Geoffrey Christian, may have been badly injured . . . . Ordering an immediate investigation into what happened . . . . Nothing immediately to suggest that there was any third party involvement . . . . Robert Salstice, the Foreign Secretary and Deputy Prime Minister will lead the government until the Prime Minister recovers . . . . The car in which the Prime Minister was travelling will be subjected to an intensive forensic assessment once the Prime Minister has been carried to safety."

"Thank you, Sir Edwin. That seems fine to me. What are we doing at this precise moment?"

"The joint security operations are in emergency session trying to see if there has been anything that could have suggested an assassination attempt. A forensic team is standing by to examine that car. Westminster Bridge has been closed off to the public, and we are trying to keep cameras away. We are reassuring the local Muslim communities throughout the country that the police will respond immediately to any signs of threatening behaviour. We have temporarily closed all airports, ports and the Eurotunnel. The army is on standby, but is not being visibly deployed at the moment. We think that would spread panic. Beyond that, we are trying to fend off the press who is demanding that we admit that the Prime Minister is dead."

"OK. Make sure that all the department heads are assembled for a meeting with me directly after the broadcast."

"They are already conferring together, Sir. We are having to recall a few urgently from meetings they were having around the country. Most of them should be back within three to four hours, ready to join you after your Cabinet meeting this afternoon."

"It sounds like you have everything under control."

"As you know, Sir, we rehearse for this sort of thing. No British Prime Minister has ever died in office since Spencer Perceval was assassinated in 1812, but we have still rehearsed the possibility three times a year just in case. The procedures are tried and tested. We have even anticipated an assassination attempt by Middle-Eastern terrorists, so we are not in any way caught with our guard down. I will be here to meet you when you arrive."

❋   ❋   ❋

The emergency Cabinet meeting is a cross between a wake and the Ides of March. Everyone knows that Geoffrey is dead. He is profoundly present in his absence, his ghost hovering over us. Robert Salstice is in his chair, managing the meeting with due decorum. To give him credit, he appears truly shocked. Roger Danby is preoccupied.

The main topic of conversation is what happens about replacing Geoffrey as Prime Minister with nine months, twelve days to go before the final date for the next election. We cannot go immediately to the country because it will take us two months, give or take, to elect a new leader of the Labour Party. The party election process will be kicked off this evening. Robert suggests that we hold an election as soon as possible after we have someone in place, say in three-and-a-half months' time. What do we think?

We concur. Names of candidates will have to be declared to the party chairman, Matthew French, within eight days. Robert will be meeting with the leader of the opposition and the leader of the Liberals in ninety minutes time to agree an election date and any immediate response. They have already been informed that the Prime Minister is dead. There is no known threat to the country at this time, but the economy will be destabilised by the inevitable uncertainty. Financial institutions become very anxious in such situations. We must exude calm, and communicate clear plans, which have been co-ordinated with Number 10, to the public. There must not be any alarm.

"We are looking to you, Adam, to pull everything together," Robert urges me. "We need to be kept fully informed. As soon as you know what happened to the car, you must let us know."

"Of course, Mr. Deputy Prime Minister."

"Good. In that case, we can adjourn, unless anyone has anything else to say."

"Oh, Adam," Robert continues. "Please keep your blog in your pocket for the time-being."

"Of course. I don't have time to write one anyway at the moment."

"You can send out a short holding message, if you wish, but clear it with this office first."

"Thank you, Deputy Prime Minister."

"Good evening. It is with great sorrow that we regret to inform you that it has been announced by Number 10 that the Prime Minister, Mr. Geoffrey Christian, has died as a consequence of the injuries he sustained in a car accident on Westminster Bridge in London this morning at about 11:30. The time of his death is not known as it took emergency services nearly four hours to cut him loose from the car. The emergency services found him dead when they reached him. It is not clear yet whether he had died instantly or not. Geoffrey Christian is the first British Prime Minister to have died in office since Spencer Perceval was assassinated in 1812 by a John Bellingham, who had become indebted as a result of Mr. Perceval's government's trading policy. There is no evidence that Mr. Christian died from any other circumstance than a tragic accident. Mr. Robert Salstice, the Foreign Secretary and Deputy Prime Minister is deputising as Prime Minister until a new leader of the Labour Party has been chosen. He called an emergency Cabinet meeting this afternoon, but it is not yet known whether he will call an early general election, or whether he will allow the present government to continue for a full term until a general election is due to be held in nine months' time. Tributes and condolences have been pouring in from around the world. His Majesty the King has just made an official statement regretting Mr. Christian's death. He described him as a deeply trustworthy and loyal Prime Minister to his country; a steady hand on the tiller. The US President, Mr. Kieran Peterson, said that he had lost a close personal friend whom he had rapidly grown to respect and trust since his own recent accession to office. The Russian President, Mr. Oleg Gregovich, said that he was deeply saddened by the news. Pope Benedict XVI has made a statement from Austria, where he is currently on tour, that he would pray for Mr. Christian's family, and for the people of Britain in this difficult and tragic time."

The wheels are off. The steering system has been examined. Indeed, every single micron of the car has been scrutinised. The forensic experts have inspected the front offside tyre minutely, where the puff of smoke was seen. There appears to be a tear in the rim, without any indication as to how or why this might have happened. It does not look like it has been impacted by a bullet, there is no exit point, there was no bullet inside the tyre itself, and no sign of damage to the wheel other than that inflicted by its collision with the curb. The wheel and the tyre have now been handed over to the car manufacturers for a full assessment. They have responded immediately that they will work jointly with the tyre manufacturers, Michelin, to try to explain what happened, but that, on first inspection, the damage is considered most unusual, and indeed inexplicable. The rim of any tyre would not normally become damaged in such a way under any circumstances. Such damage has never been encountered before.

The press is still hinting darkly that Geoffrey was indeed assassinated, and that Youssouf ben Abdul is in someway responsible. However, with not the slightest evidence of wrongdoing, the story is failing to take off, which is a relief to us and to Muslim communities throughout Britain.

Youssouf is an intriguing man. Where does his power emanate from? He is steadily building his constituency, even outside the Middle-East into India, Russia and China, as well as towards us in the West. He appears to have links with al-Qa'eda, but also with Hamas, and Hezbollah, and Gaddafi in Libya, Iran, Syria, the Dalai Llama, even the Pope. He is a consummate politician. He is less and less in their pockets, and they are more and more in his.

What is his ultimate purpose—to work towards his own vainglory, to "save" the Middle-East, to save the world? He appears to be almost creating a new religion, without ever explicitly saying so. The most quoted of his interviews took place five months ago with a journalist from al Jazeera. He was uncharacteristically at ease with his interviewer, and therefore more expansive, more human than he had ever been before.

His interrogator asked him what his ultimate vision for the Middle-East might be. He replied by saying that he did not have a vision limited to the confines of the Middle-East. He preferred to take a world view, the centre of that world view being that there is only one religion because there is only one God. That God is infinitely multifaceted, so there is scope for an infinite number of insights. The major world religions represent key strands of those insights, yet they must be considered truthfully as strands of only one religion, the one true religion of God himself. There is no need, or justification, for religious wars between different factions, Jew against Muslim, Christian against Jew, Hindu against Muslim, Buddhist against Christian. These wars reflect and amplify purposeless and destructive factionalism. We must focus on what is common, what lies at in the fundament of the one true religion, a faith in the world and in everything within it, whether animate or inanimate, whether kind or unkind, whether beautiful or ugly, whether altruistic or selfish, whether forgiving or spiteful. We must respect every single element of the earth, and honour it for its merits, for its role in the ultimate purpose. That was the intended message of Christ. That is the message of any true prophet. That is the journey we must all embark upon.

"Does this argument come directly from God, or what you believe to be God, or is this your interpretation of the scriptures?"

What you must understand, he continued, is that God has never written down what he believes. He has always worked through the agency of human beings, some reliable, some unreliable, some downright subversive. You must regard the articulation of religion as being through the lens of the world's rulers who have had a primary interest in consolidating their own power. So, their depiction of God has been more a reflection of their own conscious and unconscious desires than any true reflection of God as a supremely intelligent being. In the earlier developments of each religion, the ideas and beliefs were independent of political imperatives, and indeed inimical to them. For as long as their advocates were being threatened, and tortured, and publicly executed, there was more chance that their pronouncements were connected to the truth, although they were inevitably filtered through the beliefs and prejudices of their evangelists. Once a hierarchical structure was established, you can be sure that the Church, or the religious establishment, was walking in step with the desires and the political interests of the local ruler. If the representative of God strayed from the path of power, it meant humiliation, demotion, death. As religious people are as political, vain, ambitious and venal as the rest of us, they tend to seek accommodation with their local ruler rather than conflict. We therefore should not be surprised that the true faith of God has become distorted by the exigencies and tastes of political power. In order for a king to remain a king, or for an emperor to remain an emperor, it is expedient to create an enemy. That enemy is necessarily described as being inexorably after whatever you have and may wish to keep. He may also be of a different race. Preferably, he is of a different religion. It is in the interests of kings, presidents and tyrants to fan the flames of controversy, and to demand allegiance to the one true faith of the king himself, not of the living God.

This is why God is always depicted as a violent, vicious, resentful creature, with limitless power to destroy his enemies and his detractors. This represents an idealist projection of the fantasies of the rulers of men, not a true reflection of the creed of the living God. Why would a supremely intelligent being want to behave like some hellish amalgam of the insanities of Mao Tse Tung, Joseph Stalin, Adolf Hitler, Napoleon and of any other megalomaniac autocrat? What sort of God would that be? What depths would he be aspiring to? This is not God, this is man torn along in the wake of the full sweep of empire.

The truth, as indeed revealed to me directly by the living God, is that man must learn to live in harmony and in balance with all creatures, with all things, to honour the core design of the earth and of the heavens, of this planet and of the cosmos as a whole. Christ proclaimed "Love God, love thy neighbour", but he was God adapting his message to the times. I say simply "Love thy neighbour", and understand your neighbour to be anything that lies within your reach, every atom, every molecule, every entity. That is the guiding principle of the one true religion which is the sum of all religions.

"But aren't there fundamental differences between the religions? Surely you cannot cook up a pot and blend them all together?"

Their similarities are more significant than their differences. If you define the central belief as being a respect for all elements of the earth, all true religions converge on that point. Thereafter, to be sure, they promote different formulae to achieve that end, they focus their concerns on different aspects of the earth. The Christian belief has little time for the rights of insects. The Janist belief expressly desires to protect the lives and well-being of all sentient creatures. Gaia talks about the survival instincts of the entire universe. What we have to understand is that the belief that is the most inclusive is the best. The true faith is not about what is good and what is bad, it is not about oppositions, it is about synchronicities and serendipities, it is about the ultimate purpose of anything we can identify, it is about the value of every element of creation in the eyes of God. He loves and cherishes his entire creation. Everything is precious.

"And yet, Youssouf ben Abdul, you are probably most associated with a dangerous, intangible, undefined threat emerging from a particular point on earth, with affiliations with movements that fall far short of that ideal. Why is that?"

"As God's apostle, I am a potter. I have to work with the cosmic clay. I have to adapt what there is, starting with what there is. I cannot decide to embark from some remote, mythical, ideal place where everything is perfect. I have to operate in the here and now. God cannot control the intentions and the actions of every element of the universe. What would be the point? What would be left to do? He has to work and live through the agency of all these elements. He has to be an artist, urging a change towards the better, towards the course upon which the universe is designed to travel. I am an instrument of that purpose. I am a work of art. I may be dispensable. You can tear me up, you can set fire to me, you can blow me up, you can destroy me. I may be eternal. Whatever my current state, on this earth or as a faint memory, I may exert my influence. Once an imprint has been made, it never entirely fades from view. Its essence weaves around the world, seeking an outlet. That is true of ultimate good; that is true of ultimate evil. They are the same. Their merits are contextual, their strategy is identical."

"So what do you foresee happening next?"

Youssouf faced straight to camera. "I don't know. I cannot explain it all. That is your decision, your solution."

"And will there ever be peace in the Middle-East?"

Youssouf inclined his head. "Will there ever be peace in the world? I doubt it. We can only play our part. We can only act in hope. We can only intervene. As Bill Shankly once said, 'If you are not interfering with play, you should not be on the pitch'."

"Who is Bill Shankly?"

"He was a football manager whom I greatly admired as a child. You can tell your worldwide audience that I used to be a Liverpool fan. Maybe they did have an instrument of God on their side after all."

❄ ❄ ❄

It has been a week horibilis, as the late Queen might have put it. It started with Geoffrey's death, and it hasn't stopped. For the first time, despite Yasemin's warnings and pronouncements over twenty years, I feel the clammy, leaden hand of destiny on my shoulder, stones in my stomach. This may well be when whatever it is that is intended for me happens. I will know if I become Prime Minister, because there is not the slightest hope of that at the moment, and I am not sure that I am really talking about hope here.

Yes, one part of me would like to be Prime Minister. That is the natural ambition of any politician, especially once he or she becomes a member of the government. But something terrible awaits me. I can feel it, and I have seen it. God will ask of me something more than I will be able to bear, despite whatever support he may offer me. According to my vision, I will be asked to betray him. How? How do you take a God unawares? In which case, how is it that he does not avoid the consequences of your betrayal? The logical conclusion, therefore, is that he will have chosen his own fate, and mine.

It is the story of Judas Iscariot all over again. Judas betrayed God. Judas was destined to betray God. Christ might not have been crucified had Judas not betrayed him. Judas' betrayal was written into the divine narrative. What choice did he have? What future did he have? What a reputation he has!

I am trying to discover how I will betray my God. I am willing myself into the future, to foresee events. It is not happening. It may yet happen to me, but I cannot make it happen. I am staring at a blank screen.

Yasemin says she knows everything, without being able to tell me anything. "You will find out when it is time," she keeps repeating.

The real shock for me was on Tuesday, when I woke up to discover Yasemin by my bedside. In a flat empty of anyone other than me, she awakened me. I thought for a second that Arab terrorists had stormed the building. Not very PC of me, although I can be forgiven for being scared rigid.

"I am here," she said.

Once I had recovered I said "I am delighted that you are. What are you planning on doing today? How did you get in?"

"I have a key."

"How on earth did you get a key?"

"God is the Great Locksmith who has the keys to everyone's heart and to everyone's front door."

"He must have one hell of a bunch stashed away somewhere."

I regretted using the word "hell" in that context.

Yasemin smiled encouragingly, tolerantly. "He has, as you say, one hell of a bunch. All clearly marked, though."

"So what are you doing here?"

"I am moving in with you. You have a spare room, haven't you?"

"So you are not completely moving in."

"No, not in that sense. Not yet, anyway."

"How long are you moving in for?"

"Oh, a couple of years at least."

"I look forward to that. Do I get any say in the matter?"

"No. Yes. You can say yes."

"But not no."

"No."

"I wouldn't anyway."

"I know."

"It is rather awkward, though, to be honest. Sit down."

She perched on the bed. Her presence was already very homely, very reassuring.

"It has all been anticipated and catered for."

"So, it does not interfere with your mission that I be seen here in apparent adultery with a young woman of Middle-Eastern origins, maybe, who knows, a recognised associate of Youssouf ben Abdul?"

"If they dig hard enough, they will indeed find out that I have met Youssouf on several occasions."

"Is Youssouf God, or God's prophet."

Yasemin put a finger to her lips, and shushed me. "Adam, don't fret yourself. All in good time. Youssouf is a great man, that is all you need to know."

"But is he God, a prophet, a Middle-Eastern troublemaker, or a terrorist?"

"Yes, he is a couple of those."

"The categories were meant to be mutually exclusive."

"They are not."

"So you still will not give me any more details."

"No."

"Was Geoffrey assassinated, can you tell me that?"

"He had to die."

"Why?"

"It was his time, and yours."

"I was afraid you might say that."

"You must embrace your destiny, Adam, not fear it. It is a great destiny. You are truly beloved of God. You have a place by his side for eternity. It is what most human beings are meant to crave, isn't it?"

"Not an agnostic like me."

"Adam, you are not an agnostic. You are a true believer in denial."

"Not for long, apparently."

"That doesn't matter. The future does not hinge on your faith, only on your deeds."

"So, do you have your case with you?"

"Yes, all my earthly belongings are here."

"Then I had better get up and make breakfast."

"I will go and settle myself into my room."

"I'll see you in a minute."

Tasha was seismic when she learnt that Yasemin was shacked up with me. She immediately resigned as my ghost writer, and removed herself from my life. She called me a traitor, a vile userer, a crook, a predator, and a typical politician.

Within three hours, I was contacted by her PR agent who informed me that Tasha was considering leaking our story to the press in lurid kiss-and-tell interviews. She didn't use the word "lurid", nor the words "kiss-and-tell". I asked what I could do about it. Nothing, she replied. I have been asked merely to inform you, so that it doesn't come as a complete surprise. Mrs. Wolf (Tasha) wishes to treat you with greater respect than you have shown her. She will not stoop to your level, she says.

Sure enough, two hours later I was flattened by a barrage of press inquiries relating to my adulterous affair with Mrs. Tasha Wolf. I resolved to make no comment, initially, however when I was asked by the first journalist, from The Times, whether I was denying it, I said "No, I am not denying it."

"Are you admitting it?"

I had a split second to make a choice between cheating husband and dishonestly evasive minister. "Yes," I confirmed, "I have had carnal relations with Mrs. Wolf on four occasions."

"Where did these take place?"

"At her home."

"Is her husband aware of these events?"

"I am sure that he is now."

"But not previously, to the best of your knowledge."

"You may be straying into private matters," I warned him.

"Talking of the which, is it true, minister, that you have a young girl of Middle-Eastern origin staying with you?"

"Yes."

"Has she not recently arrived in this country from the Middle-East?"

"Yes, I believe so."

"How long have you known her?"

"Twenty years."

"Since she was a small girl, then?"

Not this again.

"Yes." Well, Yasemin has never been that tall, and she is very slim. You could call that small.

"So, she is a friend of the family would you say?"

"She is a good friend."

"Would you care to describe your relationship with her?"

"She is a good friend."

"Nothing more?"

"Nothing less."

"I don't know quite how to put this. Mr. Home Secretary, but is it not rather inappropriate for you to have a Middle-Eastern woman staying with you at this time?"

"Why would that be?"

"Given the circumstances of the recent death of the Prime Minister."

"What has that got to do with anything?"

"It has been rumoured that his death may in fact have been as a result of the actions of some Middle-Eastern agents."

"Only because you have decided to spread that particular rumour. You plural, rather than you personally. There is not the slightest evidence that the Prime Minister died from anything other than a tragic, freak accident."

All of which got me the headline "Melton engages in Middle-Eastern Relations" from The Times, "Cheat and Double-Cheat!" from the Sun, and "Minister confesses" from the Mail.

It also got me Robert Salstice on the phone within seconds of publication. "Adam, what on earth are you up to?"

"Are you referring to the newspaper interviews or to the investigation into Geoffrey's death?"

"I was referring to your bringing this government into disrepute."

"At least I haven't lied."

"I would have greatly preferred it if there hadn't been anything to lie about."

"Well, I am afraid that is as it is, Robert."

"I was planning a reshuffle anyway, Adam. I am afraid that you will be in it."

"What are you offering me next, if anything?"

"The Environment."

"I presumably cannot do any harm there."

"No, I think it will be a role more suited to your talents."

I think that was an ow!

Yasemin laughed when she heard the news, all of the news. "Tremendous publicity," she commented. "It's as well that I am here. Without me, you would be a sordid old gimpo caught with his pants down. Now you are a romantic danger to your country. We can do something with that."

"I don't relish the Environment, I can tell you. That is the governmental equivalent of being moved sideways into Training."

"You won't be there for long. Take a rest. You have challenging times ahead."

A few minutes ahead, as it happened. Tessa appeared on my doorstep, accompanied by the children, both of whom were looking pale and distracted.

"Can we come in?"

"Of course. It is lovely to see you."

Tessa did not reply.

"Hello, again," she said antagonistically to Yasemin. "So I was right then, was I?"

"No, Mrs. Melton, you were not."

"We'll see."

"Only if you are looking through honest eyes, and you don't let your prejudices deceive you."

"I don't think that I am the one who has been doing the deceiving around here."

"I wouldn't say that."

"What do you mean?"

"You know what I mean."

"No."

"You have been having a rather intimate relationship of your own, haven't you, Mrs. Melton? Does the name James Protheroe ring a bell?"

I don't think I can ever recall Tessa being so utterly thrown by a statement or by an event in all our years of marriage. The children were puzzled too, not wishing to hear any of it.

"Come on boys," I suggested. "Let's go off and eat something. Your mother and Yasemin appear to have a lot to discuss."

"We've eaten," countered Ben.

"Then we'll have to go off and find something else to do."

❋　❋　❋

Now that the dishonour is spread more evenly between us, banked up more strongly on Tessa's side in fact, relations have improved between us to the point of empirical cordiality.

I have learnt that Tessa's affair with James Protheroe, who is a client of hers, as well as being serviced by her in other ways, dates back to those trips around the world that Tessa made. Exotic stuff.

When Sandy was diagnosed with schizophrenia, it threw Tessa into a maelstrom of guilt and cast the suspicion of divine retribution all over her, although it did not end the affair.

She is now free to pursue James as she pleases, although it is not yet resolved as to whether it pleases him. He has a wife and four children of his own, and he is self-proclaimedly a devout Catholic.

I asked Yasemin whether any of this was God's will. "No," she said. "It is irrelevant to the situation."

Sandy and Ben have been allowed to stay with me for several sleepovers. They have really taken to Yasemin and call her their Guardian Angel. I believe that they are more comfortable with Tessa and I living apart than living together. Children sense when things are going wrong, and get confused by the deceit.

I have been sorely tempted to remove Sandy from his drugs, but have decided not to do so out of a belated complicity with Tessa's instincts.

It is so comfortable living with Yasemin again. As before, she keeps disappearing, but I am now confident that she will return. I no longer want to possess her, except physically, which she is still refusing, although she allows a fair degree of intimacy between us, and demonstrates unceasing affection.

On the political stage, all is riotous. The election of the new Labour leader has entered the stabbing in the corridor stage. Votes are being counted by all sides, both among the MPs and the constituency electors.

Robert Salstice has done me many favours over the last couple of months. My removal to Secretary of State for the Environment has opened up the way for my successor as Home Secretary, Paula Redwood, to make a monumental hash of things. She seems to have unravelled herself over the Middle-Eastern question with ill-judged remarks swinging between hawk and dove inflaming all sides, and she has certainly upset Sir Edwin, according to Susan. He has become positively nostalgic for our golden days together, she reports to me.

Robert himself has not fared too well either. He has revealed himself to be, at best, a stand-in—indecisive, vindictive, anxious, adrift. None of the political pundits is backing him for leadership in his own right. According to them, the race lies between Nathan Ketts and me. My blog, which I now write myself in Tasha's absence, is swinging things in my favour. The country, it seems, appreciates my honest, direct style.

You may not credit this, but 'honest' is my new label, having replaced 'reforming' since my affair with Tasha. The public warmed to my immediate and open confession of my affair; Tessa's affair with James has leaked out; and it has been revealed that Tasha had seduced several men before me over the last couple of years, and one woman. I am now more plucky victim than love cheat.

The press have rather taken to Yasemin too, but they just cannot seem to capture her on film. Funny, that.

❋   ❋   ❋

Part IV
Prime Minister

Chapter 13

I have just won two major campaigns back-to-back, and I am sitting here in my office at Number 10 eloquently pleased with myself, accepting celebratory phone calls. I did it! Yasemin, we did it! Outside there are television and radio crews, and other motley reporters cordoned off at the end of the street. My face is being flashed up on TV by the minute. I can be as drunk as the proverbial skunk, and today nobody cares because they will read it as euphoria. Hallelujah!

Which isn't to say that I have forgotten what is in store for me. That premonition flows like a fresh, cold, troubled, subterranean stream through the bottom of my soul. Anyway, as the old joke goes, how could I forget? I still don't know what it is.

I won the first round two months ago. It was Nathan Ketts and I competing on charm and chumminess. Both of us are smart enough to erase all policies from the agenda. In the end, my arrival at the Environment was the clincher. I immediately announced a whole series of radically progressive initiatives which I had not the slightest intention of seeing through personally, which made the previous incumbent, namely one Nathan Ketts, out to be a right laggard. So, the move that was designed by Robert to label me as a downsliding has-been, instead provided me with the platform to remind people how energetic and creative I am, in a thoroughly-researched, populist sort of way, of course. Poor old Nathan was, by now, hemmed in at the Foreign Office which, as I discovered at the Home Office, is not a department you can do anything ambitious or inspirational with, and certainly not within a few weeks.

So, there I was, Mr. Energy, Mr. Voice-to-the-People through my blog, Mr. Vibrant-but-Calm, and even Mr. Polite-to-my-Rivals. I kept repeating what an excellent Foreign Secretary Nathan was proving to be, sincerely praising him for how well he had settled in, begun to get his feet under the world table, a credit to the nation, i.e. don't move him; leave him where he is. On the other hand, I portrayed myself as punching light at the Environment, there to effect a quick turnaround after years of neglect, and then up and off, free to be the next

Labour Party Leader and Prime Minister. Nathan tried delivering a few snide, knocking soundbites against me, and some obviously disingenuous praise, and only succeeded in looking shifty and untrustworthy. Silly boy!

On arrival in office, I instantly called a general election for two months' time, the perfect period for the people to get an appetiser of me, a teaser leaving them hungry (or at least prepared) for more. So, I have been the PM for a couple of months already, but it didn't count for me because it could have ended there. I got to meet the King, who was as bumbling, and charming, and touchy as ever, I rattled off a few Prime Minister's Question Times, where I got the government benches rocking with laughter at the expense of the Leader of the Opposition, Max Allsop. I am not sure he knew what hit him. It must have been like being run down by a speeding juggernaut whose driver is high on alcohol, drugs and ambition. And then it was straight to the hustings.

My other distinct advantage lay in my predecessors. Let's face it, Geoffrey may have come to a gut-wrenching end but, like old Spencer Perceval before him, that is sadly about all he will be remembered for. His skills were internal political management skills, nothing in the public domain where flair, charm and quicksilver rhetoric are urgently required. Following on from him, Robert was simply wet, whatever he expected himself to be. He was never even half a contender. He was a man entirely in the wrong place, and maybe on the wrong planet.

So "Rejoice!", as my illustrious predecessor, Lady Thatcher, would say. "Victory!" I feel like Harold the Really Great, the one who would have marched up to Stamford Bridge, beaten up his brother Tostig, and his mate Harold Hardrada, despite that enormous great Norwegian on the bridge itself, slicing everyone to ham, and then marched south on William the Bastard, and driven him into the Channel where he would have drowned in his suit of armour as the miserable megalomaniac, psychotic, dead Frenchman this island simply didn't deserve. What do you call a cross between a lucky cat and an ecstatic dog? A dog with nine pricks! That's me today. That's me every day for the moment.

❋   ❋   ❋

Yasemin and lie in bed together at Number 10, celebrating carnally, as I am sure many others have before us. We are back to being an absolute couple again, for as long as it lasts. My adultery has been expunged, and we are free to be intimate again.

Having said that, I am feeling very crowded in here as Yasemin sashays on top of me, very oppressed. The weight of history is upon me. This house has seen every Prime Minister since 1730, when the rather portly Sir Robert Walpole took office. I am lying in a room which must have been occupied, if not always slept in, by every succeeding Prime Minister (I must look up the history). I am surrounded by eminent ghosts and their spouses, commenting discriminatingly on my sexual technique. Do I need this? What is Mr. An Empty Taxi Drew Up and Clem Atlee Got Out saying? Is Winnie considering poison or calculating where to put his cigar? Is Lady Thatcher contemplating a U-turn out of the room? Is Lloyd George consulting The Fathers? The face of Mr. Disraeli has just hovered into view, and I am losing my momentum. "What's up?" Yasemin asks. "And could you reboot it? I am oh so nearly there." I cut out the Prime Ministers, and think of Emmanuelle Béart instead. It works. My font flows into Yasemin's cascade with perfect synchronicity, like champagne into a glass.

❅   ❅   ❅

Not that the outside world is much to be happy about. The Middle-East is bathed in rocket fuel, waiting for the sun to rise.

True to his promise, Youssouf ben Abdul has created his own foreign policy and is winding up everyone he has ever heard of. His main target is China for its dismal human rights record in Tibet and elsewhere. He has called on the Chinese President, Mr. Tan, to repeal the death penalty in his country (China formally executes a hundred times more criminals than any other country on earth), and to respect the rights of all of its citizens. He has also demanded that he recognise Taiwan. You can imagine that this has made President Tan beyond livid. Oleg Gregovich in Russia could have been expected to be delighted by the castigation of his old enemy, except that Youssouf has turned on him too for his "colonialist policy of aggression and exploitation" in Chechnya. And President Peterson is under attack for his unthinking, callous support for the "revolting Saudi dynasty", the source of most of the unrest in the Middle East. Except that Youssouf seems to be trying to cap even that. Not only is he blazing away against almost all foreign governments, he is having a pretty torrid time at home too. Despite arguing for an ecumenical unification of all faiths, he has recently outraged traditional Muslims by denouncing Sharia law as a barbaric corruption of the teachings of the Koran. All you can say for him at the moment is that he seems to be succeeding in uniting the Sunnis and the Shias against him, which is certainly a death-defying achievement. I cannot see him lasting long. It is only a question of who will get him first. Is he Yasemin's God? If so, he may need all the help I can give him if he wants to stay alive, and no contribution from me whatsoever if he prefers to go down in a blaze of glory. Perhaps I am off the hook. Perhaps destiny has disappeared on a diversion, and I can lay down my head in peace, and merely grow older at an accelerated rate, as appears to happen to all British Prime Ministers.

Acceleration is the word. A British Prime Minister lives his life at warp speed. It is like playing Crazy Taxi, you only win by driving down the pavement, and forcing all the pedestrians off into the road. Perhaps that is what Geoffrey's driver was trying to achieve after all.

Talking of the which, we are still clueless. Michelin came back to say that there was an abnormal impact to the rim, which would have meant that the tyre would have burst instantly, but the surrounding structure is robust, and so the damage could only have occurred as a result of an inexplicable intervention. At the same time, there is no sign of any hostile activity. No traces of bullets, or of explosives, or of chemicals, or of laser beams, or of sonic impulses. If a weapon was used, it is not one that we have any knowledge of.

All of which has set the conspiracy theorists racing from the blocks to denounce the United States for something or other. Only they, or the Russians, could have the technology to perpetrate a crime no-one else can detect. And they seriously doubt that Russia would have this technology either, so over to you President Peterson. Naturally enough, the President is baffled. Why would his government want to assassinate a British Prime Minister who was entirely accommodating? It doesn't make the slightest sense, and his Chiefs of Staff haven't any inkling of what the technology could have been either. The coroner's inquest ruled it to be death by misadventure, and I struggle to suggest what else it could have been, unless divine intervention played its invisible hand, which is ominously possible.

Contrariwise, I had President Peterson fulminating against Youssouf ben Abdul this morning. "Something must be done with that bastard, before he gets us all killed," he raved down our private line. I would not be surprised to wake up and to find that he has been erased from the earth. President Peterson, the CIA or whoever must have some friends they can call on, and no-one would miss him at this precise moment.

So what happens? I have just turned on the television to catch up with the real world of affairs, and there is an interview with Youssouf ben Abdul where he states his intention to visit Britain and to meet its new Prime Minister. Oh great!

※   ※   ※

I am sitting in the Cabinet room, with my back to the fireplace, seeking the advice of my Cabinet team relating to the request by Youssouf ben Abdul to visit Britain.

I have just completed the inevitable reshuffle to reward allies and curtail the power of opponents. It is a delicate balance. Several of my allies are, quite frankly, idiots, and I cannot appoint them all to high office without fearing for the consequences. Conversely, several of my opponents are either highly intelligent and streetwise, like Roger Danby, or party big hitters, such as Nathan Ketts. As the old saying goes, it is better to have the bastards on the inside of the tent peeing out, than on the outside of the tent peeing in. On the other hand, you don't want to keep someone on the inside of the tent who is a copious incontinent either, so Robert Salstice has to be exiled directly to the Lords as Lord Robert of Tristan de Cunha, or whatever he comes up with.

Roger Danby remains in the Cabinet, but as Foreign Minister. I have appointed my young friend and ally from the Home Office, Julian Fleming, as Chancellor of the Exchequer. Nathan Ketts is moved across to the Home Office, and Paula Redwood is dropped like a stone down a well. Thereafter, there is a sprinkling of new faces among the more established ones.

Everyone is agreed. Youssouf ben Abdul should, on no account, set foot in this country. 'Period', as they say in the US.

Except that the US does not appear to be saying 'period' at all. Completely to the contrary, President Peterson has specifically requested me to approve Youssouf's visit.

I lean back in my chair at Downing Street. "Why would that be, Mr. President?" I enquire.

"Well, to state it bluntly, Mr. ben Abdul has alienated so many world leaders in such an even-handed manner, including myself, that he really poses no further threat to us. He remains a force to be reckoned with in the Middle-East, but a nothing anywhere else. He must realise what he has done, and that it is in his interests to cultivate at least some friends among the greater powers. After all, the man is no fool, or so I am assured. No politician either, not like you or me. Given that he needs us, it is most likely in our interests to accommodate him. He may yet prove useful out there."

"So why do you not invite him to the US?"

"I could not guarantee his safety, and it is the UK he has asked to visit, not the US."

This rat smells.

"I am not at all sure that the King would agree to meet him as he is somewhat offended by Mr. ben Abdul's unorthodox theological opinions. If he refuses an audience, that will be perceived as a snub, which will result in us scoring an own goal. An own goal is where you score against your own side."

"I am aware of the allusion."

"I apologise, Mr. President. It is a habit of mine. I always like to spell out acronyms and colloquialisms."

"Understood, Mr. Prime Minister. So, are you minded to invite him?"

"At present, my entire Cabinet is resolutely opposed to the idea. I polled all its members earlier today. I am not sure how I can talk them round, particularly in the short term. On the other hand, giving due weight to the special relationship that exists between our two countries, I will do what I can."

"With every respect, Mr. Prime Minister, I would strongly counsel that you should not wait too long. The iron is hot, which means it is the time to strike."

I laugh. "Thank you, Mr. President, for that explanation."

I am met with a silence down the other end of the phone. Apparently he wasn't explaining anything.

I report our conversation to Yasemin over dinner. We always try to have dinner together. I keep evening official engagements to a minimum. I will do up to 6:00 p.m., and after 9:00, which gives me adequate time to deliver an after-dinner speech without having to endure the dinner itself.

"You will invite Youssouf," she says. "He must come here. It is mission-critical."

"Why?"

"It just is."

"Yasemin, what is going on here? Why do both you and the US President want Youssouf here so badly, when it defies all logic? What do you both know that I am totally in the dark about?"

"Closer to the time, as ever, Adam. In the meantime, get him here, whatever strings you have to pull."

"Can you give me a good excuse?"

"His nephew is gravely ill, and is over here for specialist medical treatment. Youssouf is like a father to him. It would be a compassionate visit."

"Is this true?"

"Yes, it is true."

"What is wrong with his nephew?"

"He is being treated for cerebral palsy at the Bobath Centre in London."

"Well, that does give me something to work with. By the way, and on a completely different topic, we have been invited by the people who live in our old house in St. John's Road in Reading around for dinner. What do you think?"

Yasemin grins. "I think we should go. What a lovely news story."

"That is what I thought."

✳   ✳   ✳

Mr. and Mrs. Paul and Susan Plumb are standing nervously on the doorstep as our car pulls up. It is raining lightly. Against all advice, I have dispensed with security once we are in the house. My bodyguard hovers as we are ushered out of the car by our driver, Samuel. Several members of the press corps crowd round us, taking pictures as we introduce ourselves to the Plumbs. I suggest that they take some photos of me alone with the Plumbs, a recommendation which is forthrightly endorsed by Yasemin, to make sure that they are rewarded for their efforts. They react with affronted surprise, presuming arrogance on my part.

The house has changed since I left it fourteen years ago. The stripped wooden floors are carpeted once again, the furniture is much heavier and expensive than mine used to be and, as you would expect, it has been made painstakingly tidy for our visit.

The Plumbs, in their anxiety, have a tendency to hover, which means that we bump into each other twice, like a children's crocodile concertinaed to a sudden halt. I decide to put them at their ease by describing the house as it used to be. I then introduce Number 10 as it is now. The rise in the level of interest as I do so is discernible. Yasemin follows up with the "womanly" details. She is charming on these occasions, as she is at any other time. She is a perfect politician's wife.

"Anyway, you will see Number 10 when you visit us for the return match. We will give you a full tour." Their jaws drop open a split second before they begin to smile like silly buggers. Actually, they are perfectly nice, and possibly interesting too if they could find a way to relax with us. They had the gall to invite us here; they must have something about them.

They want to wait on us as if we were maharajas. We mess up their plans by mucking in. They have the tiniest red wine glasses I have ever been offered. They are almost too small for shorts. You couldn't drown a fruit fly in them, let alone a whole wasp. Everything in the house whispers caution. Mustn't let that alcohol get out of hand, they must be thinking every time they crack open a wine box (they have one closeted behind their kitchen door). Today they are serving their wine in bottles, some over-priced Bordeaux chateau, from the looks of the label. Not connoisseurs, but they desperately want things to look right.

I try to avoid talking politics on these occasions as parading all around my vocation rarely induces conversation, unless I am confronted by someone, usually a rosy-faced male (or a woman with a horse), who has been dying to have the opportunity to give the Prime Minister, any Prime Minister, a piece of his carefully-nurtured and prized mind for years. On the other hand, I am not especially gifted at small talk although, God knows, I have had the practice, so we end up squeezing the subject of our mutual accommodation dry.

At the end of the first course, a beautifully presented carpaccio of beef, intricately woven, I grab some plates to take them through to the kitchen. I need the air. Yasemin stands up too. Paul tries to persuade me to hand over the plates, which I resist, and in the ensuing negotiation I lose track of where Yasemin has gone. I win my exchange with Paul (I am ever the winner), and see Yasemin by the sink washing up. "That is going a bit over the top", I comment.

"What is?" I turn, and there is Yasemin by my side. I exclaim and drop the plates, as I catch sight of myself drying a dripping cup Yasemin handed me over twenty years ago. My heart pounding, I scan the four of the two of us wildly. "It's OK, Adam," the Yasemin by my side consoles me. "It is only history. We were very happy then too, can't you see?"

My younger self does not appear to have seen me, but the Yasemin at the sink suddenly swings round and winks at us.

Paul and Susan have raced each other into the kitchen to see what is going on. "Is everything all right, Prime Minister? What happened?"

I pull a sheepish expression. "I am terribly sorry. I have dropped your beautiful plates. I should have let you carry them through after all. I will get them replaced immediately I get back to Downing Street, if I may keep one as a sample."

"No need to worry," Susan declares magnanimously. "We are honoured that you dropped our plates." A cheeky grin crosses her face. "It will be a fun story to tell our friends, the Prime Minister turning our home into a Greek restaurant."

A much ruder thought crosses my mind. I could grab hold of those ridiculous wine glasses, and turn it into a Russian restaurant. The open fireplace is still there in the dining room, I notice.

"Adam had a sudden flashback from our time here together," Yasemin explains ingratiatingly. "He is much more emotional than he appears, aren't you, dear?"

"Oh, how terrible for you," empathises Susan. "Mm," Paul concurs.

"Well, the only solution now is to feed me up."

The Plumbs set to.

❀　❀　❀

This whole Youssouf thing is really troubling me, not only because it could be dangerous, but also because I am niggled that there is obviously something going on and I cannot identify it.

What could be in it for the UK if Youssouf visits here? He turns up, some people will meet him, others won't. He will pose a massive security risk, both to us and to himself, so we will have to mount an equally extensive security operation. Everyone will get restless. The native Brits will complain that yet another renowned troublemaker and sponsor of terrorism is being allowed into this country, all the better to make the Muslims restless. The Muslims will indeed become agitated as they have to endure heightened local and national racism, and some of their more radical spokesmen will mutter curses.

In the worst case, he will be assassinated, and we will forever on be suspected of complicity. No, actually, that is not the worst case. That would be if he arrives here, and as soon he touches down he makes a speech that incites riots all across the country. He then has a thoroughly hostile meeting with me during which he issues many threats, and he promptly walks out of the door and gives an impromptu press conference during which he harangues Britain for all our colonial and imperialist crimes, past and present, thus igniting another forest fire of riots. Before returning home, he is attacked by a crazed farmer from Norfolk who has had it with these dagos, who stabs him. He lingers on for another three days before dying, and we have to ship him home in a coffin shrouded in some Hamas or Hezbollah flag, or something, with full honours. All the currently factionalised Muslims will close ranks against us for the foreseeable future, and everyone else will laugh at us. That would be worse.

The positive side of his visiting us would be that we will have shown compassion for his personal circumstances with his ailing nephew, and we can always play that one up in the press, at least in the Mail. We will also prove once again that we are a haven of tolerance of those with views not necessarily aligned with our own. The spirit of Britain harbouring great and radical thinkers, like Karl Marx and Sigmund Freud, will be reinforced, thus siphoning off some of the wailing against our current asylum policies.

Taking both sides of the argument into account, no way does Youssouf come to Britain. And that is to leave out of the equation the considerable political capital I would have to expend to persuade my Cabinet colleagues to change their minds and allow him in.

What about the US and our special relationship? Why on earth does President Peterson want him here? He could be trying to set up an indirect line of communication to Youssouf, I suppose, via me. I become pally with him. Peterson wants something from him, like "lay off the US," and I am the go-between. That is enticing, but it doesn't ring true. Perhaps he wants to lure Youssouf to these shores so that he can slap in a quick extradition order, and whisk him off to the US. Nowadays, the US does not even need to show cause to have an extradition succeed in our courts. It just needs to spell most of his name right. Then what? Youssouf arrives in the US to the President's greater triumph, he is held in some murky detention centre for several years, and may or may not stand an unfair trial thereafter. In the meantime, he is removed from the politico-religious scene in the Middle East, and the US has demonstrated its power once again.

Can you imagine the consequences to the long-term resolution of chronic unrest in the region? My fear is that the US government probably can't. It tends to be a bit thick, or at least a bit thick-skinned in its foreign policy.

What is Youssouf after? It may simply be that he is seeking political credibility, and he has decided to start with one of the minor major world powers. He can practice on us before moving onto the Americans, Russians and Chinese whom he is currently softening up with corrosive rhetoric. We know that his ambitions lie wider than the Middle East. He has said so.

What if he is God? I cannot persuade Yasemin to tell me who is God and who isn't. If Youssouf is God, then he appears to be on a quest to unify all the different and competing religions into one World Religion, for which he should no doubt be applauded for his doomed courage. You might be able to build global hegemony around the US culture, but I cannot see it ever happening at a religious level. He cannot want to come here to encourage our nominal C of E Christians to become more passionate in their church-going, and the radical Muslims, Sikhs and Hindus to become more tolerant (presumably the Buddhists are in the bag anyway on that one). Does he want to be extradited to the US so that he can shame some of his nuttier fundamentalist disciples into cooling it? That might be tougher than to create a World Religion.

What would I want if I were Youssouf the God, if I have the temerity to ask myself the question?

I am afraid that, even today, I tend to default to a brand management analysis of the world. Think of selling his World Religion like vodka. What would be his objective?

He has a strong brand, that is for sure. Religions invariably have. There are two main active ingredients to the essence of a brand. Think of a brand as being like a person. The first question is "Do you trust that person? Do you respect them?" This is irrelevant of whether you actually like them. Youssouf engenders great authority. When he opens his mouth, you listen. He is almost mesmeric.

The second question is "Do you like that person? Are you proud to be associated with him or her?" This is where you want your brand to be polarising. You want some people to love it, others to loathe it. That is a mark of a truly differentiated brand—think McDonalds, or Benetton, or The Body Shop. In the Middle East, Youssouf has his absolutely devoted disciples, and others who are baying for his blood, in roughly balanced numbers.

So he is in possession of a power brand. What would I want to do with it, if I were he? Expand, of course. Penetrate and dominate new markets. Which markets? It has to be China. Where else do you have 1.3 billion lost, nominally communist, souls inhabiting a country that will inevitably grow to dominate the world within the next fifty years, not long in a blink of infinity? How do you get to China, figuratively speaking? By getting there physically speaking. President Tan would love to get his maulers on him for the rioting Youssouf is promoting there with his inflammatory rantings. The UK and the US gets the kudos of landing him there, which is good for trade.

Tell it not in Gath, but economically I am 80% with Marx (Karl) who argued that the cashflow in all economies has a tendency to leak, and therefore to shrink. When it does, you get a recession, and potentially a depression. The way to avoid it doing so is to top it up again, typically by expanding the economy. How do you do that? You move into new markets, and grow those markets. Western markets are relatively saturated, although if you could persuade those pesky, fiscally conservative, continental Europeans to borrow as much against as many credit cards as the Brits, there is still plenty of headroom for a bonanza for a few years to come. The great opportunity is China and then Asia, then Russia, then Africa. President Peterson must be torn between the desire to have the US continue to dominate the world politically and economically, and the realistic understanding that without world economic growth, and with a huge and widening budget deficit, America will have enormous problems keeping control of itself.

So, is that the scenario? Youssouf arrives here. He then leaves for China, where he will do some bandstanding to spread his message, President Tan will get his revenge, and President Peterson and I will gain preferential access to Chinese markets? It looks like a Devil's compact to me, except that its instigator may be his antithesis.

How would Youssouf get to China in this scenario? He is hardly going to apply for a visa and buy a ticket for Beijing for a spot of sightseeing. It would have to involve forcible (if voluntary) kidnapping, drugs, the intense co-operation of the US and UK security services, and Youssouf turning up on a plane, trussed, gagged, sedated and packed into a food trolley marked as containing servings of chicken, prawn and ham and pickle sandwiches.

And the consequences for Britain? World outrage? Not much. It will be a deniable operation that we can palm off onto the Chinese, American or even French secret services (people will believe anything about the French).

For me? In all probability, I will never need to be involved. I can be as shocked and horrified and remorseful as the next person. I will have it on my conscience to a degree, but I suspect that God is willing this particular piece of theatre and, as Groucho Marx declared "These are my principles and, if you don't like them, I have others."

What would be in store for Youssouf? A long, long time in prison under extremely rough conditions until he finally emerges blinking into the light, Mandela-style, as an old and venerated man, having accumulated a large and devoted following.

Joy all round, in fact. I must run it past Yasemin.

Chapter 14

There is a fireball tearing through the Middle East. It disappears underground as it crosses India, only for it to re-emerge in the Far East.

Israel and Syria are virtually at war over the Lebanon, which Israel has decided to occupy yet again. President Peterson and I tried to dissuade President Ramon of Israel from such an intemperate action at this time of inflamed tension throughout the whole region, and other Western leaders did the same. His response was that this was exactly why they had decided to do it, to show their Arab neighbours that Israel would never be pushed into the sea by them. "We need to demonstrate that we have a more deadly army than they can ever imagine for themselves. It is a political and military necessity. If you do not agree with me, withdraw your troops from around the world, President Peterson, and disarm. We may follow your lead." Presidents of Israel do not chuckle, however President Ramon recognises a trump when he has one, and rejoices in using it.

There is a civil war brewing in Jordan, partly as a reaction to Israel's occupation of the Lebanon. The king is under pressure to abdicate, as Amman is subjected to intensifying rioting and disorder, characterised by rebel militia storming through the capital with their artillery mounted on the backs of their trucks and jeeps.

Iraq is a basket-case, as it has been since 2003. Every day there are more massacres, as the Sunnis and Shias blow each other apart for old times' sake.

In Iran, they are reputedly stockpiling nuclear weapons by the day, catalysing President Peterson's war-like ambitions. In response, they use the same argument as President Ramon: if the US would like to decommission its nuclear weapons, they will do the same. They wouldn't, of course, but they are odds-on betting that the US won't either. Yesterday, they stoned to death a fourteen year old girl. She claimed to have been gang-raped by three of her cousins at a wedding, an assertion for which Amnesty International unearthed considerable bystander evidence, and consequently fell pregnant. She was allowed to give birth to the baby, and was executed a week later. The world has registered its condemnation.

Egypt is showing its own signs of emerging instability. There have been two minor explosions in Cairo over recent weeks, one in Alexandria, and an attempted coup five days ago.

In Libya, Gaddafi appears to be dying of cancer. He has visited clinics in all of Paris, London and New York for tests and remedial treatment.

In the Far East, there is a civil war in Indonesia, Malaysia overthrew its President last week, and even Singapore seems to be wobbling as riots take place over the jailing of two opposition leaders for their criticisms of the government.

In Sydney, in the early hours of this morning there was a huge explosion at the opera house. Several staff were killed, and one of its signature shells has buckled like a floppy ear. Australia is in shock.

Yasemin and I are having breakfast, before I embark on a frenzied itinerary. Who would have guessed that the most intellectually disconnected of US presidents, Ronald Reagan, would prove to be one of the wisest in relation to his work schedule. I become more and more of a Reaganite by the hour.

My favourite Ronnie Reagan story is of his visit to the Coors beer family during his re-election campaign in 1984. He arrived there in the evening after "one hell of a day". He had criss-crossed the country for a breakfast meeting, a mid-morning speech, for a lunchtime speech and television broadcast, for another mid-afternoon appearance, and for an early evening rally. He turned to his hosts with a mock stagger and announced "I could murder a Bud."

"Why can't God stop all this?" I challenge Yasemin, not referring to the Coors story. "Why this endless suffering and turmoil?" It is an age-old question.

Yasemin takes me by my right hand. She has become increasingly solicitous and affectionate over the last few months, and hardly ever goes off in search of souls to save. I get the strong impression that she is concentrating on saving mine; that she will need all her powers of support to usher me through this next section of my life. It is a realisation that increasingly scares me as the imminence of my destiny begins to trace out its message on tablets of stone located between my heart and my stomach. No-one remains at the top of the world for long, unless you are Gaddafi. When they raise you up to the pinnacle, it is only for the better to hurl you down again. All leaders follow the King Kong trajectory, from discovery in some obscure constituency, to mass publicity and fame, to being attacked at the top of their tower by the best technology their opponents can bring to bear until they are beaten down, and die in obscurity again.

"Imagine. Imagine you had to calculate just one second of the world, perhaps this second, for every creature and element within it. You would not only have to understand every detail of their past, but also every permutation for their future, which necessarily includes every possible mutual effect. How much computer power do you think that would require?"

"It would be impossible, of course, even if you could get the base data."

"We can assume that God has the base data, but even he does not have the computing power, and certainly not to repeat this feat second after second for many billions of planets in the galaxy. That is why he cannot intervene directly in the world. He cannot calculate its effect. He is as likely to provoke more harm than more good. Yes, he could exercise his powers and wreak widespread destruction, but what would that do? This is his world, that he created, that he feels responsible for creating, that in fact he deeply loves to the core of his being. He cannot destroy it, so he cannot destroy any part of it, even down to the most evil of individual creatures. In his infinite wisdom, he has decided that all cosmic phenomena must live out their destiny. All he is willing to do is to try to influence the structure of the cosmos from time-to-time, as he is doing now, attempting to persuade the human race to live in greater harmony by promoting one World Religion, and by demanding that people respect all other creatures, and all other elements of the universe."

"So he is Youssouf ben Abdul."

"Yes, he is."

"My time must be close, then."

"Yes, it is."

"What does he expect of me? Can this finally be revealed to me?"

"He will do that himself when he visits you."

"Is that why he wants to meet me?"

"Yes. He knows, obviously, the unbearable sacrifice he is requiring of you. He is coming to thank you personally and to renew your courage and determination."

My whole body has become a tablet, frozen to stone.

"However, he is not asking of you what he is not prepared to suffer himself."

"How exactly does God suffer?" My voice is shaky with emotion, anticipation and fear.

"In his human form, he suffers as you do. If you cut him, he bleeds. If you flay him, the flesh is burned off him. If you nail his hands to a cross, it is the same as if you were to have your own hands nailed through. In his human form, God is human, he feels as a human, he suffers as a human, he experiences the physical agony of being human. There is no difference."

"Surely he can distance himself from all that. Even mystics can do that, walking across hot coals without burning their feet or suffering any pain."

"What would be the point of his being human if he did that? His very purpose is to share in your pain and your suffering, to empathise with the human predicament, and to try to steer the world towards a better course. He has to do that from among you, shoulder-to-shoulder with you. There has to be complicity, solidarity. It is the one chance there is, that people understand his suffering as their own, and resolve to live better lives."

"It didn't work last time around, did it? If that was the last time around?"

"No, it didn't, not all of the time anyway. You could say that there has ultimately been some improvement, depending on your perspective. That is why he has decided to try again, to push the mountain just a little bit further over to the left."

"Is that left in a political sense?"

"No, because from the other side of the mountain, it is to the right."

"And you cannot tell me what he expects of me?"

"No, I can only tell you that it will be unbearable, and you would do much better than to try to anticipate it. God knows best; trust him."

"Trust him to destroy my life in the interests of the world."

"That, surely, is the role of a leader, and it depends on how narrow a definition you form of your life."

❋   ❋   ❋

Yasemin urges me to arrange for Youssouf to visit Britain, to visit me. This is going to be a difficult one.

Where to begin? The person I will ultimately have to persuade is Nathan Ketts at the Home Office. Will he co-operate? Er, no. He is smart, and fly, and has no personal loyalty towards me. I have no leverage.

So, I will have to approach Roger Danby, even less enticing, but more feasible. He might at least succumb to pressure from the US. I arrange for a teleconference with President Peterson. Roger will double-check everything, and the State Department must confirm the President's intent instantly for my message to be persuasive.

"Hi, there, Adam." Through his protocol weavers, the President has insisted that we converse more informally, and on first name terms. Who am I to refuse?

"Hi, Kieran." There you go.

"Good to talk to you."

"And you."

"What can I do for you today?" He makes it sound as if he does me favours every day rather than, in this case, my doing him a favour.

"I have decided to invite Youssouf ben Abdul to Britain."

"That is great news, Adam, great news."

"But I need some help to persuade some of my colleagues."

"Fire away."

"I will be talking to Roger Danby, our Foreign Minister first."

"I know Roger."

"He will almost certainly check that you have indeed requested me to talk to Mr. ben Abdul, to act as a bridge between the Middle East and Europe."

"Yeah . . . ." He sounds cagey.

"Would you be willing to brief your State Department officials accordingly?"

"What should I tell them?"

"That you and I have spoken, and that you are eager that I invite Mr. ben Abdul to Britain for talks."

There is a momentary hesitation. "Well, er, Adam, this is your call; your initiative."

"I have no personal desire to see the man."

"It will do us a great service."

"Then, can you help me?"

"Let me be frank with you, Adam. My concern here is that this must not be regarded in the least degree as a US initiative. If it comes to be viewed that way, it will fail. Mr. ben Abdul will not come."

"There is no need for it to be announced to the public that it is a joint US-British initiative, or anything. I just need your officials to confirm to Roger Danby that you are highly supportive and encouraging of the initiative."

"And he is then attacked by your press for wanting to invite Mr. ben Abdul, and what does he say?"

"He says that he believes that, on balance, it would be a good thing for Britain to commence a dialogue with Mr. ben Abdul as a more moderate voice in an extremely chaotic and volatile region."

"And he wouldn't mention us at all?"

"I would ask him not to."

"You see, Adam, I cannot say that I know the man as well as you do, but my bet is that he will. Placed under the slightest pressure, he will declare this to be a joint US-British initiative, and then the whole thing is blown sky-high. It is not that I disapprove of the visit, not at all. I believe that it will be extremely important for us to negotiate with Mr. ben Abdul, but the US cannot be seen to be taking the lead."

"You must understand, Kieran, in that case, that the invitation may never be issued."

"You will find a way, Adam. I have every confidence in you. Good luck! Excuse me, but I have an urgent call scheduled with the Chinese President, Mr. Tan."

"Well, Kieran, if you change your mind, please let me know."

"I am convinced you can handle the matter, Adam. As I say, good luck to you!"

Oh well, I am going to have to try Roger without him. I ask him over for 5:00. He is available. I would prefer to visit him for this sort of discussion, to place him at his ease on his home ground, but that would appear weak.

"Good evening, Roger."

"Good evening, Adam."

"What's new?"

"In the last half-an-hour, not much. The big event of the day is the Sidney thing. Only a few dead, but it hasn't half rattled them. They are treating it as their version of 9/11."

"I can imagine they would."

"And they are expecting a follow-up within the next 24 to 36 hours, either in Melbourne or Perth."

"What are we doing to help?"

"What help can we really give them? They are in touch with MI6, sharing data, but we have not picked up anything on this. We are not even sure that it was an international incident. It could be home-grown."

"You think so."

"It is possible. We usually pick up traces if something big is about to happen, and there hasn't been a thing. Not a whisper."

"Have you spoken to the Australian Prime Minister?"

"Yes, we spoke earlier today. Bob says he is shaken, too, although he sounds like his normal calm self . . . ."

Tea arrives, and interrupts our flow while Lucy pours it.

"Thank you, Lucy."

"So, Adam, what did you have it in mind to discuss with me?"

"I wanted to sound you out on the idea of Youssouf ben Abdul coming here after all."

"I thought you might be coming to that conclusion."

"What makes you say that?"

"I heard a few rumours to that effect."

"You did."

"The quotidian of government is paved with rumours. I am sure that you have your ear as much to the ground as I have."

"So what do you think?"

"Why do you think he should come?"

"Well, the immediate pretext is that he has a nephew who is dying of cerebral palsy over here, and he wants to see him. They are very close."

"And this nephew cannot return to the Middle East to see him?"

"I assume he is too ill. I haven't checked."

"Who is paying for the treatment over here?"

"Again, I assume that the family is. They are pretty wealthy, I believe."

"I heard that he was being treated on the NHS."

"Ah."

"Anything else?"

"The other point, Roger, is that we need to have people who are amenable to our interests over there, and President Peterson and I believe that we have perhaps underestimated his potential in the past."

"How can he help us? He is a somewhat isolated figure at the moment, having alienated almost everyone with his indiscriminate criticism of anyone and everyone, or indeed of everyone who is anyone."

"Our joint assessment is that he will continue to be a key player in the region for many years to come, and that his influence will increase over time."

"That is not our assessment, as you have seen."

"I am working on hunches here, Roger. The President, I would guess, is working off something rather more substantial."

"The State Department's analysis almost exactly matches ours."

"Is that so?"

"Yes, it is so."

"So your advice is that he should not come?"

"He definitely should not come, Adam. If we want to retain some influence in the Middle East, he is the last person we should be buddying up to. And not only will we alienate most of the leaders in the Middle East we care about, you mustn't forget that this is a practised troublemaker we are talking about here. We will end up with riots over here, and cold shoulders over there. What does the king say?"

"I haven't discussed this with him yet."

"I am not surprised. He cannot stand the man."

Which leaves me Nathan. I ask Jo to book a meeting with him tomorrow morning, if he is available.

I explain the situation to Yasemin later in the day.

"You had better find some way, Adam," she says, with a steely tone in her voice I have never heard before. "We are depending on you."

❈   ❈   ❈

Forty-five minutes with Nathan, and I feel like a complete fool. He sat there humouring me throughout. He made me feel this small. The trouble with being PM is that you have nobody to go to when you want to complain about a colleague's condescending behaviour, except Yasemin.

"Can't you fix it?" I ask her.

"How do you expect me to do that?"

"No, how do you expect me to do that?"

"You are the Prime Minister, Adam. You are there because you are good at fixing things."

"Not including this apparently."

"We will think of something."

"We will have to."

"Who else could approve Youssouf's visit?"

"The king."

"Would he?"

"I very much doubt it."

"When are you seeing him?"

"Tomorrow, as it happens."

"Ask him."

"I am going to have to."

"The king is an intelligent man. Why would he not want to meet another intelligent man?"

"Some of the things Youssouf has said about religion have upset him."

"What exactly?"

"The king takes his role as Head of the Church of England very seriously."

"And . . . . ?"

"I think he feels his position is being interfered with."

"So the representative of God in this country feels that God is interfering with his position?"

"He doesn't know that Youssouf is in fact God, does he?"

"Can't be much of a church leader then."

"Does anyone know who he is?"

"Yes, many people have recognised him. That is why he gains so much respect while saying things that rock people's foundations. They recognise his authority to do so. They know that he has the right, and the wisdom."

"Well, the Church of England never was much about religion."

"Nor was any established church. They are all about power, ambition and politics."

"Doesn't that infuriate God?"

"Not so much. He is the ultimate realist. He knows how things work, and even appreciates the irony of it all, having God's representative on earth more beholden to a ruler who thinks he is God's anointed on earth, leaving God to play gooseberry."

"If I were God, I would be chucking thunderbolts."

"It is just as well that you are not God, then. You are psychologically unsuited. Stick to being in his service, and find a way of getting him over here. Your task is mission-critical. He must come."

"Surely he has other ways of getting what he wants. He must have a plan B."

"No, Adam. This is the only way. Timing and sequence are critical. This path has been booked for many years."

"Perhaps I could have been given more warning, to prepare the ground."

"Things will happen as intended. The only question is how."

"I have had more reasonable bosses in my time, Yasemin. Some of them have even recognised the limits of what is possible."

"Everything is possible, Adam. Don't give up."

As timing goes, Tessa calls at that minute. Jo checks that I will take the call and patches her through.

"Hello, Adam."

"Hello, Tessa. How are things?"

"I need to talk to you."

"Sure. Next week sometime? I'll have Jo work out an appointment."

"I would prefer it to be today, if possible."

"Today?"

"Yes. There is something I have discovered that I need to discuss with you urgently."

"Is it to do with one of the boys?"

A hesitation. "Yes."

"Should I be concerned?"

"Yes. I would not be asking you over in such a hurry otherwise. I would not even be talking to you, I suppose, although I miss that. I am feeling rather nostalgic today."

I glance over at Yasemin who is staring passively at me.

"I'll see what I can clear, and come back to you within an hour."

"Thank you, Adam. Please make it a priority, and please come alone. I don't want to deal with any complications."

"I am sure that Yasemin will understand. I'll call back shortly."

As luck would have it, I am due to see Nathan again this afternoon between 2:00 and 4:00 to discuss asylum seekers, a topic close to Nathan's heart and far from mine. I cancel, postpone or whatever, the meeting with a certain amount of glee.

"Is Tessa OK?" Yasemin inquires.

"At this moment, Yasemin, you tell me."

"I don't think she is, Adam."

I search her face. "Woman's instinct or angel's instinct."

"I use them both together. They are inseparable. I cannot tell you which."

"What is wrong with her?"

"That I don't know. I am only going by the tone of her voice. Almost heroic."

"She said it was to do with one of the boys."

"I think you'll find it is more to do with her."

I am chauffeured to the Barnes house for 2:15, and we draw up outside the home where I lived for over ten years, where we both lived, where Tessa still lives, which I pay for, which the children regard as their one true home.

Tessa is waiting for me, and opens the door as I approach it.

"Hello, Adam." I hang back out of respect, but she kisses me on both cheeks. "Come in."

There is no real change to the house as far as I can see, except that I no longer belong to it.

"Sit down, Adam. Tea?"

"No, I'm OK thanks, Tessa."

"I am going to have some. Are you sure?"

"OK. I'll join you."

I wander through to the kitchen in her trail, and watch the once-familiar ritual of Tessa making tea.

"How is it going with James?"

"Fine. Good even."

"Does he love you?"

"Enough."

"Do you have what you want?"

"I did. Not now, it seems."

"Why not now, Tessa."

Tessa puts down the teapot, its lid hinged open.

"I went for tests yesterday afternoon. I have had a small lump in my right breast for a little while. The tests say that it is malignant. I shall need to have a mastectomy, and radio and chemotherapy. They say that it is a particularly aggressive one. I need you to take care of the boys so that I can concentrate on beating this thing."

"And James?"

"James is not their father, Adam."

"I was not shirking the responsibility, Tessa. I was only paying you the respect of treating you as an authentic family, however much I may feel otherwise."

"I would very much prefer it, Adam, if you would take care of Sandy and Ben. You and Yasemin can have the chance to play happy families too."

"Tessa, before we get into that, I want to say how sorry I am. You must be scared."

She is standing apart from me, at a stranger's distance. I move towards her to offer her a conciliatory hug. She steps back. "No, Adam. I don't need your sympathy."

"Of course you have my sympathy, Tessa. We are still bound together in some ways, whether we like it or not."

She shrugs her shoulders. "I have put it in my past. I had, anyway."

"Perhaps that was not the place to put it."

"Whatever."

"Whatever. Do the boys know?"

"Not yet."

"Should we tell them together, and plan as a family?"

"They would appreciate that."

"OK. I'll call around again tonight. About eight?"

"Yes, that would be fine."

"I won't be interfering with Sandy's social life?"

"Tonight he will have to put it on hold. I am sure he will understand. Sandy being Sandy, he'll know already."

"He has turned clairvoyant?"

"I took him off the Risperdal two months ago. It's all right. He is coping with it. The voices tell him everything. Luckily they are still friendly voices."

"I thought he was behaving a bit other-worldly the last few times I have seen him. I did not want to ask."

"It is as well that you didn't. You might have damaged his self-confidence. He insisted on coming off all his drugs one day. I fought him at first, but he was as determined as only a teenage boy can be. You have been missing out on that. You have had it easy."

"You are right, Tessa. Running the country day and night is a cinch in comparison."

"I think it probably is, especially when you are having to deal with the fall-out of an upcoming divorce single-handedly. Just think, Adam. We may not need a divorce now. Just hold your horses for a while, and you can marry Yasemin without even that stigma."

"I am not planning to marry Yasemin."

"No? Why? I would certainly have married James. I may yet."

"Yasemin is not the marrying type, and there is no need."

"You could time it for a few months before the next election, Adam. That should be worth a few votes."

"I doubt that I will seek re-election. We'll see."

"Why is that, Adam? All the opinion polls are very positive about you. You have a golden touch."

"It certainly does not feel that way at this precise moment. I would rather come back and be with you, in fact."

She gives me a very queer look. "You miss me?"

"Of course I miss you. This wasn't my idea, after all."

"It was your idea to have an affair too."

"I am not so sure that it was."

"Whose was it then? God's?" She raises her eyes to heaven.

"Quite likely, come to think of it."

She turns away to continue making the tea.

"Adam, don't be so pathetic," she tosses over her shoulder. "Take some responsibility."

I laugh dismissively. "I don't think anyone can accuse me of avoiding responsibility. Every second of my life is responsibility, and has been from before we met. I wear responsibility like I wear my skin."

Tessa turns and hands me a cup. "Come and sit down, Adam."

"Tessa, I am worried about you."

"So am I, Adam. I don't think I am going to make it. I am not sure that I even want to. It is the pain I am most frightened of."

"Surely you want a life with James and your children."

"Our children, Adam."

"I know that. I was approaching it from your point of view."

Tessa considers. "Yes, I do, but this is one more bloody thing. I am exhausted by work, I am exhausted by us, I am exhausted by the boys, and whatever relationship I have with James, which is generally fairly good, however it does not replenish my batteries. I am being dragged down. The treatment will drag me down further. I am not sure that I have enough to live for. To beat cancer, you really need to be trying."

"You will beat it, Tessa. You are a very determined woman. I do not see you giving up."

My mobile rings. I glance down at the screen. It is Jo. "Sorry, Tessa." I answer it. "Yes, Jo."

"I am really sorry to interrupt you, Adam. It is your father. He has just had a major heart attack. The hospital is suggesting that you get up to Huntingdon right away. Yasemin says she will come and pick you up."

"I'll be here."

"I am really sorry, Adam. Your father sounds such a nice man on the phone."

"He is."

"My sincere wishes for his recovery."

"Thanks." I turn to Tessa. "We have a bit more time, if you are OK with that. I need to go up to Huntingdon now. My father has just suffered a heart attack."

"Poor Tim. I have always liked your father. What a shame. I really hope he recovers. Poor you. What a day for you."

"No, poor you, Tessa. I may be suffering too, but only by proxy after all."

✳   ✳   ✳

My father dies before I manage to reach him. Yasemin holds me tight. "I am really sorry, Adam. I really liked Tim. You can console yourself with the fact that he has gone to a better place."

"If you weren't an authority on the subject, darling, I would take that as a cliché."

"He is a good man, Adam. That does not go unrewarded."

"And me?"

"Yes, you are a good man too. Not as good as your father, though. He is a very good man."

"It is strange that you refer to him in the present tense."

"He doesn't cease to exist just because he is dead."

"I was wondering about that. I had better make some funeral arrangements, I suppose."

"Jo can do that for you."

"I would prefer to do that myself, as a last gesture towards a very good man, as you say."

"Adam, you are too busy for that. You have at least one extremely urgent issue to attend to, and probably several more, not least that you have to help your two sons settle in with us."

"Perhaps they can make the arrangements. It would distract them, and it would be some great practical training. A project."

"They would probably rather chat up some girls with the news that they are now living at Number 10 Downing Street. That should open things up a bit."

"Well, if only to keep a balance, and to keep their feet on the ground at least some of the time, they can sort this out too. Sometimes, I think I am a genius."

My mobile rings again. It is Jo again. "Yes, Jo."

"Adam, I am really sorry to disturb you, but there is a breaking event that will need your personal attention, I think. Mr. ben Abdul has just arrived at Heathrow Airport, and is being held under detention there as an illegal immigrant. Immigration are asking what they should do next."

"OK, Jo. I'll be back in London as soon as I can. My father died a couple of hours ago . . . ."

"I am so sorry, Adam."

"Thanks. There is no more for me to do here immediately. Can you arrange for Nathan to meet me as soon as I arrive back at Number 10."

"I'll do what I can."

"Perhaps Roger could join us too. I am going to need some wise counsel on this one." I turn to Yasemin. "It looks like your friend Youssouf has found a solution."

"I was sure that he would, given that you couldn't."

"A black mark for me, then."

"No, you were trying." She smiles consolingly. "You are only human after all."

❋   ❋   ❋

Roger and Nathan are on my doorstep within five minutes of my return to Number 10, having bided their time catching up with each other at Julian's residence next door at Number 11

"Thank you both for being on call. Come in."

We file through to the sitting room. Yasemin retreats diplomatically upstairs.

"So, where are we Nathan on Mr. ben Abdul's impromptu visit?"

"Can I check one thing first, Adam?"

"Sure, Nathan. Fire away."

"Did you have any prior knowledge of this whatsoever?"

"No, I didn't."

Roger watches me warily, possibly sceptically.

"Thank you for clarifying that, Prime Minister. What appears to have happened is that Mr. ben Abdul boarded an Emirates flight bound for London in Dubai this morning. He did not have a visa, but airline officials decided that they would prefer to pay the fine in this case rather than be seen to thwart Mr. ben Abdul's intentions. He is not a man it is particularly pleasant to cross either personally or politically. We will obviously arrange for Emirates to pay the maximum punitive fine for deliberately contravening the Customs & Excise Management Act. We are also considering prosecuting them for illegal trafficking."

"I think that might be an over-reaction, Nathan, unless you have evidence that Mr. ben Abdul intends to stay."

"At the moment, we know that he is being held at Heathrow Airport pending our decision on what to do with him next. Mr. ben Abdul has not elaborated on his intentions, beyond his determination to see you. It could be that he will ask you personally for political asylum. The Middle East must be getting uncomfortably hot for him. Someone is bound to bump him off sooner or later."

"So what do you think we should do now, Nathan?"

"I think we should return him to Dubai immediately."

"What do you think, Roger?"

"I agree with Nathan entirely."

"Thank you." I hesitate. "I know that it will send the wrong messages all over the place, but I am minded to see Mr. ben Abdul. I was swinging that way yesterday, as you both know, and it would seem to me verging on the abusive to refuse to see him now."

"What do you mean abusive?" Roger explodes. "He is here illegally. It would be abusive to agree to see him. It would be to condone a blatant breach of European Law, in fact. You cannot possibly grant him an audience, Prime Minister. I will resign if you decide to do so. I cannot have this."

"I will resign too," Nathan adds, bristling.

I hold up my hands. "Let us calm down and review the big picture for a second here. Mr. ben Abdul is a highly influential man in a Middle East which is becoming more dangerous for us by the minute. Given his repeated and stated desire to hold urgent discussions with us, Mr. ben Abdul can be considered, on the face of it, as a potential ally. Things may not be as they appear, of course. Currently it seems that he has isolated himself from most Middle-Eastern governments, viewed as a firebrand whom they cannot control. Nevertheless, things change quickly over there, as you well know. My hunch tells me that he is too politically strong a character to be ignored. At the very least, if we insult him in full view of the world, we are offering ourselves as hostages to fortune to those Middle-Eastern governments who want to embarrass us, and to stir up hostility against us, to further their own agendas, including full-scale nuclear armament. I would not be at all surprised if they did not denounce a slight to Mr. ben Abdul as a personal outrage for them and their people, whatever they may actually believe. My granting a short, personal interview with Mr. ben Abdul strikes me as the lesser of two evils, and we could still have him back on a flight to Dubai first thing tomorrow morning."

Nathan scratches his head distractedly. "What about the plan to kidnap Mr. ben Abdul should he arrive in this country?"

"Whose plan is that?"

"I thought it was yours."

"Mine? Why on earth would it be mine? It is the first time I have heard of it."

"I am sorry to be so frank, Prime Minister, but I thought that it was something you had cooked up with President Peterson, to lure Mr. ben Abdul to this country, to kidnap him, and to ship him off to China or somewhere to be dealt with."

"That is ridiculous. The thought has never crossed my mind, and I have had no such conversation with President Peterson."

"So, forgive me, Prime Minister, who has authorised MI5 and MI6 to work directly with the US secret services on this one?"

"Certainly not me."

"They say that they have your approval, communicated via the US State Department."

"Who says that, exactly?" I grimace. "You must take me for an incredible fool, Nathan, to believe that I would sign off on something like that."

"That is what they say."

"What who says?"

"Rod Bricknell at MI5 and Joanne Judge at MI6."

"This is an absolute lie. I cannot imagine what they are up to." I look at my watch, then shrug. "I don't care what the time is. I want to see them both immediately, whether they have to get out of bed or not. I want a full explanation." I pick up the phone. "Jo, can you come in here please?"

"Yes, sir."

Jo knocks and enters. "Jo, I need to see Rod Bricknell from MI5 and Joanne Judge from MI6 absolutely immediately. Please tell them to be here without delay."

"Yes, sir."

"In the meantime, Nathan, please have Mr. ben Abdul brought to see me as quickly as possible, whether you both resign or not. I want him out of the country by lunchtime."

"Yes, Prime Minister. I may have been overly hasty in my threat to resign. I apologise."

"And you, Roger."

"I am afraid I over-reacted as well, Prime Minister. I too apologise."

"Apologies accepted."

❋   ❋   ❋

Rod Bricknell arrives first. He was still at work. I make him wait. Joanne Judge arrives fifty minutes later. Jo ushers them both through to my office.

"Good evening," I greet them frostily.

"Good evening, Prime Minister," they reply together. For them it is no longer the evening.

"Sit down, please."

"Thank you, Prime Minister."

"Please tell me what is going on in relation to Mr. ben Abdul."

"As per your request, Prime Minister, we have been co-operating fully with the US secret services to arrange for Mr. ben Abdul to be passed over to the Chinese authorities on leaving this country."

"And how is it that Mr. Ketts, the Home Secretary, heard about this?"

"We did not realise that you intended to keep it a secret from your Cabinet, Prime Minister."

"I want to keep it a secret from everyone. Therefore, I want you both to go back to Mr. Ketts first thing tomorrow morning, and tell him that the information you provided to him was false. Understood?"

"Yes, Prime Minister."

"Mr. ben Abdul will be leaving the country within twelve hours."

"Yes, sir. Do we continue to co-operate with the US secret services?"

"Of course. However, it is critical that our involvement is denied resolutely and at all times. The story you will tell is that the US secret services misled you as to my sanctioning of the operation. You co-operated with them in good faith, believing their assertion. That you have learnt from me, in this meeting, that I mostly certainly have never sanctioned anything of this nature, and that I have made you personally responsible not only for withdrawing all co-operation with the US on this operation, but also for ensuring that Mr. ben Abdul gets home safely. Unfortunately, as it turns out, the US secret services had an additional plan that they had kept from you, and they succeeded in their mission anyway. Understood?"

"Yes, Prime Minister."

"And I am appalled that you should have discussed this matter with anyone."

"Yes, Prime Minister."

"Please leave. I am most disappointed. Put the record straight without delay."

"Yes, Prime Minister."

"You may go."

I turn my back.

I hadn't told you about that bit, had I? Whoops.

❋   ❋   ❋

What do you do when you come face-to-face with someone, or perhaps more accurately something, you believe to be God?

I have been terrified of, and exhilarated by, this very moment for weeks. Every cell of my body is consciously, pre-consciously and sub-consciously anticipating it. Shivers run up my spine, around my rectum, across my stomach, up and down my arms and legs.

The door opens. Jo ushers him in. "Mr. ben Abdul, Prime Minister."

A small man crosses the threshold into my private sitting room. He glances up at me humbly and gives me the traditional greeting of placing his hands together in supplication. I suppose it avoids being touched. I wonder if he is affronted that I am not affording him the normal reception we would give to a head of state, and instead inviting him into my intimate domain, as seems more appropriate to welcoming the living God. If it concerns him, he does not show it.

I respond to his salutation in kind, bowing deeper and longer than I usually would, and ask him almost appeasingly to take a seat on the sofa opposite to the one I intend to occupy.

He nods in recognition of a due act of hospitality, and then insists wordlessly on my sitting next to him. He intrudes closely into my private space, a hair's breadth away from touching me. His breath is sour. He has amber, intense, probing eyes.

So what do you do when you come face-to-face with something which could well be God incarnate? My first instinct is to ask him to heal my son, straight out, no preliminaries. Please, Your Holiness, lift this terrible affliction from my son's shoulders. He is a good boy. It is not fair. Sadly, I cannot say that. That would definitely be lèse majesté. Sandy is suffering greatly. I look for an opportunity to at least mention him. I will put the issue between us, and see whether he picks it up. It is such a small thing for him.

Then I stare at him. I examine his eyes. Could these be God's eyes? They are beautiful, poetic, empathetic eyes, but are they God's? Give me a sign that they belong to something beyond a human being. His hair is not well kept. It is rough, and frayed with split ends. Shouldn't a God have perfect hair, the magnificent mane of a Greek god? His teeth are tinged with yellow, and a canine tooth is missing entirely, leaving a gap. Give me a sign. There is the irony. Everyone beseeches a simple sign that God exists, "Just give me a sign, oh Lord, and I will believe in you and serve you all my days!" I have possibly the living God within inches of me, I have his undivided attention, I can examine every inch of his visible body, and I am still asking for a sign, not that he exists, but that he is who he claims to be, although he has never, to my hearing, ever claimed to be God, or the Son of God, or anything supernatural. That he is whom Yasemin claims him to be.

How did he get into his skin? Does it peel off to reveal an intense act of light? Has he occupied someone else's body? Did the original Youssouf die, and God decided to borrow his body?

My body remains electric. Is this my direct reaction to the being in front of me, or merely my speculation of being in the presence of the supreme being rendered into my flesh, my bones, my muscles and my organs, and my nervous system? Am I leaving anything out?

Youssouf leans forward gently. The ends of our hair may even be embracing each other. "How is your son, Prime Minister? I hear that he has been ill."

Is this the sign I have been praying for, or is it Youssouf the man and the politician making polite introductory conversation?

"My son is distressed . . . ." How do I address him. My Lord? Sir? Youssouf? Mr. ben Abdul? Your Excellency? ". . . . , Sir."

"He will be whole. Indeed, he is already whole. His suffering is a gift few are capable of receiving."

As a politician, I immediately reach for my statistics. "1% of the population of the UK experiences schizophrenic episodes."

"Your son is not schizophrenic, Prime Minister. He hears voices. The clinical diagnosis of psychoses is not an exact science. Not everyone who hears a voice is hallucinating. We all dream. Some dream when they are awake. Some tap into other dimensions and over-hear or participate in real conversations. Your son, Sandy, is one of those. He has an extraordinary gift. You have been persistently depriving him of it with your regime of medicines. Risperdal does indeed banish other worlds at least temporarily, but it is a poisonous answer to an extraordinary talent. I am glad your son has had the burden of these drugs removed from him, Prime Minister. Believe in his voices, reassure him that he is not in any way going mad, accompany him step-for-step on his journey, and he will sleep more peacefully at night."

"Why me?" I am unsure as to what my question actually refers to.

"Because you are the man who would become Prime Minister of your country. You are the necessary link in my earthly destiny. My mission is in your hands. The Angel Yasemin has explained this to you."

"So what must I do?"

"You must send me to my death. My willing death, I hasten to add. It is an assisted suicide more than a betrayal. It is not a betrayal at all, in fact. It is an act of supreme loyalty, of supreme goodness."

"I must be your Judas Iscariot?"

"His motives were more mixed than yours. He would probably have done it anyway. I relied on that. I built his weakness into the universal narrative. In your case, you would not naturally betray me, but you will honour me. You will show the ultimate act of courage, in the full realisation that it will bring you disgrace, incarceration, humiliation and ultimately death, and yet for you to rise up and be by my side for eternity. That is the devil's compact I am offering you." He laughs.

"The devil's?"

"A manner of speaking. I don't believe in devils. They are a human construct. I have never met one personally, and seriously doubt that they exist anywhere in the cosmos."

"What can I ask you?"

"Anything you like. Anything which is in your heart."

"Is this all worth it? Will my sacrifice be worth it? I feel that I am being treated as the son of God here, the man to be crucified in order to purge the sins of the world."

"There is an element of that."

"And will the world be a better place for it? Will all the cruelty and the suffering go away? Will we be transported to an earthly paradise, will the Garden of Eden be re-established?"

Youssouf chuckles. "That is my Pascal's Wager. If there is a 5% chance of things improving, it is worth shooting for, it is worth a little sacrifice, even of others, such as yourself, principally of yourself, come to think of it, together with the unfortunate inhabitants of Beijing."

"Why of Beijing?"

"Because they are the ones ultimately at risk. It is a matter entirely outside my control. It lies within the sinews of the universe. If I am tortured by the Chinese authorities, if I am executed, their symbols of power will come crashing down, as the walls of Jerusalem came crashing down after my previous death at the hands of the Jews. The Chinese government has a choice, and it will know it has a choice. It is a matter of free will. It can choose to kill me, and destroy itself, or it can honour me and draw down more of the Kingdom of Heaven upon the earth. Either way, my will shall be done. Either way, China shall become a holy nation. Either way, the people will believe. It is a question of how—the easy way or the hard way. Human beings tend to prefer the hard way. It is a design fault I cannot rectify now."

He reaches out and holds both my hands.

"Now do you believe that I am who I am?"

"Yes, My Lord."

"Good. Then we are in business. I must leave you now, but I shall never desert you. I shall always be by your side and in the fullness of your soul. I walk your path with you, and I will greet you into my heaven. Adam, you will be honoured among men, albeit that you will indeed be reviled by men. That is your destiny. You can choose your pride for your reputation, or you can choose the eternal truth and the greater wonder of the universe. I know that you will make the correct choice, despite the almost overwhelming doubts you will face in your own Garden of Gethsemane. Stay well. Love your wife. Love your sons. And love your world as well as you love your wife and your sons."

He kisses me on the lips. I jolt back on the sofa, taken entirely by surprise. Youssouf smiles almost mockingly. "That is a sign from God. No head of state does that!"

He gets up to go. "Oh, and another thing . . . ."

"What is that?"

"Please lodge a protest in front of the United Nations over China's genocidal policy in Tibet. It will help fan the flames of God's truth."

You have to hand it to him. He is one tough negotiator, and I am one damned human being. How quickly you can destroy your earthly life, and with what carelessness.

Part V
The Fall

Chapter 15

"Mr. Melton, you have been brought in front of this court, charged with causing the death of a child while driving under the influence of alcohol. Do you have anything to say before this court proceeds to pass sentence?"

I shake my head. Tessa regards me mournfully.

"In that case, I shall proceed to sentence. Mr. Melton, you have caused the death of a child. That this child was your son makes this case doubly tragic. You are already undoubtedly greatly punished by that fact for your extreme foolishness in getting into a car, for leading your two children into the car, knowing that you had consumed sufficient alcohol as to be unsafe to drive. You deliberately placed your children at unnecessary risk of death or injury. You equally placed any member of the public in your path at the same risk. From the facts of the case, it cannot be established whether the accident was your fault or not. It may well not have been. You say that you were avoiding what appeared to be a dog running out into the road in front of you. Eye witnesses confirm that a dog did indeed cross the road immediately in front of your car. Having said that, if you had not been adversely affected by the alcohol you had consumed, maybe you would have reacted to the incident with more skill, thereby avoiding the dire consequences that ensued. That we cannot determine. What we can determine is that you are a man of the utmost standing, a former Prime Minister of this country, someone everyone in this country should have the right to treat as a role model. You have failed your country in this respect. You have acted foolishly. You have acted fatally. You have brought to an end the promising life of a child, of your own child. Under these circumstances, I have no choice but to sentence you to an exemplary term of imprisonment. Mr. Melton, you have our utmost sympathy. Nonetheless, I sentence you to seven years imprisonment."

❇   ❇   ❇

Within a matter of months I was pitched from being a potentially memorable Prime Minister to being a destructive wreck, convicted of the drunken killing of his young son.

I am now sitting in a cell in Wandsworth Prison. That much I already knew. I am three years through my sentence, which will no doubt soon be commuted for good behaviour, if not by Tessa or the general public at large.

I am reading about the earthquake in Beijing. They believe that over one million people have been killed. Beijing has been left a bigger wreck than I.

When Youssouf ben Abdul left Britain that morning, he was taken in a plane to China. Yasemin accompanied him. I had never anticipated that. Their arrival in China was kept a secret for two weeks. It was rumoured that they had snuck into Tibet to provoke a public uprising. Then, on 11 June, there was a major demonstration in Lhasa, apparently led by them, although the whole event was almost certainly staged. There was some shooting from within the crowd. The police fired back, and eleven people were killed. Youssouf and Yasemin were tried for causing the deaths of these eleven people, found guilty, and immediately executed. I do not know whether they were tortured, although I do know that they did not confess to the crime.

At the moment of his death, the image of Youssouf ben Abdul appeared on every television screen in the world, whether the television was switched on or not.

Youssouf ben Abdul was instantly pronounced God reincarnate throughout the Middle East, and subsequently amongst many Chinese people. The Chinese authorities were brutal in attempting to stamp out all such inferences, and yet only succeeded in amplifying the message.

Our delegation at the UN denounced China for conducting a systematic genocide in Tibet, and was roundly applauded.

All seemed well except, of course, for me personally. I had lost Yasemin forever on this earth, without any warning whatsoever. I grieved her loss for the second time.

It is reported in The Telegraph here, as an aside to the main story of the earthquake, that two million people in China claim to have received body parts from Youssouf ben Abdul. In China, they recycle the organs of executed criminals. The component parts of Yasemin must be treading their separate paths too, come to think of it. Over a million people claim to have at least one of his eyes. Over 500,000 people claim his heart. 10,000 people even claim his testicles. Needless to say, the figures are far in excess of any transplant operations that have taken place since his death.

Then, three months after their execution, it was leaked to the press that I personally had arranged for Youssouf ben Abdul and Yasemin Karin to be kidnapped and flown to China. There was some initial scepticism in the press, as no-one believed that I would let Yasemin go like that (and I wouldn't have done, if I had understood what was happening). However, the rumour persisted, fanned no doubt by either Nathan or Roger, or both.

I was obliged to deny directly to parliament that I had played any part in the affair. I stuck to my script, that I had been made aware of the plan a few hours prior to my meeting Mr. ben Abdul, and to his subsequently leaving the country under duress, and that I had ordered that the plan be foiled by both MI5 and MI6. For a further two weeks, Rod and Joanne supported my claim in public, although I suspect that they were briefing the press differently in private. I was placed under immense pressure to appoint a select committee to investigate the affair, which I did. Under pressure from the committee during a two day interrogation, Rod then Joanne confessed that I had personally ordered them to provide all assistance as requested by the American secret services.

I had no alternative but to resign.

There was an immediate demand that I be prosecuted for conspiracy to kidnap, and even treason, given the suspected true nature of Youssouf ben Abdul. I escaped that, but not the airing in public of every aspect of my corruption, including my duplicitous insistence that China be denounced by our delegation for acts of genocide in Tibet.

I was well and truly and irrevocably disgraced. Tessa insisted on the boys returning to live with her. They looked devastated by the chain of events, by the fall of their father, and by the emergence of my hidden, putrescent character. I hired a cottage near Esher under an assumed name, and hid.

Then, one afternoon, after I had downed a bottle and a half of an excellent 2006 vintage of Château Roumanières "Les Garrics", Tessa phoned me on my mobile to say that she had to go into hospital as a matter of emergency, and would I pick up the boys from Barnes and drive them over to her parents, who would look after them, in Chesterfield? I should have declined, but instead agreed. I got to Barnes in record time, bundled the boys into the car, and off we went. I had not even left Barnes when I braked to avoid the dog. Ben was in the front seat, still putting on his seatbelt. He was hurled through the windscreen in a split second. I leapt out of the car and ran over to his huddled body. He was already dead.

As I crumpled onto the road beside Ben, Sandy covered me with his own body. His sobs breathed down my cheek.

"I didn't realise it was going to happen today," he protested, "until a few seconds ago. I should have stopped it. I could have stopped it. Ben, forgive me. Dad, forgive me. Mum, forgive me. I hate you, you useless, fucking voices! Go away, all of you!"

A vertiginous fall towards grace for both of us, Sandy.

❄   ❄   ❄

About the author—
Tim Roux

Born near Hull in the UK in 1954, Tim was called to the Bar before working for over 20 years in business strategy and strategic brand marketing for a major multinational corporation.

With degrees in both law and social sciences/psychology, and having worked as a volunteer for Amnesty International for several years, he is fascinated by the complex issues surrounding personal rights (human, civil and animal), and much of his writing is centred on these themes.

Tim has a wife and two children, and lives between the UK, France and Belgium running Valley Strategies Ltd. which leads a community of expert consultancies in bullet-proofing business strategies.

Other books by Tim Roux are:

Little Fingers! (2007), or *How good can a killer get?* Following her mother's suicide, Julia Blackburn vows to understand her tragic life. She knows one person she must confront—Mary Knightly. She knows where to find her. She hasn't a clue what she did. And she knows nothing about her mother's rapist. Will she take revenge? Will she get away with it? At its heart, "Little Fingers!" asks the troubled question: who does the greater wrong—those who ruin many lives with impunity, or those who kill to stop them?

Blood & Marriage (2007), or *From Kingston-upon-Hull to the first genocide of the 20th century.* Driving down the Mediterranean to inspect the family papers held by his cousin in Narbonne, David Lambert reviews his own troubled times against the backdrop of his family who fled Germany in the 1880s on pain of death for mutiny and desertion, to face genocide, espionage, bombs, bullets, tragic accidents, murderous designs and that curious fruit cordial Great-Grandma used to make. Classify under genealogy, or something.

Shade + Shadows (to be released in 2007), which is about Alan Harding, an alternative healer with a particularly unusual basis for his therapies, who marries the former wife of a controversial ambassador who survived an assassination attempt by Middle-Eastern terrorists. When his wife, Jane, is kidnapped as retribution for her husband's crimes, everyone assumes that the kidnappers are referring to the ambassador's activities. However, the good doctor has his own dark secrets . . . .

✻   ✻   ✻

About the artist—
Sharon Hudson

I first came across the work of Sharon Hudson, the San Francisco Bay artist, when I was looking for an e-card to send as a commiseration for the death of my niece, Clare, to whom this book is dedicated.

I was immediately struck by the warm immediacy of her paintings. She herself uses the word "sensual" to describe them; I would prefer the words "intimate" and "private". Many of Sharon's paintings are nude portraits, yet it is the serenity and ease of their subjects that strike you more than their naked bodies.

I subsequently used "Sheherazade" for "Little Fingers!" (2007), and "Alliance" for "Blood & Marriage" (2007).

"Seated Nude in Hat" is a straight art school charcoal, but I wanted something simple and "honest", and choosing it for "Girl on a Bar Stool" was fortuitous in that it provoked not only the title, but also a significant part of the story.

If you would like to see more of Sharon's work, and I strongly recommend that you do, you can visit her virtual gallery at http://www.byhudson.com.

Tim Roux, February 2007.